PRAISE FOR ADRIANA LOCKE

"Adriana Locke creates magic with unforgettable romances and captivating characters. She's a go-to author if I want to escape into a great read."

— *New York Times* bestselling author S. L. Scott

"Adriana Locke writes the most delicious heroes and sassy heroines who bring them to their knees. Her books are funny, raw, and heartfelt. She also has a great smile, but that's beside the point."

— *USA Today* bestselling author L. J. Shen

"Adriana Locke is the master of small-town contemporary romance. A one-click author for the masses, [she has a] perfect blend of wit, sexy banter, and well-developed characters [that's] guaranteed to leave readers satisfied. A book by Adriana is sure to be the romantic escape you're looking for."

— *USA Today* bestselling author Bethany Lopez

"No one does blue-collar, small-town, 'everyman' (and woman!) romance like Adriana Locke. She masterfully creates truly epic love stories for characters who could be your neighbor, your best friend— you! Each one is more addictive and heart-stoppingly romantic than the last."

— *USA Today* bestselling author Kennedy Ryan

"Adriana's sharp prose, witty dialogue, and flawless blend of humor and steam meld together to create unputdownable, up-all-night reads!"

— *Wall Street Journal* bestselling author Winter Renshaw

T0036134

Nothing But It All

OTHER TITLES BY ADRIANA LOCKE

The Exception Series

The Exception
The Connection: An Exception Novella
The Perception

Landry Family Series

Sway
Swing
Switch
Swear
Swink
Sweet

The Gibson Boys Series

Crank
Craft
Cross (a novella)
Crave
Crazy

Dogwood Lane Series

Tumble
Tangle
Trouble

Carmichael Family Series

Flirt
Fling
Fluke
Flaunt
Flame

Stand-Alone Novels

Sacrifice
Wherever It Leads
Written in the Scars
Battle of the Sexes
Lucky Number Eleven
Like You Love Me
The Sweet Spot
The Proposal

Nothing But It All

ADRIANA LOCKE

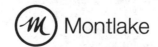 Montlake

Published by Montlake, Seattle

www.apub.com

Amazon, the Amazon logo, and Montlake are trademarks of Amazon.com, Inc., or its affiliates.

ISBN-13: 9781662512438 (paperback)
ISBN-13: 9781662512421 (digital)

Cover design by Letitia Hasser
Cover photography by Regina Wamba of ReginaWamba.com
Cover image: © Angelika Kaczanowska / Getty; © Taleju / 500px / Getty;
© Gary Yeowell / Getty

Printed in the United States of America

To my daddy:
What I wouldn't give for another summer of mushroom
hunting, berry picking, and fishing with you. Those
long days that I thought we were doing nothing, I know
now we were doing nothing but it all.

PROLOGUE

LAUREN

"You promised me you'd come home tonight, Jack."

Ice pelts the windows. It's been a continuous assault on both the glass and my nerves—my very last one—for the past thirty-six hours. Fog paints a barrier between the inside of the kitchen and the snowy outside world as the electricity flickers. *Again.*

Cabin fever has officially settled in for the winter. The kids are in desperate need of time apart after being home from school for seven days in a row. I'm in desperate need of adult conversation, a moment of peace, and maybe a large glass of wine. But, by the looks of it, I won't be getting any of those things tonight. Or ever.

"Jack?" I ask, gripping the phone entirely too hard.

"Lo, *I'm sorry.*"

"You said that last night and the night before that too."

"I know, but—"

"Damn it, Jack."

I grit my teeth, flexing my jaw so hard it aches.

I used to handle this better. For years, I lied to myself and said things would change. *He's putting food on the table. He's keeping the electricity on—when it's not storming. Jack is providing a great life for me and the kids.*

It won't always be this way.

"Do you even want to be here?" I ask. "Do you want to come home at all? Because it's really starting to feel like I'm a roommate that's taking care of my part of the rent over here and not your wife."

"What the hell? What do you want me to do, Lauren? What choice do I have? I'm working my ass off for you and our kids, and you call me and act like I'm—*what?* Out here having fun?"

I laugh, the tone edged in as much anger as his voice is in frustration. *What choice do you have? A lot more of them than I do.* "Well, I happened to catch your social media post this afternoon. Let's just say your lunch at the wings place was a hell of a lot more fun than mine. I had cold chicken nuggets because the kids started fighting and Maddie knocked over a glass of lemonade that I had to clean up."

"The guy I was with—I built two of his cars. Superchargers, carbon fiber—all of it. He spent a shit ton of money in the shop this past year and probably single-handedly paid our mortgage payments. What was I supposed to say? 'No, I can't go to lunch with you because it'll piss off my wife'?"

I pace the kitchen, struggling to keep my voice down. The last thing I want is for the kids to hear me shout at their father. *Again.* But the fact that I don't even have the luxury to express my own damn emotions in my own damn house compounds my frustration with . . . my life.

I'm not pissed he's having lunch with a customer. I'm resentful that I don't have a life outside these walls.

"Maybe," I say, working hard to stay calm. "I mean, I would've worded it differently. Something like, 'I would love to go to lunch with you, but I haven't been home for dinner in a month. So I'm going to pass so I can get out of here before my family is asleep for once.' But, you know, that would mean that you wanted to come home."

"Will you fucking stop it?"

I gasp. "No, *I won't fucking stop it.* I am so . . ."

I search for the right word.

My bones ache and my eyelids are heavy. Sleep sounds as nice as the haircut I desperately need. But I'm too exhausted for either one.

"I'm *tired*. Lonely." My bottom lip quivers, and that frustrates me more. "I miss you."

He sighs.

My heart sinks even further.

I stare at the picture next to the cookie jar sitting on the windowsill. Jack has an arm around me and another around our daughter, Maddie. Michael stands next to his father with a goofy grin on his face. We look so happy, so comfortable. So much like a family.

When did things change? When did we stop being that and start being . . . I look around the dark, empty kitchen. *This?*

It's a question that's been licking at my subconscious for weeks now.

The first time it entered my mind, I was crying in the shower at midnight. I had been up since five that morning hustling Michael off to a wrestling tournament, sat in the bleachers for nine hours to watch him on the mats for a total of thirteen minutes, and coordinated with my best friend, Billie, to get Maddie picked up from cheer camp, since the tournament had run late. A red blister had formed on my forearm from trying to fry chicken for dinner—a dinner that no one ate—and the back of my ankle was raw from the trash can scraping it as I hauled it to the road for pickup. In the midst of it all, I realized I'd forgotten to pick up chocolate to finish the dessert I had to make for the grand opening of Jack's new auto shop location the next morning.

I stood in the shower, tears of exhaustion running down my face, and took an inventory of my life.

I had one friend, whose friendship hinged on how often she could come to my house because I was too busy taking care of everyone else's lives to do anything with mine. The health I'd prided myself on now involved blood pressure medicine. The person in the mirror was unfamiliar, and the version of me inside my head was a stranger.

When did I start being this *Lauren Reed?*

"I can't do this anymore." The words fly out of my mouth well before I realize they're on the tip of my tongue. "I'm serious. Something has to change, Jack."

My eyes widen. The thundering of my heart makes me light-headed. *What am I doing? What does that mean?* I'm not sure. But the relief that washes over me is undeniable.

"What are you saying?" His tone cuts me through the line. "What are you getting at?"

"It means that I'm drawing a line in the sand. I—"

"*I'm working to take care of you, damn it.* You wanted to stay home with the kids. I'm giving you what you asked for—what's best for our family."

"But when did I say I didn't want *you?*" I ask, my voice rising as tears gather in the corners of my eyes. "I didn't know it was going to be a trade-off. I thought we'd still see each other, you know. Have a life together. I never realized I was going to turn into an employee."

He exhales harshly. "That's not true."

"What in the world do you think I'm doing here all day?" I catch myself and lower my voice. "Who does your laundry? Who runs Maddie to a million things every week and makes sure Michael's wrestling stuff is taken care of? Who shoulders the food preparation, grocery shopping—making sure the bills are paid? I'm happy to do all of that. I love taking care of you guys. But I also want to feel like I'm more than the woman that lives in your house."

"Do you want a thank-you? Is that it?"

"*No,* I don't want a *thank-you.* I want . . ."

More.

My shoulders fall forward as I give up the argument. *What's the point in saying anything? Nothing changes.*

He's not going to understand, and I'm foolish to even try.

"I appreciate you, Lo. You're the best mother in the world. I just . . ." He blows out a hasty breath. "Why do we argue like this?"

My heart cracks, deepening the caverns that have been forming for years. The man who used to heal all my wounds now only injures me more. I don't think he does it on purpose. I just don't think he cares enough to listen. But maybe that means it *is* on purpose. *Who knows?*

"Is it because I'm not home enough?" he asks.

"Yes. No. *Maybe?*" I sigh, wishing I hadn't called him in the first place. "Maybe we've spent so much time apart that we don't remember how to get along."

"We never had to try to get along before."

I frown. "Maybe that's saying something."

Jack groans, defeat thick in his voice. "I love you. Okay? I do. And I'll try to do better. I'll start moving shit around so I can be home in time for dinner. All right?"

My lips twitch, wanting desperately to smile. I want to believe him with every fiber of my being. But every time I try to raise my hopes, the memory of each failed attempt to do better resurfaces.

"All right," I say, shrugging. *"But something has to change."*

"I heard you."

"Good."

There's a long pause.

"I gotta go, Lauren. Love you."

"Love you. Goodbye."

The call ends.

The kitchen is dark, lit only by the occasional bolt of lightning and the dim bulb over the stove. The stillness settles over me like an old friend.

A pile of dishes sits in the sink from dinner. The floor is sticky from Maddie's lemonade spill earlier. Loads of laundry are stacked in the mudroom off the door on the left, waiting on me to give them attention.

But why bother? It'll all be here for me tomorrow. And the next day. And the day after that.

Nothing will change.

I take a long, steadying breath.

Unless I change it.

A swell of sadness and anger rises from my soul.

"I'm giving you what you asked for . . ."

"But you're not, Jack. I didn't ask for *this*."

I know what must be done, but I hate it all the same. The thought of moving forward without Jack somehow feels even lonelier than staying right where I am. But if I don't try to do something—if I don't try to fix the only thing I can, which is me—then this is exactly what my life will look like twenty years from now. That makes me sick. Defeated.

I have to try. I have to start somewhere.

After all, my husband has decided what he's doing with his life.

It's time for me to make a few choices too.

CHAPTER ONE

LAUREN

Two and a half years later . . .

I'm not funny, Billie. I'm mean and people think I'm joking."
My best friend throws her head back and laughs. I want to point out
that she's making my point for me—she thinks I'm joking and I'm not.
Instead, I stand in the middle of my home office with my hands on my
hips and residue from a powdered doughnut on my lips.

"You are not mean," she says, rolling her eyes. "Stop it."

"No, trust me—I was mean. I-meant-it mean. He didn't even have
the wherewithal to ask me for my driver's license." My nose wrinkles
in disgust. "Who doesn't card a woman buying wine? Isn't that a law? I
don't care if I'm clearly over forty or not. It's just rude."

She grins. "You must've not been too mean. He asked for your
number."

I swipe an armful of bubble roll off my desk. "He wasn't serious."

"Um, I think he was. Younger men and older women are *a thing*
right now. And, let's face it, you're hot. All that gym time is showing."

"Calling him a 'man' is way too generous. He was barely old enough
to sell me the alcohol. Hell, I could've been his mother."

"So?"

"*So*, what would I do with that?" I ask, the thought of dealing with a twentysomething's bullshit exhausting me. "If I *was* in the market for a boy toy, *which I am most definitely not*, I wouldn't choose someone without basic manners. Besides, there's not a teeny-tiny part of my soul that has any interest whatsoever in raising another man."

If Billie notices the extra energy that I use to stuff the Bubble Wrap into the appropriate bin, she doesn't mention it. And that's the thing I love most about Billie Wickerson. She knows when to let things go. Unlike me. I hold on to topics—ideas, kindergarten finger paint projects, *people*—for way too long.

Containers and packing material litter the floor. A stack of cardboard sits neatly by the door, since Billie took extra effort and broke down our empty boxes. She said something about recycling and it being good for the environment. I replied with something about being low on time and wanting to get it out of my sight. I appreciate her environmental activism, but as a mother and new small-business owner, I have priorities. That list includes keeping my two teenagers alive and healthy, corralling my business that exploded overnight, and keeping our house clean enough so that if child protective services comes knocking, they won't gasp in horror.

I have to worry about the teens. Someone else is going to have to worry about the trees.

"Did you see the video Maddie posted last night?" I ask.

Billie smashes another box flat. "No. I was putting together a proposal for work because I spent yesterday immersed in CrimeTok instead of doing what I get paid to do for eight hours a day."

"That sounds like a good use of your time."

"Hey, if you want to get away with a crime, I'm your girl."

I laugh.

"I mean it," she says, shrugging. "First, don't take out a life insurance policy or change any dollar amounts. Big red flag. *Huge*. Game over right there." She points at me. "Two, leave your phone at home.

Three, never, *ever* use bleach. Peroxide is a better choice. And four, if you have to put them in a lake, puncture the lungs so they don't float—"

"*Oh, my gosh.* Enough." My face screws up as I continue to chuckle. "I'm concerned that you know all of this."

"Be concerned now. But if you need help, you know where to find me." Her bright-blue eyes sparkle with mischief. "Now, tell me about Maddie's video."

Right. "I was working late last night. Couldn't sleep. I have this custom order that will never end. This woman sent me a literal wardrobe box full of pictures, mementos—and thirteen feathers—that she wants me to scrapbook. I can't even wrap my brain around all of this, let alone get it into some semblance of a story. I close my eyes at night and see silver feathers and pine needles."

"Weird."

"Tell me about it." I pause to take a quick drink. "Anyway, Maddie always records as she walks in on me working. It's kind of her thing now. All of her videos start that way. So, she comes through the door just as I'm tugging on this package of a thousand tiny buttons. It opens and they go flying—I mean *flying*—across the room. My jaw drops, and some of them fly into my mouth and I start choking."

Billie laughs.

"It was a whole thing. As I was trying not to asphyxiate, Mads put the video to music, posted it on my social pages, and we woke up to over one hundred thousand views this morning."

"That's amazing."

"*I know.* I have no clue where she gets her Maddie Magic from, but she's taken my scrapbooking from a hobby to a real business. I can't keep up with orders anymore. I've been turning people down." I close the doughnut bag. "I need these next two weeks off to get a business plan together. I wasn't prepared for all of this."

Billie collapses in a chair by the window and watches me smugly.

"What?" I ask.

"Lauren. Babe."

"What?"

"You know damn good and well where Maddie gets her skills. *From you.* She might've gotten those big brown eyes from Jack—and Michael might be Jack through and through—but that girl is all you. I see it even more these days."

I give her a simple smile. She winks back.

The last two and a half years have been some of the hardest but most necessary of my life. Admissions were made. *I wasn't happy.* Truths uncovered. *I wasn't setting a good example for my kids.* Dreams acknowledged. *I wanted to live a life I recognized and loved.*

I chose to give my husband the opportunity to make good on his promises. I had to exercise patience, never my strongest virtue, while I waited for him to come around. To be an active participant in our family again. To remember I exist as a woman.

As the days and months wore on, it became clear—if I wanted to be happy, that was my responsibility. I couldn't wait on Jack to change. *I had to change.*

So I did.

I started a business, although serendipitously. I discovered that I like sushi. Exercise became a part of my life, I bought red lipstick for fun, and most importantly, I changed my mindset. I became *me* again.

"Your scrapbooking business was just featured on the national morning news," Billie says, shaking her head in awe. "*A scrapbooking business*, Lo. Who does that? *You.* You do that. You're a big fucking deal."

My cheeks flush. "I'm not a big fucking deal. I was on the screen for, what, sixty seconds?"

"It doesn't matter. You're the biggest fucking deal I know. You're the biggest deal in Maple, Ohio."

I laugh. "Like that means anything. A thousand people live here."

"Stop downplaying it. Be proud of yourself."

I grab the last of the Bubble Wrap and stuff it in the bin. "I am. It's just . . . surreal, I guess."

The afternoon that Maddie caught me dancing while shaking glitter onto a project caught me by surprise. I said no when she begged me to let her upload it online. Absolutely not. The only reason I ever agreed was because she did all the laundry and dishes in exchange for the video. If I thought I was surprised that she'd recorded me, that was nothing compared to my shock at the video going viral the next day.

"I'm so proud of you," Billie says now, beaming. "I just want you to know that. I tell everyone that my best friend is a superstar."

"Will you stop it? You're making me all . . . *feel-y*."

She laughs, getting back to her feet. "The horror."

"You know what I mean."

She smiles at me. I return the sentiment.

I'm amazed at the things I've been able to achieve over the last year. Once Maddie put my scrapbooking online—videoing me and uploading to social media sites—my hobby blossomed into a business that I'd never had the courage to dream for myself. The more projects I complete, with those customers then showing off my work and tagging me on their posts, the more requests I have. It's wild and amazing—and so fulfilling.

"Thank you for saying that," I say. "I appreciate *you* very much."

She waves a hand through the air before continuing her box smashing.

I stretch my arms overhead, feeling the pull all the way down my back. Sore muscles still surprise me every time they ache. Billie insisted that moving around and getting into a "me routine," as she calls it, would help me feel better all around.

She wasn't wrong.

Early-afternoon sun streams into the room, filling my small corner office with light. The room was a guest bedroom until a month ago, when I decided to put the space to better use. I had to. My scrapbooking work had started to take over the entire dining room. Not that we use that room much anyway, but I hated walking in the front door and seeing the mess. So I talked Michael into helping me build shelves and a brand-spanking-new desk, and voilà! I have my very own office space.

It's not the brick-and-mortar store of my dreams, but it'll do. *For now.*

"Where are your kids?" she asks. "I need Michael to help me carry this to the garage. I'm not putting this stuff in my new car and hauling it to the recycling center for you."

I glance at my phone. "He should be picking Maddie up from Elodie's. He worked at the farm stand this morning and was grabbing her on the way home."

"I'll leave this until he gets back, then." She tosses a stray piece of cardboard on the pile. "What are you doing tonight? Want to grab a drink and some dinner?"

"Can't. Maddie has a cheer party tonight, and Michael has been begging to go to this party that's apparently held in a cornfield. By his level of enthusiasm, I'm pretty sure he shouldn't go."

Billie's eyes go wide. "Oh. *Right.* The annual Montgomery summer party is about this time of year."

"I didn't grow up here, remember? What does that mean?"

She sits again. I drop into my office chair and let my legs dangle over the arm.

"The Montgomery parties are *legendary*," she says.

I cock my head to the side. "So, my son shouldn't attend."

"Correct. But don't you dare tell him I told you that."

"*Great.* We'll fight about this tonight." I sigh, wishing for a split second that Jack were around to help with this stuff. "If I had the time back that I spent arguing—or 'negotiating,' as they like to call it—with my children, I could be a lot more productive."

"Speaking of negotiations, did you tell them you aren't going to Story Brook this year?"

I groan.

My stomach tightens as I replay the conversation with the kids a couple of days ago about our annual trip to Story Brook. The disappointment etched on their faces. The unbelievability of the levity in my voice as I explained that their dad's shop and my scrapbooking business were both exceedingly busy, and we wouldn't be able to go to the cabin this summer.

It was better than telling them that Jack and I had had a fight, ending with us agreeing not to go. *How could we ever spend two weeks in a small cabin without killing each other?* These days, we barely last five hours. I refuse to put us through that.

"They took it fairly well," I say. "Better than I expected. They were disappointed and initially had a lot of big emotions about it, but Michael calmed Maddie down, and . . . it was okay. They understood."

Somehow.

"They're growing up," she says. "They can't be oblivious to what's going on with you guys. I know you try to hide it, but you're a terrible liar."

"I am a terrible liar, and they are growing up. But I'm not sure they aren't in the dark. I mean, Jack's never here, and when he is, he's doing his thing and I'm doing mine. We aren't even passing ships in the night. We're more like trains operating on different continents."

My eyes close briefly as I fight off a wave of sickness.

I hate that this is what we've become—that the only way we're happy is when we're apart.

"So, are you just going to keep living like this?" she asks, brows pulled together.

"I don't think Jack gives a shit if we're married or not. Hell, he sleeps in his office at the shop half the week. The other half, he sleeps in front of the TV or in the guest room." I shrug. "The kids are the only reason I stay with him. Mom guilt is a real thing."

"It's a stupid thing."

"You'll understand when you have kids someday."

She gives me a look. "Why should you feel guilty?"

"It's like . . . how can I put my happiness over theirs? Doesn't that make me a bad mom? Can't I just wait until they're out of high school?"

"No, you can't. What are you teaching them? You're telling them it's okay to be unhappy? Would you want either of them sacrificing their happiness for someone else?"

"No."

"*Exactly.* So stop with that guilt nonsense." She pauses until she's satisfied that her words have had time to sink in. Then she continues. "How did Jack's dad take the news of you not going to Story Brook?"

"Also, fairly well, from what Jack told me." I shrug. "Harvey hasn't been feeling the greatest, so he said he was good with staying home." My heart sinks. "I hate disappointing him, though. I love that old fart."

Billie's smile is lopsided.

My spirit wobbles too.

Harvey Reed and I have grown close in the twenty years that I've been married to his son. He says I remind him of his Myra—a woman I never had the opportunity to know. She's where Jack gets his love of fruit and beef jerky and his predisposition to wake up looking gorgeous, if Harvey is to be believed. What did Jack inherit from his father? His ability to compartmentalize too well, if I'm to be believed.

"Does Harvey know you're thinking about divorce?" Billie asks quietly.

Hearing her say "divorce" causes my heart to stutter.

"No," I say, taking a deep breath. "Harvey doesn't know anything is wrong at all. We've been careful to hide it. I think the kids instinctively know not to share anything with him, if they *are* suspicious that something's amiss between me and Jack."

"Harvey will probably take your side."

I laugh. She's right. He probably would.

"Forget the kid at the grocery," I say. "If I'm getting a boy toy, I'm getting one like Harvey."

"Old?"

"*No.* Someone that likes to be home, eat cherry pie, and adores me."

"Maybe that's where I'm going wrong," she says. "I've been looking for abs, money, and no mommy issues."

"Yeah, you need to refocus. Abs are great, but they're no good if you never get to see them."

"Fair." She laughs. "Okay, besides age, dessert, and adoration, what else would Lauren's perfect man be like?"

My lips are parting to respond when the hair on the back of my neck stands up. Billie smirks and stares over my shoulder.

I hold my breath as a voice rings out behind me.

"Oh, I can't wait to hear this."

Great.

CHAPTER TWO

LAUREN

Jack.

His Tom Ford cologne mixes with the distinct scent of his sweat. It floats through the room with a confidence that used to be a huge turn-on. Now it's annoying.

I used to joke with him—years ago, when we had fun sex and not get-it-over-with sex—that all he had to do was work out for a few minutes or mow the lawn. The scent of his body was the match to my libido's fuse.

He squeezes the back of the chair, causing his knuckles to graze my shoulder blades.

"What are you doing here?" I ask, still facing Billie. "Eavesdropping is a nasty habit."

"It's a pleasure to see you, too, Lo."

I roll my eyes and turn to face him. His brown eyes deepen as he holds my gaze. Despite my frustration—*my lord, he's handsome.*

Unlike me, he's unbothered by our unofficial separation—because that's what our life really is. We're both here for the kids and maybe convenience, but this isn't a marriage and hasn't been for a long time.

Jack's hair tapers down the sides, and the back blends into the skin at his nape. It's brushed up with a slight part, as if he woke up and ran his fingers through it. *Has he seen a barber?*

He leans forward, his gray T-shirt darkened by his perspiration, and smiles.

"I didn't say it was a pleasure to see you," I say, leaning away from him for good measure. "You can't just sneak in my office like that."

He winks. "I just did."

Smart-ass.

"I'm meeting the kids here," he says, lifting a brow. "I assume you've heard about the party Michael wants to go to."

"I'm trying to figure a way around that without a fight."

"I took care of it."

Really? "How?"

"Asked him if he wants to go to Hocking Hills for a couple of days. I'd already planned to be gone from the shop for two weeks when you decided we weren't going to Story Brook."

I glare at him. *That's not what happened.*

He holds my gaze but doesn't miss a beat. "So I figured I'd kill two birds with one stone. Spend some time with the kids and keep Michael out of trouble."

"Is there a reason you had to personally tell me that? Texts were suddenly inefficient?" I ask.

His forearms flex as he grips the back of my chair even harder. "No. Not really."

Billie hops off my desk. The movement causes me to twist around to look at her and catch her wide, shit-eating grin.

What's that all about?

"Hey, Jack," she says, her voice entirely too sweet.

"Hey, Bills."

"How are ya?" she asks.

He shrugs, looking confused. "Fine. Shitty. Great. Whatever. *Why?*"

She hums. "You're all of those adjectives but not . . . 'suspicious'?"

Slowly, the confusion melts from Jack's face, and a deep smirk graces his lips.

"Will someone tell me what's going on?" I ask, my heartbeat picking up.

Neither of them looks at me. They just stare at each other in amusement.

"Hello?" I say, waving a hand in the air.

"Tell her," Billie says, nodding toward me. "Stop lying to Lauren and tell her why you came inside."

"I just wanted to say hello."

Billie bursts into a fit of laughter. *"You lie."*

Jack tilts his head and looks at me through his dark, thick lashes.

"You know that would never happen, right?" Billie asks.

"Yes. I do. So I figured I would prove it so I'm not lying on the couch in my office tonight, wondering."

What? "Can someone explain?"

"Fine. I'll tell her," Billie says. "Your husband saw my new car in the driveway and didn't recognize it. He wanted to see who was here. Didn't ya, Jack?"

Oh. Satisfaction at Jack's reaction, *and the fact that he was jealous*, erases all traces of my irritation.

Cheating on my husband is out of the question; it's never crossed my mind. I don't necessarily want to be with someone else. I'd just rather be alone than half-alive.

"That's what I'm talking about," I say, teasing him. "You can't just walk in here. I could've been in the middle of something."

His eyes blaze. "That would've been great. I would've gotten here just in time to help you out of it."

"Stop it," I say, smacking the top of his hand. "You know I wouldn't do that."

Jack runs his tongue along his bottom lip. "You didn't answer her question."

"Whose?"

"Billie's."

My brows tug together. "What question?"

"What kind of guy would be your perfect man? What does Lauren Reed think is hot?" he asks, his gaze pinning me to my seat.

I'm going to kill Billie.

I'm not sure what kind of game Jack is playing. *What does it matter what I think is hot?* I have no clue why he's pushing the topic, but I do know I'm not going to sit here and let him think he's putting me on the spot or getting the best of me.

I go with the first thing that crosses my mind.

"A man standing at the sink, shirtless, doing dishes." I groan for effect, leaning my head back so the ends of my hair swish against his forearms. "That image stirs something inside me that I thought was dead."

He flexes his arms, effectively shooing me away from him. "You're pushing it, Lo."

"Oh, what do you care?" I ask, sitting up. "It's not like you're interested in what turns me on."

Jack's hand drags across the top of the chair, the side of his palm skimming the skin exposed around my tank top. "You'd love for that to be true, wouldn't you?"

"On that note, I'm going to go. Jack . . . be smart," Billie says. "I like you, big guy. It would pain me to have to help dig your grave. But have no doubt—I would. And I'd get away with it." She walks toward the door. "See, Lauren? It's only concerning when you don't need it."

Jack holds his hands up, palms out in defense, making Billie and me laugh. The sound catches me off guard. There hasn't been much laughter between the three of us in a long time.

"Be careful going home," I say.

"I will. Call me later." She backs toward the doorway, stepping over her pile of cardboard. "Bye, guys."

She waves and then disappears into the hallway.

The energy in the room shifts as soon as Jack and I are alone. It's hotter. *Thicker.* The humidity amps up another level, and my skin dots with perspiration.

Jack moves until he's a few feet away, putting some much-needed space between us. I can't quite read what he's thinking, but whatever it is, it causes his eyes to host a golden sparkle that makes my stomach knot.

"What are all of those boxes?" Jack asks, nodding to the mess.

"Scrapbooking supplies." I stand and begin to shove the remaining items into containers. "If you haven't heard, my business blew up over the last couple of months. I was on a huge morning cable show recently."

Jack takes a Coke out of the mini fridge next to my desk. "I heard something about that."

I lift a brow. *What the heck does that mean?* "You heard something about that?"

"Yeah," he says, his eyes finding mine. "I heard my wife was hot from every fucking person that came into the shop."

I hold his gaze, my cheeks warming. *"Oh."*

"What did you think was going to happen?" A grin flirts against his lips. "Beauty and brains always catch men's attention."

What?

My brain misfires as it tries to wrap itself around his statement, but he doesn't give me time to figure it out.

"The guys were showing me some of the comments on your social media posts," he says, the grin vanishing as quickly as it appeared. "Who are those fucking people?"

It's my turn to grin. "Customers. Maddie calls them my fans."

"Do you read those comments? Because some of those 'fans' need to take a step back."

"You think that's bad?" I ask, lifting a brow. "You should see my inbox. There are men, and a woman or two, that go into explicit detail about the things they'd like to do to me in my craft room—and not all of them are legal."

I don't know if it's possible to open a can with force, but the snap of the tab dominates the small room.

"Well, I hope it makes you happy," Jack says before taking a drink. He watches me over the rim of the soda. "God knows that's something I can't do anymore."

"Typing out a response on social media does take more effort than you're willing to give."

He narrows his eyes.

"Oh, don't get pissy," I say, rolling my eyes. "I've forgotten what your dick looks like. I'm not comparing them or anything, if that's what you're worried about."

"No, Lauren, that's *not* what I'm worried about."

I hum as if I don't care. And I don't. Not really.

"You need to ban those idiots," Jack says. "People are ridiculous. Who knows who might show up late one night with bad intentions? I want to go to sleep knowing that you and the kids are safe."

Damn it. I blow out a breath as my urge to argue with him—the survival mechanism I've developed over the last few years—wanes.

When he acts like this, I'm reminded of the man I fell in love with. The sweet guy who sat with me outside a bar while I hurled my guts up on my twenty-first birthday. The handsome man who got down on one knee in a rainstorm, because it had rained all weekend, to ask me to marry him at Story Brook Lake. The protector who swung me in a circle when he found out we were having our first child.

Why did things have to change?

Jack slips his T-shirt up and over his head. *Has he been going to the gym again?* "I talked to Dad this afternoon. I told him Michael and I might stop by on our way to Hocking Hills."

"How is he feeling?"

"His blood sugar was a mess. I was a minute from calling an ambulance when he said the number was back down." He squeezes his forehead. "He's more of a headache than the kids."

For you, maybe.

My irritation subsides as I take in the pain on Jack's face.

His biggest fear is that something will happen to Harvey, and he won't be there to help him. But his dad refuses to move out of the house he shared with Myra and is fiercely independent, so there's not much Jack can do. *And I hate that for him.*

Jack's gaze holds mine before he rips it away.

"Thank you for breaking the news to him about the cabin," I say, taking a deep breath to steady myself. "I didn't expect you to do that."

"I'm sure you didn't."

I pause and look at him. "What does that mean?"

He sets the Coke on my desk and then turns to me. His muscles shine in the light beaming in through the windows. *Good grief.* He leans forward, his eyes glued to mine.

My breath catches in my throat.

"Has it ever occurred to you that I'm not incapable?" he asks.

I force a swallow down my throat. "Incapable of what?"

He glares at me.

"Don't look at me like that," I say, instantly defensive—the moment stolen. "I don't know what you're talking about."

"You act like it surprises you that I'm capable of anything."

"Oh, I know you're capable. I just have low expectations."

"And that's a fucking problem, don't you think?"

I stand taller. "What? The fact that you're capable or the fact that I've given up hoping you will exercise that ability when it comes to me?"

He walks across the room and stands in front of me. The intensity of his gaze makes my knees wobble. I have no idea what he's going to say, nor do I understand why he's making a point to argue this now. *Isn't it moot?*

I search his eyes longer than I should—long enough for my heart to soften. Long enough to remember exactly why I avoid seeing him at all anymore. It just makes things harder. It pulls me back into a vicious circle of caring, then hurting, ending in disappointment.

"When are you and Michael leaving?" I ask.

His jaw pulses. He stares at me for another second, then two. Finally, he sighs and swipes his shirt and the can off my desk.

I exhale in relief.

"I'm going to grab a shower, and then we'll head out once he's back and packed," he says, sending a whoosh of his cologne my way.

"Make sure he tells me goodbye."

He looks at me over his shoulder. I can't quite read the look in his eyes, and that's probably for the best.

"And take his inhaler," I say.

"Of course."

And with that, he walks out of the room.

CHAPTER THREE

Jack

"Did you tell your mom goodbye?" I ask.

Maddie snaps her seat belt in place. "You're just dropping me off at my cheer party. I'll see her in two hours when she picks me up."

I level a look at my daughter.

"*Oh, right,*" she says with appropriate fourteen-year-old sarcasm. "Like she'd let us out the door without telling us goodbye. But here's the question, Daddy—did *you* tell her goodbye?"

She bats her mile-long lashes, a feature she got from her mother, my way. But there's a special brand of smugness to her this afternoon that I can't quite put my finger on.

I watch her warily. "*Yeah.* I did."

Before I can follow up on my response, Michael flings open the back door. He tosses a backpack in the cab before climbing into the middle and closing the door.

"I got all of our luggage and camping gear in the truck bed," he says. "And all of Maddie's stuff for cheer."

I glance in the rearview mirror. "You know we'll just be gone a few nights, right?"

"Yeah."

"That's a lot of crap," I say, switching my gaze to my son. "Are you sure you only got the stuff I told you to get out of the garage?"

Maddie waves a hand through the air. "I packed you some extra food and just . . . little things. You know, mosquito spray and peanut butter crackers. Can't let my boys get hungry."

Her boys? Can't let us get hungry? She's usually willing to let Michael starve.

I have no idea what that's about, but I'm not going to ask. Her mother has already exhausted me.

Lauren's coy grin. *"You can't just walk in here. I could've been in the middle of something."*

I grip the steering wheel so hard that my knuckles turn white.

I've never considered that Lauren might have an affair. She would never do that, but I'm well aware that she could have her pick of men. I'm not at home much these days, so seeing a strange car in the driveway had sent jealousy snaking down my spine.

"Where's Snaps?" Maddie asks, peeking into the back seat.

I blow out a breath. "He's still at the shop. Michael and I will pick him up on the way out of town."

"Cool. I left Mom the keys to my truck in case she needs to go anywhere," Michael says. *Whoa, did he use the entire bottle of body spray after his shower?* "So we don't have to worry about that."

"Why would she need your truck?" I turn on the engine and then roll down my window a crack to get some fresh air before we all choke to death. "She has a car."

"She probably won't. It's just in case, because her driver's-side front tire has a slow leak," Michael says. "I put some stop leak in it a while ago, and it seemed to help. But it's started going flat again."

It is? "Why doesn't she come by the shop and get a new one?"

"Why don't you take it to work one day and fix it while you're there?"

I lift a brow. "I've been a little busy." *And I didn't know it was flat until now.*

"Well, she's been kind of busy too."

"I'm aware. I saw her office."

Michael grips my headrest and pokes his head into the front. "Did you notice the new shelves? She's had me in there for the last week building crafting tables and shelving units. If that's what adulting looks like, I'm done. Seventeen forever, man."

I laugh at the look on his face—one of abject horror at the thought of manual labor for the rest of eternity.

The day Michael was born was one of the best days of my life. He wailed, wrinkling his nose, and screamed for all he was worth. I stood beside Lauren's bed, gobsmacked that this heroine had just birthed a nine-pound baby, while Michael protested at the top of his lungs. When they put him in my arms, I swear he screamed louder. But when I placed him on Lauren's chest? *Silence.*

He has had an affinity for his mother from that day forward. He's her fiercest protector, her biggest fan. I used to tell myself that he got that from me. But lately, I'm not so sure that's true, and that's hard to justify.

The last few weeks have been different with the kids now out of school. Michael has hung around the shop. Maddie and Elodie have walked up to get money to go to the movies or to get a milkshake. As the days have passed, I've found myself wanting to go home. I've thought about pulling out the grill and seeing if Lauren will make her potato salad. Or seeing if she wants to take a drive at sunset like we used to.

But I haven't done either thing.

If I go home, Lauren ignores me. If she's not ignoring me, she's making it clear she's annoyed. And she's not really to blame.

But here we are, and I don't know how to get us anywhere else. *Do I leave her happy and stay out of her way? Or do I press my luck and potentially make things worse?*

Michael slinks back into his seat. "I borrowed your drill. The battery is on the charger if you go looking for it."

"Why didn't you ask me for help?" I pull out of the driveway. "We could've worked together and done it in half the time."

"Correction: we could've done it together in a third of the time. I had no idea what I was doing. But you're never home and she needed it done, so I just figured it out."

Wow. Okay.

I glance quickly at him in the rearview mirror and then back at the road.

What else don't I know?

I make a right onto the highway toward Maddie's gym.

"Are you okay, Dad?" Maddie asks.

"Me? Yeah." I exhale harshly. "Just thinking about your mom. I'll never understand that woman."

"She's not hard to understand, you know," Maddie says, sliding her sunglasses down her face.

"I beg to differ."

Michael grips my headrest. "I wouldn't worry about her too much. Mom is pretty self-sufficient. It's not like she's sitting around waiting on someone to take care of her, you know?"

"Sit back," I say, shoulders tensing.

What the hell is happening?

There's a cloud of uncertainty swirling around. *Why do I feel like I've missed a conversation?*

"Where are you guys going camping, anyway?" Maddie asks.

"Hocking Hills," I say, thankful for the topic change. "But first, we're going to stop and see Pops. It'll only cost us a little time to circle up there on our way."

Michael shoves his knee into the back of my seat. "Can we get some food on the way?"

"You seriously just ate," Maddie says. "I saw you down three Lunchables."

"I'm a growing boy."

I grin. "What are you hungry for?"

27

"You know what *I'm* hungry for?" Maddie asks. "A chili dog from Schmidt's with cheese and onions. *Yum.*"

"Schmidt's in Story Brook?" I ask.

Her smile is bright. "Yup. Doesn't that sound good?" She smacks her lips together to drive home the point.

"I'll take that, Dad," Michael chimes in from behind. "Two of them—no, three."

I shake my head, wondering what's gotten into the kids. They know we aren't going to the cabin this year.

But of course, they want to.

Hell, I do too.

It still hasn't soaked in that we won't be there. I've gone to Story Brook every summer, give or take a couple, my whole life. Lauren and I went the year before I proposed and have gone each June since Dad gave us the cabin next to his as a wedding gift.

But Lauren was quick to dismiss our tradition this year—too quick, really. I thought she'd change her mind. She even had some of her supplies packed and in the garage when she called the trip off.

"I was thinking more like a place to eat that's not three hours away," I say.

"Maybe Pops wants to go get one," Maddie says, using the sweet voice she's learned from her mother. *One I haven't heard from Lauren in a long time.* "I bet he would love to go."

"I bet he would too. But things are just . . . different this year," I say, irritated. "He probably has other plans by now and wouldn't go even if I asked him to."

Maddie giggles. "He would if *I* asked him to."

"He's not gonna change his mind for you. What do you think— that you have him wrapped around your little finger or something?" I joke.

Maddie and Michael burst out laughing.

"You know, Dad, I bet it killed Pops that we're not going. He's gone every year for, like, eighty years." Maddie twists around in her seat as far as the seat belt will let her. Her eyes sparkle. "But I have an idea, and I think you'll love it."

I look at her out of the corner of my eye. "I know just by the sound of your voice that I won't."

She punches me in the arm. I pretend that it hurts.

"Ignore her," Michael says. "Just follow me."

"Follow *you*?" I ask. "You two are up to something *together*?"

"We weren't, but I think we're on the same page now," Michael says.

Maddie nods. "I think so too. It's brother-sister intuitiveness."

"Let's set the stage," Michael says. "Campfires at dusk. Can you smell the burning oak wood? The sun on your face on the beach. Watching the girls dive into the water in bikinis." He pauses. "I mean, you can do that now since you and Mom are getting divorced."

My gaze whips to him in the rearview. My blood runs cold. *"What did you say?"*

Maddie's face falls. She slumps against her seat and sighs. "We know."

My stomach drops. A bitter, vile taste coats my tongue.

"We're not ignorant," Michael says, his voice void of the playfulness of a moment ago. "We're just surprised it didn't happen before now."

"I . . ." *The fuck?* I clear my throat, unsure what to say. "We haven't filed for divorce. Why would you say that?"

"I saw the appointment written on the business card on Mom's desk. So it makes sense you guys canceled the trip," Michael says.

What? An appointment? For what?

Lauren scheduled an appointment with an attorney?

My mind races, my cheeks blazing. Surely she didn't do that. *Why would she do that?*

The weight of the kids' gazes is on me, waiting for a response. I want to heave.

Divorce? What the fuck?

My brain short-circuits, trying to process every interaction I've had with my wife to determine if there's any truth to Michael's suspicion.

Lauren and I talk every day. We haven't really fought in ages.

A chill races through me.

When did Lauren stop calling me each night?

A flurry of goose bumps breaks out across my skin, and I think I might be sick.

My palms sweat, and I wipe them on my thighs.

Should I go back to her? Call her? Text her?

But what if I bring it up, and Michael's gotten it all wrong?

What if I bring it up and she confirms it?

I heave a breath.

"Your mother and I are *not* getting divorced," I say, gripping the steering wheel again.

"I hope you're right," Maddie says.

"I'm sure there's an explanation," I say, my throat dry.

Michael sighs. "Probably. But when you look at it from our side, Mom doesn't bring you dinner to the shop anymore. You haven't really said much about her scrapbooking stuff, and that's honestly pretty weird."

"And," Maddie says, chiming in, "you two are never on the same page. If we wanted to pull a fast one on you guys, we could. But we wouldn't. I'm just saying we could."

I glance at her out of the corner of my eye again.

"Something is going on if we aren't going to the cabin," Michael says.

Shit. My stomach wobbles. *I think he's right.*

"This is between the two of us," I say.

"Yeah, like it won't affect us at all," Maddie scoffs beside me. "This isn't just between the two of you. It's between the four of us."

"I told you we aren't getting divorced, Mads."

"Okay, let's regroup, Maddie," my son says, taking control. "Dad says they aren't getting divorced. He would know. So let's focus on getting that chili dog."

Maddie stares at me for a long moment and then switches her attention to Michael. "I can't go. I have a cheer party, remember? But you guys should get Pops and go."

I slow the truck and turn on my signal. *How did I miss this?*

"So, will you?" Maddie asks, her voice filled with hope. *"Please?"*

I flip down my visor and sigh.

Story Brook is my favorite place on earth. There's magic there, a spot for relaxing and appreciating life. I've always loved sharing it with my family.

But my family includes Lauren. I can't go without her. But if I ask her to go after she's said no, she'll just accuse me of not hearing her. Again.

My stomach twists so hard I groan.

"I mean, you can do that now since you and Mom are getting divorced. We're not ignorant. We're just surprised it didn't happen before now."

Lauren set up an appointment with a divorce attorney. What the hell?

"You've already taken time off of work. And Pops would love it," Maddie says, refusing to give up. "It would be good for him. *He needs this trip, Dad.* You know it."

Damn it.

She's right—Dad does need this trip. He's forever regaling anyone who will listen with tales of trekking through the woods with the kids, looking for wild berries. He talks about the time that Lauren left food on a picnic table, and he and Michael were sure they saw a bear. The stories of sitting around the campfire while lightning bugs flicker around the forest are a part of our family lore.

He lives for these two weeks every summer.

I probably broke his fucking heart by feeding him two lies as an excuse, and that's nothing compared to what he's going to do when he learns Lauren and I are having problems. He loves her maybe more than he loves me.

"There's no good reason to go fishing and not go to Story Brook Lake. You can fish there," Maddie says. "You already have a place to stay with running water. Snaps will have so much fun running around the yard. It covers all the bases."

Her freckles shine just like her mom's. "Why do you care? You're staying with your mom this weekend anyway."

"You'll understand when you get there," she says.

"What's that supposed to mean?"

"I'm just being optimistic, Dad. I'm manifesting. There's power in manifestation."

"Who have you been hanging around with?" I ask.

"Daniel," Michael says, gagging.

I lift a brow at the mention of my daughter's so-called boyfriend. "So, Daniel is still a thing?"

"Daniel is the love of my life," Maddie says, dreamily.

"What do you know about love? *You're fourteen,*" I say.

She crosses her arms over her chest. "I don't think age has anything to do with it."

I hum, not wanting to delve into this topic with my daughter. I have my own problems to worry about.

"You can't control who or when you fall in love," she says, a knowing twinkle in her little eyes. "I could say I don't love him. I could pretend. But that wouldn't change anything, would it? Because once love is there, it's always there."

Oh, I see. I chuckle, the sound ending on a near growl. "Can we not do this?"

"Do what?" Maddie asks innocently.

"You know what I'm talking about, Mads."

She reaches across the console and flips on the radio. Once the music is on, I let out a haggard breath.

My neck is pinched. The spot just behind my eyes is beginning to throb. My jaw pulses.

Lauren thinks she's filing for divorce?

I scrub a hand down my face.

That's not happening.

The enormity of the situation falls heavily on my shoulders, and I struggle to make sense of what to do now. If there were signs—and apparently there were—I missed them. But I thought all this was what she wanted. She was happier with me not home. She understood that I have to put in the hours to keep the shop running and our bills paid.

Didn't she?

My insides rage with conflicting memories and emotions at odds with one another. The one thing—the only thing—that I know for certain is that I'm not losing my wife.

I blow out a breath.

I need time. I need a few days to think.

"Kids," I say, watching the road.

"Yeah?" Michael says.

I turn to Maddie. "We'll bring you a chili dog when we come home."

My daughter wraps her arms around my neck, nearly making me crash the truck into a ditch.

"This is a great decision, Daddy. You're going to be so happy you did this." Maddie presses a hard kiss on my cheek. "Thank you."

With a shake of my head and a small smile that doesn't quite reach my eyes, I resign myself to reality.

At least being away will give me a few days to get my head sorted . . . and figure out where things went wrong.

And how to save my marriage.

"Put your seat belt back on, Mads," I say.

Looks like I need to buckle up too.

CHAPTER FOUR

LAUREN

I can't hear you, Mads. Stop moving the phone around," I say, yawning.
"Sorry. Is that better?"

"Yes." I glance at the clock. "Why are you up so early?"

She laughs. "It's nine o'clock, Mother. It's not early."

"Speak for yourself. I didn't get to sleep until four this morning."

"Sucks for you. Anyway, can you come and get me in an hour or so?"

What?

I climb out of bed and rub my eyes. The house was too quiet last
night to sleep. With Michael gone with Jack, and Maddie texting halfway through the party that she was going home with Elodie, the silence
was loud. Too loud. I finally got up at midnight and worked until after
three. Then I lay in bed for another hour before I could doze off.

My brain was active, bouncing back and forth between the past
and present. It's probably because Jack was home during daylight hours
yesterday. Because for a moment with Billie, things had felt almost
normal—or what normal used to be, anyway.

Nostalgia was a bitch in the lonely, dark hours of the night, and
it took everything in me to fight it. To not drown in its depths. To
remember that I'd pulled myself out of that state of mind for a reason.

"Mom?" Maddie asks, shaking me out of my reverie.

"An hour? I just got up—literally. I haven't even had coffee yet."

She sighs like only a teenager can. "I need to get home."

I slip on a pair of Jack's shorts under his T-shirt that I sleep in and make my way down the hall.

"What do you have to do that's so pressing?" I ask, pausing to adjust the thermostat. *It's freezing in here. Who turned the air-conditioning so high?* "You'll just get home and complain about being bored."

"No, I won't. I promise. There's a bunch of stuff I want to do today."

Early-morning sunlight filters through the curtains and casts a pretty glow over the kitchen. It's been my favorite room of the house since the moment I walked in with the real estate agent almost twenty years ago. I could envision myself standing at the sink, laughing with Jack. It was easy to imagine this space filled with warmth and traditions—and love.

I get a cup of coffee brewing and find my hazelnut creamer behind the juice.

"Let me get some coffee in me and jump in the shower," I say. "I have glitter stuck to my palms from last night."

"So, an hour? An hour and a half?"

I blow out a breath. "I'll be there by eleven."

"Perfect. Love you, Mama."

"Love you, Mads. Bye."

"Bye."

The line goes dead.

I shake my head, making quick work of my caffeine in a cup. Then I take a seat at the table. I sip my coffee and watch the traffic out the window.

The stress I've carried on my shoulders since Jack left yesterday begins to subside.

It's funny how I used to not get a second to breathe. I would've paid someone for ten minutes to take a shower alone. Now, the moments I do get to myself are tricky. They're an echo chamber of memories—and that's not always a good thing.

"No, Lauren, that's not *what I'm worried about."*

"What does that mean, Jack?" I ask aloud. "What *are* you worried about?"

I take another sip of my coffee.

I can't help but wonder sometimes what might've happened if I hadn't made the conscious decision to disconnect from Jack. I had to—I know I did. I had to start living a life instead of playing a role in his. But I can't deny that by backing away from trying to mold our relationship into what I wanted, I probably put the final nail in the coffin.

It's a double-edged sword. If I had kept putting my life—everything from cleaning the gutters, to my health, to finding my personal joy—on the back burner until Jack was ready, maybe my marriage would be on better terms. At least, it's possible I could've put my head in the sand and pretended to be happy. Obliviousness can be bliss. But while that might've infused my relationship with Jack with a shot of energy, it would've drained me.

And that's the decision I had to make—us or me.

Is it wrong to pick me too?

More fire. More passion. More time spent together besides meeting at a sports event and grabbing fast food on our way home—if he doesn't have to go back to the shop.

Is that so terrible?

My phone rings again, making me jump.

Harvey? Jack's dad's name flashes on the screen.

My stomach sinks as I pick it up.

"Hey," I say, my brows furrowed. "What's going on, Harvey?"

"Hey, sugarplum. How are you doing today?" His voice is crackly, betraying his attempts at hiding his penchant for cigars. "You doing okay over there?"

"I'm good. Getting my day started."

"You're just now getting started? It's halfway through the morning."

I laugh. "I don't need your negativity, sir."

He laughs too. "I haven't heard from ya in a while, and I was startin' to get worried. Afraid you're getting too big-time for me. I saw you on the television."

"You did?"

"Yeah, and I'm damn proud of ya, Lauren."

I swallow a lump in my throat.

My father-in-law has no way of knowing just how badly I need to hear those words. Then again, maybe I didn't, either, because I didn't plan on blinking back tears already today.

"I got other things I want to talk to ya about, though," he says.

"Sure. What's that?"

Harvey coughs, the sound rough and raw.

"Are you okay?" I ask him.

"That's why I'm callin' ya. I wanted to know if you could do me a favor."

I lean against the counter and sigh.

Harvey Reed doesn't ask me for much. He doesn't ask anyone for much. Truth be told, he doesn't accept much of anything, whether he asks for it or not. So if he's calling for a favor, it must be important.

"Sure," I say. "What's up?"

"Well, I messed up pretty good, and I'm in a bind."

"What did you do this time?" I ask, smiling. "You didn't get into a fight over college football with old man Travers at the diner again, did you? I'm not calling down there and convincing them to let you back a second time. I warned you."

He chuckles. "No. No. Nothing like that."

"And you didn't accidentally mow just a hair over the property line just to annoy your neighbor, right?"

"Nah, I just blew the cuttings into his yard, the old prick."

"You're no spring chicken, Harv," I laugh.

"You aren't, either, sugarplum."

I gasp. "That's rude."

"That's the damn truth, and you know it."

Still laughing, I take my mug back to the coffeepot and refill it. "So, what do you need? Want me to come over tonight and watch *Jeopardy!* With you? I'll bring a meat-and-cheese tray," I say, taunting him with his favorite snack.

"It's called a 'char-cute-rie' board these days. Get it together."

My laughter trails off. "Sorry. I'm not as hip as you."

"Yeah, yeah, yeah. Anyway, I need you to please go by my house and grab my insulin and bring it to me."

I pour half the bottle of creamer into the mug. *Fuck it.* "Where are you? The diner?"

"No . . ." The pause lingers, going on too long for it not to intentionally be a cliff-hanger. Then: "I'm at Story Brook."

I stare straight ahead. *Is he kidding me?*

"I decided to come up here this morning and get some fresh air. Hell, we own these cabins and haven't been up here since Christmas. Kinda stupid to let them go unused, if you ask me," he says. "Maybe do a little fishin'. Might see if Mrs. Shaw is around and do a little face-sucking."

My head shakes back and forth as I grin. "You better hope she's on the pill."

His laughter is fast and loud—so loud that I have to pull the phone away from my face. It's infectious. I find myself laughing too.

"She's about as old as I am," he says, as if I don't already know. "I reckon she lost the ability to have kids about thirty years ago."

"You never know."

"I do have high testosterone. I bet I still have some swimmers."

"Harvey, *stop it,*" I say, my tone light with humor.

"Fine. But will ya bring it to me or not? I don't want to have to ask that husband of yours, because he'll give me shit about being here in the first place. He forgets that I managed to raise him and not get him killed. So I don't know why in the hell he thinks I can't be trusted alone at Story Brook, but that's what's in his head."

"He's probably worried you'll knock up Mrs. Shaw too."

Harvey chuckles.

"I suppose I'll bring it," I say, sipping my drink. "I mean, it's three hours there and three hours back. It's not like I have anything to do today."

"Didn't figure you did. And if you did, it doesn't hold a candle to seeing this old face."

"That's true."

He sighs. "Can you not tell Jack about this? Or those kids of yours. I hate to tell ya, but they're little snitches. I lit a cigar a few weeks ago, and they told their dad within ten minutes of pulling out of the driveway."

"You don't need to be smoking."

"Honey, that's the least of my worries. I had a pound of bacon for breakfast. Now, will you stop at the store and bring some stuff for a char-cute-rie?" He says the word in his fanciest accent. "I have some beer up here. We'll have a little picnic-y."

"No beer."

"You're no fun."

"I'll have to tell Maddie, because I'll have to bring her. Jack and Michael went fishing this weekend."

Harvey coughs again. "Yeah, Jack said something about that. Why didn't Miss Maddie Moo tag along?"

"She had cheer, but I'm pretty sure she wouldn't have gone with just the two of them anyway."

"Well, bring that little darlin' with you. It'll be good to see her too."

I sigh. "We'll see you at . . ." I glance at the clock on the stove. "I don't know. Around three o'clock? Maybe four?"

"Sounds wonderful. Thanks, sweetheart."

"You owe me."

"I always do. Oh—one more thing?"

I grin. "What?"

"Maybe bring me a few groceries? I figure I might stay up here awhile, and I got nothin' to eat."

"You better be glad I love you."

"Don't I know it."

"Bye, Harv."

"Bye, kiddo."

I slide the phone across the counter and take another sip.

Why can't Jack be as easy to deal with as his father?

CHAPTER FIVE

LAUREN

I'm going to be out of service in a second."

"Yet another reason why this trip is wholly ridiculous," Billie says, the words punctuated through the phone with a deep sigh. "I know you love Harvey and all, but this is a little above and beyond."

Bright afternoon sunlight blazes through the windshield. The warmth is welcome. The strain on my sleep-deprived eyes, not so much. I flip down the visor and turn right onto a pothole-filled gravel road leading toward the cabin.

"One day, you'll understand," I say.

"Maybe."

I glance over to the passenger's seat and smile at my daughter.

Maddie's head bops back and forth, her long hair swishing against the leather seatback. Her lashes are as long as her brother's and flutter happily to the beat of whatever is playing through her AirPods.

"I still can't understand why you couldn't have Jack do it. It's his dad," Billie says.

Because besides Jack and the kids, Harvey is the only family I have, and I'm having a hard time thinking about letting that go.

"Maddie was thrilled to get to come to the cabin—even if it's for one night."

"I bet Michael will be pissed he missed it—even for one night," she says.

I take a deep breath. "He'll understand. He's with Jack. I bet they're up to their eyeballs in fish and firewood."

The words sound a whole hell of a lot breezier than they feel.

Despite my best effort to brace myself, coming to the cabin without Jack and Michael hurts my heart. I keep growing excited for all the things we'll do—the beach days, bonfires, and game nights around the kitchen table. The realization that those things aren't going to happen, ever again, is sharper than I anticipated.

A part of me wishes I'd ignored it, that I'd sucked it up and gone through with our plans. But I know why I didn't. It was to protect the kids from watching their parents melt down after a day or two. That's not one of the final memories of our family together that I want them to have, let alone the memory of our last summer at Story Brook.

"So, are we talking about Jack or not?" she asks. "Not sure if that was an opening and you wanted to go there, or you were just stating facts."

I chuckle.

Billie has been my best friend for twenty years—the same amount of time that I've known Jack. I met them on the same night, my twenty-first birthday, in a Cincinnati dive bar. Billie held my hair while I spewed tequila into a bush and cried. I was certain that I had alcohol poisoning because I'd prepared for my first night of drinking by spending too much time on medical websites. *One can never be too careful.* She cleaned me up and sat me down . . . next to the most attractive man I'd ever seen—drunk or not.

Jack didn't gag at my vomit breath or laugh at my mascara-streaked cheeks. Instead, he told his friends to go on without him and handed me bottles of water while promising that I wasn't going to die. He did it all with a smile that set my insides on fire a whole lot more than the tequila had.

I'm pretty sure that Billie and I both fell in love with Jack that night. *We both thought he was perfect for me.*

"Considering my current company, I was just stating facts," I say, glancing at my daughter again.

"Shit. Yeah, yeah. I forgot you were with Maddie."

"Exactly," I say, turning onto the long, winding road toward the cabins. "I'm losing you, Bills. I'll call you when I'm back."

"Have fun. Text me updates and let me know you haven't perished in the wilderness."

"Wait! What do you have going on? You started to tell me yesterday before I mentioned the child that asked for my number. I don't want this conversation to be all about me."

She snorts. "Your life is infinitely more interesting than mine these days."

"Share."

"Well, I have a presentation Monday on social media and its effect on marketing to a bunch of men in suits that probably don't even care because God knows they won't listen. We'll have the same problems and discussions next month and the month after that and the month after that."

I smile. "Good luck. I know you'll be so interesting that they won't be able to do anything but listen to you."

"Right."

My grin grows. "Also, wear a low-cut top. That might help too."

"I want them listening, not staring."

"Oh, they'll be staring anyway. You're a hottie."

"Thanks, babe."

"You're welcome. Now, I gotta go. Bye, Billie."

"Bye."

The call disconnects from the car. Billie's voice is replaced by a hit from the nineties blasting a bit too loud. I toggle the switch on my steering wheel to lower the sound.

The foliage grows darker and thicker as we make our way up the hill. Pathways that Jack and I used to take the kids on when they were little are nearly overgrown. I only know they're there from memory.

My heart tugs as I sort through the moments stored away in my head. Michael attempting to ride his bike down the trails at thirteen years old, only to wreck into a tree and separate his shoulder. Maddie stopping every five feet to pick flowers, making our hikes infinitely longer.

Jack and I stealing weekends here during college and getting snowed in over Christmas break.

I smile at the memory.

"Hey," I say, reaching over and shaking Maddie's leg.

She pops out an AirPod. "Yeah?"

"Talk to me. You're the one that was jazzed to come up here."

"Can't you see I'm busy?" She rolls her eyes with the dramatics of a daytime actress. "Kidding. Daniel made me a playlist. He said every song reminds him of me."

It's my turn to roll my eyes. "He did, did he?"

"*He did.* Isn't it *so* romantic?"

"There's nothing romantic about a fourteen-year-old boy."

"Because you don't remember what it's like to be a fourteen-year-old girl."

I lift a brow. "Do we need to talk about the birds and bees again?"

"I don't know. *Do you want to ruin this trip?*" She waits a beat before sighing happily and swaying to a song that I can't hear. "I love music. It speaks to my soul."

"Good for you."

"Can I ask you something? What was your and Dad's song?"

Oh, Maddie. Please don't.

"I bet it was super romantic, wasn't it? You're the kind of mom that probably had cheesy lyrics about loving someone forever." Her eyes flicker with mischief. "I'm right, aren't I?"

I grin. "It was actually 'Livin' on a Prayer,' by Bon Jovi, Miss Smarty Pants."

She makes a face and plays on her phone. She stares at me as I drive around a fallen tree branch.

"This explains a lot," she says, scoffing.

"What's that supposed to mean?"

"Mother, this song isn't a love song."

"Child, it's one of the greatest songs ever recorded."

"Okay." She falls back in her seat. "Does it make you sad to think about you and Dad and the happy days?"

The hope in her voice stabs me in the heart. That she knows these days aren't happy is salt in the wound.

I regrip the steering wheel. "Who says me and Daddy aren't happy?"

"Oh, I don't know. Body language. That you're never together. That you bailed on our family trip this year."

Shit.

"I can't imagine not being happy with Daniel. Especially after decades, like you and Dad. I mean, how do you just stop holding his hand or hearing about his afternoon? Isn't that sad?"

"I'm sure Daniel's afternoons are *absolutely riveting.*"

She lifts a brow in her boyfriend's defense. "I'm sure they're more riveting than yours, since you sit home alone and make scrapbooks for strangers."

"Those scrapbooks are going to pay for your college tuition."

"If you say so."

My lips part to volley back—to tell her to mind her business. To remind her that I'm the one giving up my *riveting life* so she can have hers. But I stop before I plant any ideas in her head about Jack.

He might not be a dream husband, but he loves his kids. That's my problem, not hers.

"Did your brother ever text you back before we left the house?" I ask instead. "Make sure he knows we set the alarm, in case he goes back for anything. I don't need the police rolling up and us not being able to be reached."

Maddie runs a hand through the air. "Oh yeah. He said they're having a great time. The truck is loaded to the roof with . . . equipment. You know, tents and coolers and stuff."

I give her a look. *Why is she acting so weird?*

"Mads—"

"Look, Mom!"

I pull my attention back to the road—more specifically to the Firefly Cabin. Even more specifically, to the silver pickup truck backed up to the front door.

What in the actual hell . . .

My jaw drops as two male bodies that I recognize like the back of my hand exit the cabin.

My head whips to my daughter. Her eyes sparkle.

"Don't be mad," she says, holding a finger in the air between us.

"Madeline Lauren Reed, what the—"

"*Hey!* You're here!" she shouts.

The door slams shut as my daughter jogs across the lawn toward her brother . . . *and her father.*

Michael waves at Maddie, happier to see his sister than he's ever been. He also looks like he's been expecting us.

Jack, on the other hand, does not.

My husband stands on the other side of his truck, his forearms resting along the bed. His bare shoulders glimmer under a coat of sweat. And as our son and daughter reach into the back seat of the truck and haul out what appears to be the usual cabin supplies—including my designated Story Brook bag—Jack's gaze settles on me.

I stare at him through the shade from the giant oak tree separating our cabin from Harvey's. Everything seems to pause as soon as our eyes meet, as if the world is waiting to see if we will blow up on each other or act like adults.

I can't do either at the moment. My heart cracks down the center. *He came without me.*

Maddie walks around the truck, saying something to Jack that grabs his attention. He bends down as she wraps her arms around his neck like she has every day since she could move her arms. He squeezes her back just like he has every day since the warm May evening she was born.

I close my eyes. I imagine the heat of his breath, the sturdiness of his body—the comfort in his presence.

The safety . . . the permanence of us.

And I wish for one second that those things still mattered. That they still were worth all the squabbles of life.

Then I look back up, and the kids are gone. It's just Jack watching me, waiting on me to fire the first shot.

Fuck my life.

CHAPTER SIX

LAUREN

*H*ere goes nothing.

I fling open the car door, the motion a touch more theatrical than I intend. Pine-scented air drifts from the trees and mixes with the earthiness that I've loved about Story Brook since the first time I came here two decades ago. But instead of pausing, extending my arms, and making a circle while relishing the start of our favorite time of the year, I march across the lawn toward Jack.

He doesn't move. His back is against the lowered tailgate, stone-cut biceps crossed over his hard chest, like I've disturbed him on purpose.

Blood pumps through my veins. I cling to the adrenaline spiking through my system. Being angry is easier to manage than being sad.

But it stings. *Oh, how it stings.*

"What are you doing?" I ask, stopping a solid ten feet away from him.

"What does it look like I'm doing?"

I exhale, the sound ragged and rough. "Why are you here?"

His eyes narrow and slowly, *oh so slowly*, he turns toward the truck.

"Jack?" I ask, irritated.

"What do you want, Lauren?"

My name sounds so generic coming out of his mouth. *Lauren. Lauren*, like I'm an aggravating mechanic at the shop. Not Lauren like the mother of his children—the woman who's spent her life building something special with him. The woman who has given every moment, every ounce of energy, every speck of life in her to make *his life* happier.

My teeth grind together at the perceived insult. "I thought you were taking Michael camping?"

"And I thought you were doing something with Maddie?"

"So, you and Michael just come up here without her? I mean, I get you didn't want me to come. But you could've at least brought your daughter."

He jerks a plastic storage bin out of the truck and sets it on the ground with more force than is necessary. "That's strange. It looks to me like you were bringing your daughter up here without your son."

Jack wipes his forehead with the back of his hand.

"Let me clarify," I say, emotions rising so high inside my body that I shake. "Your father asked me to bring his insulin. I wasn't bringing Maddie up here without . . ." I furrow my brow. "Wait a minute. Is Harvey even here?"

Jack doesn't blink. "Yeah. He's at his cabin."

"I'm so confused. Did you come together?"

"We were going to come up last night, but by the time we got to Dad's and decided to do this, it started getting late. We slept there and then got up today, had some breakfast, and then came the rest of the way."

Oh.

I wipe a sweaty palm down the side of my maxi dress. My heart beats faster as Jack and I stare at each other, waiting for the other to flinch. To speak.

To do something.

A timeline materializes. *Jack and Michael go to Harvey's. Maddie is desperate to come home. Michael doesn't text this morning. Harvey suddenly needs insulin.*

I don't know whether to laugh or cry.

Finally, Jack sighs. "Lo, I think we've been set up."

Of course we have. My sigh is long and hasty. "I'm going to kill your kids."

"Why are they my kids all of a sudden?" He smiles. "They're only mine when you're mad at them."

"Because you're the most relatable thing I can think of when I'm mad at them."

I mean it as a joke. Any other time, Jack would've laughed. But now? He opens his mouth and then shuts it.

So I move on. "Your dad called me and said he needed his insulin. He explicitly asked me not to tell you or the kids."

"Well, *your kids,* because they remind me of you when they're being irritating"—he pauses to smile again, to soften any perceived blow—"begged me yesterday to reconsider. Maddie even called Pops from the truck before I dropped her off at the gym. She didn't mention it to you?"

"Nope. Not a word."

He tries to hide his amusement. "Those little monkeys."

"What are they thinking?" I ask. "How did they put this all together?"

"If I was betting, this started with Maddie and my dad. Michael was probably all too happy to conspire with them because that meant he got to come up here too." He leans into his truck bed and digs around in a bag. When he stands back up, he's holding a pair of my panties.

"Why do you have those?" I ask, reaching for them.

He pulls them away from me and tosses them back in the bag. "Because your daughter packed you a bag and disguised it as camping shit that she so sweetly packed for me and Michael."

I groan into the air. *This is six degrees of screwed up.*

How do I respond to this mess?

My heart tugs, pulling me toward the cabin that holds some of my happiest memories, and I hate the way my nose itches like I'm about to cry.

The world, my world, is sitting on my shoulders. Despite the kids being out of pocket and getting Jack and me together, there's still something sweet about it. They love their family traditions. *How can I fault them for that?*

But how can I stay? Should I stay? Can I stay? Harvey doesn't know about our marital issues and how tense our relationship can be. He'll notice the difference in us if we're here any length of time. *How will we get around that?*

God, help me . . .

I look at Jack. "What are you going to do?"

He gestures toward the cabin. "I'm staying here with Michael."

I nod, forcing myself not to fill in the blanks. *You were not included in that sentence, Lauren. It doesn't matter what the kids want. Jack just told you what he wants.*

I force a swallow and ignore the squeeze in my chest. "Great. I'll give your dad his insulin, and Maddie and I will head home."

"You're going home?"

My gaze flips to him just in time to see a storm rolling through his eyes. He sounds surprised, like he didn't expect me to say that.

"Yeah," I say, crossing my arms over my chest. "I mean, if Maddie wants to stay with you guys, she can."

"Oh, I'm pretty sure she wants to stay." He lifts his chin. "And I'm pretty sure they want *you* to stay too. They went to pretty great lengths to get us here."

"I really don't want to think our children are capable of that level of scheming."

"Yeah, well, you have a habit of assuming you know what people are and aren't capable of."

He holds my gaze, practically begging me to argue with him. I open my mouth, fully prepared to go to battle, but then . . . *stop.*

Maybe it's the fresh air. It's possible that I'm just drained from the three-hour drive, or the prospect of dealing with the kids about this exhausts me. Either way, I can't conjure up enough energy to fight with Jack. Not now.

"This is ludicrous," I say, refusing to follow him into an argument.

"A lot of shit is ludicrous, but it doesn't stop you."

"What's that supposed to mean?"

Before he can say another word, a puppy bolts down the steps. It lunges off the bottom step and launches a solid twenty yards in the air, ears pinned behind it, until it lands at my feet. It pants happily. I swear the little thing smiles.

Bark!

I do not return the goodwill gesture. "What the hell is that?"

"Come here, Snaps," Jack says, patting his thigh. The puppy bounds toward him. "She's not very personable today, buddy."

"You got a dog?" My mouth gapes. "You're kidding me."

He laughs. "Lo, this is Snaps. Snaps, this is Lauren." He places his mouth next to the puppy's ear. "Don't tell her anything I said about her, okay?"

"You're not serious."

He scratches it beneath its chin. "He's a cutie."

"Jack," I say, blowing out a breath in disbelief. "What the fuck?"

"I got him last weekend. A guy came by with a couple of puppies that he was taking to the rescue center. Maddie happened to be in my office, and . . . you can imagine how that went."

Maddie knew about this? I give Jack a look and then take in the little Jack Russell terrier scurrying around. He's adorable, bopping around the yard like he's had a couple of doses of caffeine big enough to kill an elephant.

"Where are you keeping it?" I ask, switching my attention back to Jack. "Don't you think getting a dog might be something you talk with your wife about prior to purchase?"

"I didn't buy him. I rescued him."

"Same difference."

Jack scoops him up, and the dog curls against Jack's chest as he stands. "What can I say? I needed something to cuddle at night when I stay at the shop."

I glare at him. "You know, that would be funny if—"

"We got everything put in the right rooms," Michael says, marching confidently down the cabin's front stairs with his sister behind him. "Want us to unload your car now, Mom?"

Snaps barks. *At me.*

I narrow my eyes. *Don't yell at me, you little shit.*

"We need to have a conversation, children," I say, popping a hand on my hip.

Maddie sighs, leaning on a wooden post that holds up the porch. *Now isn't the time for your teenage drama, Mads.*

"What about?" Michael asks, feigning ignorance.

"You know what about," Jack tells him. "And while I give you an *E* for effort on this little scheme of yours—the execution was well done—it's not cool. You two get that, right? Massive overstepping of boundaries."

I look at Jack. *Oh, the irony.*

Michael stretches his arms out with his palms in a stopping gesture. "Okay. Just everyone, calm down. Let's take a breath and appreciate our surroundings. We're in this beautiful forest together. As a family." He grins. "Let's respect this moment."

"I absolutely agree," Maddie says, giggling.

Jack watches me out of the corner of his eye. "Enough playing around. Why did you two little monsters think it was okay to trick your mother and I into coming here today?"

"Was it a trick?" Maddie turns to her brother. "I don't think we were tricking anyone. I mean, Dad wanted to come up here, and we needed to bring Pops his meds. It's a coincidence. A nice, happy little coincidence."

I point toward my car. "If you need anything out of there, get it, because I'm going home."

"Mom," Maddie whines. "No. You can't leave."

Jack stills beside me.

"I can't stay here, Maddie."

"Yes, you can."

My face burns.

I don't know how to navigate this. My defenses climb up. My shoulders stiffen as all three members of my family stare at me like *I'm* the problem.

I don't want to be the problem, and I don't want to be the bad guy. And I sure as hell don't want to stay here because Jack pities me.

"Mom. Stay." Michael stands shoulder to shoulder with his sister. "Please. You're already here—*and you're packed.* Well, we brought stuff for you. That's the part you hate, and it's already done."

I switch my gaze from Michael to Maddie and back. The look on their faces kills me.

Are they guilting me? Of course they are. They're teenagers and master manipulators. But for once in their lives, they aren't conning me into letting them have an extra hour at a birthday party or a new pair of shoes when the ones they have are perfectly fine.

They want their family together. I get it. In a perfect world, *so do I.*

"You want her here, too, right, Daddy?" Maddie asks, flashing a look at her father that she knows helps her get her way 99 percent of the time.

Against my better judgment, I look at my husband.

He's already looking at me.

Whatever he's thinking is locked away. I have no idea what's rolling around in his head. It's strange not to know his thoughts, because I always have. I'm used to knowing what he's thinking before he can verbalize it.

But as I stand under the sweltering sun with sweat rolling down my back in a steady stream, I'm not sure what's going through his mind. I'm really not certain that I want to know.

"It's up to your mom," Jack says, his words measured.

Oh, great. Thanks for putting it on me to destroy their dreams.

I sigh.

"You've already made time," Michael says. "You thought you were coming here for two weeks until a couple of days ago. There's no reason you *have* to go home. And this is our *family vacation*. You can't just leave."

I heave in a breath.

"Your mom has a lot going on," Jack says. "Don't pressure her."

"What if *I* have a lot going on and I need her here?" Maddie says, lifting her brows.

"Madeline . . . ," I say, my tone warning her to tread lightly.

"What? Can't you and Dad get over yourselves long enough to spend a weekend together? You used to do it all the time, you know? Besides, if you guys are going to end up divorced, can't you give me and Michael one last family vacation? Will it kill you?"

"If you guys are going to end up divorced . . ." My head spins, causing whatever Jack says to turn into white noise.

My hand goes to my stomach, trying to help it stop sloshing around. *They know. Of course they know. They're not oblivious.* A lump settles in my throat as three sets of eyes are on me.

To my surprise, Jack places a hand on my shoulder. I jump at the contact and attempt to hide the lightning bolt that shoots through my body. My body temperature spikes, and it has nothing to do with the sun.

I hate that he can still do this to me.

"Madeline, that's enough," Jack says, his voice stern.

Her eyes go wide at the sound of her government name coming out of her dad's mouth.

He gently squeezes my shoulder. "*Don't* talk to your mother like that."

Maddie's face falls.

"After you apologize to her, the two of you can go back in the cabin while we talk," Jack says, sweeping his attention briefly to Michael. "Then we'll deal with that little mouth of yours, Mads."

What the hell?

I don't dare look at Jack. I'm too confused at this sudden solid front to attempt to add more dubiety in the mix.

Maddie frowns. "Sorry, Mom."

"Thank you," I say.

Michael nods. "We love you. We just want one last summer together. That's all." He watches the ground as he guides his sister into the cabin.

I exhale loudly as soon as the door closes.

"Thanks for that," I say, letting my head roll around my shoulders.

"Yeah, well, no matter what's going on between us," he says, "our kids won't talk to you like that."

His hand slips off my shoulders. The side of his finger brushes down my arm, and I can't help but wonder if it was an accident . . . or purposeful.

"I appreciate it," I say.

"Can I ask you something?"

"I suppose."

He rocks back on his heels. "Do you not want to stay? Or do you not want to stay because you think I don't want you here?"

Both.

I study the scar above his right eye that he got when he was a child. He slipped and fell in the rain, bashing his face off a metal step. Somehow, since the last time I really looked at him, it's deepened. The edges are sharper. The skin is lighter.

It's easier to think about his accident than the answer to his questions. *I don't want to stay because leaving, knowing that next year we'll be divorced and I'll never get to come back, might kill me.*

He shifts. "I don't know how we would work it. I mean, I can take the couch."

"Is that what you really want, though? Or are you just throwing it into my lap and making me be the bad guy?"

He rolls his eyes.

"I don't want to fight with you," I say earnestly. "Not about this."

Jack squares his body to mine. He towers over me a good eight inches. He's close enough to reach out and touch me . . . but he doesn't.

I don't reach out to touch him either.

And I don't know how I feel about that.

"What do you want, then?" he asks. "Do you want me to tell you what to do? Because I know you, and you hate being told what to do."

"There's a difference between being told what to do and having someone cooperate in a decision, Jack."

He nods as if he's biting back a curt reply.

This isn't getting us anywhere.

"Fine," he says, his jaw flexed. "Here's what I think—you made an appointment with an attorney, according to the kids, so it looks like you want to be divorced."

What the hell? My blood pressure rises. I let that bit of information go so we don't become focused on my actions. "*You* got a fucking puppy that you keep at the shop. So that really seems like it's your home now, doesn't it?"

His eyes narrow. "Yeah. You're right. I did."

Fuck you, Jack.

"Since we're about to burn the last two decades to the ground, and we're already here, let's give them their vacation," he says, warily. "Let's make it not about us. Surely to God, we can be civil for fourteen fucking days."

My chest closes up as I stuff my emotions into the little box where I keep them.

He is right. So much of this year has been about Jack and me, and so much of last year was about us too.

Let's give them two weeks.

Jack watches me wrestle with my feelings, his gaze softening by the second. "Lauren . . ."

"I don't have enough supplies to get through two weeks. Did you bring enough clothes? Food? Toiletries?"

He grins. "You must've had a lot of that packed already because there are bags of linens and toilet paper and toothpaste in the back of my truck."

Michael must've grabbed what I'd packed from the garage. I didn't even notice.

I hold my temples, the thought of making do with heaven knows what kind of supplies causing my head to throb.

But I could do it. If they took all the bags from the garage, and if Maddie packed me some clothes, I could make it work. I already had a blank work schedule for two weeks. The refrigerator at home is practically empty. The mail is on hold. I could have Billie swing by and make sure the blinds are down and the thermostat is turned up . . .

"Dad said he had groceries coming," Jack says with a smirk. "I'm guessing that's you."

"I'm going to give your dad a piece of my mind."

Jack chuckles. "I bet he's scared."

"I'll stay on the couch," I say, my voice resolute.

"Not happening."

"It's okay, Jack."

He growls. "Can you just let me be the man, please? I know it kills you to let me try to be nice to you—"

"Fine," I say, louder than necessary. I glance at the door to make sure the kids didn't hear me. *Get it together, Lauren.* "If we do this, we aren't doing *this*. We aren't going to fight."

"Right. This is for them."

"Right."

This is a horrible, terrible idea.

Jack sighs, running a hand through his hair. "Dad doesn't know anything is wrong. He truly thinks I was working too much at the shop, and you were playing along to not rock the boat."

Oh, great.

"And, Lo . . . I don't want him to know." Jack's eyes shine with a vulnerability that slices me to my core. "You should've seen the look on his face when we pulled up to his house. He had his shit packed—practically beaming. I just can't drop this on him. Not right now. Not here."

"Jack . . ."

"I'm begging you, Lauren. *Please.*"

For the first time in a very long time, I want to wrap my arms around Jack and hug him.

It's a throwback to the old Jack—the kind, sweet man I fell in love with. When I look at him these days, I see a wall—a cold steel door locked over his emotions. But when he talks about his dad or the kids, I get a glimpse of *my Jack. The Jack I used to know.* And I know watching his father begin to deteriorate is killing him.

"So, what? Just pretend like everything is normal?" I ask.

"As normal as you can."

How the hell did I get here? Just a few hours ago, I was planning on organizing my office. Now I'm constructing a fake happy marriage for two freaking weeks.

How do I get in these predicaments?

"We can do this, right?" I lift a brow. "We can barely have a conversation without bickering, and you want to pretend like everything is fine?"

One corner of his lips draws toward the sky. His shoulders drop to the ground. He moves his head around his shoulders as if he can't figure out his next movement.

That's okay. Neither can I.

Finally, he comes to a rest facing me—a few inches closer than before. His scent drifts through the air, tempting me in some kind of dance that makes me rethink the possibility of this situation.

Jack sets Snaps down. Then he reaches out and plucks a lock of hair stuck to my neck. His fingertips dust my skin. They might as well be electrodes.

I gasp quietly, my arms breaking out in a flood of goose bumps. He notices. Of course he does. His only acknowledgment of my reaction is a slight smirk kissing his lips.

"We did this for twenty years, babe," he says softly. "Pretty sure we can do it for fourteen days."

Snaps barks.

Jack doesn't wait for an answer. He turns to the door, the puppy at his heels.

"I'm not sleeping with that dog," I say. *That's probably what this is. He wants me here to take care of the damn puppy.* "And I'm not cleaning up after it either."

Jack's head shakes as he yells for the kids, leaving me standing in the middle of the yard.

This is going to be the longest fourteen days of my life.

CHAPTER SEVEN

JACK

The cabin door screeches as it slams behind me. *That needs some WD-40.*

A warm breeze flows through the open kitchen window, across to the living room, and out of the curtains on the far wall. The air is hot and grossly humid, but the place needs a good airing out before we start the climate control. It's wild to think that we didn't have an air conditioner until five or six years ago. But the older we got, the hotter it seemed to get, and it turns out that we're no longer cut out for Ohio's hundred-degree temperatures without the ability to cool off.

Michael comes down the stairs, scooping up Snaps midstep. "Were you yelling for us?"

"Where's your sister?"

"Well, she told me to tell you that she's in the bathroom. So she's in the bathroom."

He stops at the bottom of the staircase. Despite his wariness of our conversation—and my reaction to their little stunt—the boy is happy. Relieved, almost. *At home.*

I put a hand on his shoulder and guide him toward the door. "Take a walk with me, son."

"Oh, well, I was going to head down to the beach and see—"

"That wasn't a question."

"Yes, sir."

He hangs his head and follows me onto the porch.

I scan the yard for Lauren until I finally find her sitting in her car. She looks away moments before we make eye contact and pretends to dig around in her purse.

My chest tightens, squeezing so hard that actual discomfort—pain—settles in my ribs.

As much as the kids shouldn't have done this, I'm grateful they did. It gives me two weeks to figure this out. *Because I have to figure this out.*

I'm not losing Lauren.

"Michael," Lauren yells. "Come get Pops's insulin if you're heading over there, please."

He jogs across the lawn and retrieves a small cooler from his mother. They exchange smiles, and a quick laugh, before Michael races back across the yard.

Lauren avoids my stare the entire time.

"I have to hand it to you, kid," I say as we make our way toward Dad's cabin. "I really didn't see this coming."

"What do you mean?"

"What do you mean, 'What do you mean'? This. I'll admit that I'm a little concerned with how well you and your sister pulled this off. I wasn't the least bit suspicious."

"Are you mad?"

I sigh. "No. I probably should be, considering it was completely out of line, but I understand that your intentions came from a good place. Even if you were really risking it."

"Look, I had reservations. I tried to be the voice of reason. But have you ever tried to talk Pops and Maddie out of something when they're on the same team? It's impossible."

I laugh and point at Snaps. "That's how we got him, remember? Now I have to deal with your mother about it. I was hoping to break the news in a . . . different way."

Michael laughs too. "Well, the similarities between that situation and this one are pretty striking."

Just like I figured.

"I know what you're trying to do, and honestly—I'm glad."

"Really?" he asks.

"Really. But I need you to keep your expectations in check. All right? And help temper your sister's . . . enthusiasm. She gets all wishful thinking and—"

"Dad?"

I look at him, our pace slowing.

"We just want two weeks. Two good, fun weeks. If you give us those, we'll cooperate with whatever you and Mom decide," he says, a solemn look painted across his face.

"I'm not in the business of negotiating with children who think they're going to ambush me into complying with their demands. *You'll cooperate either way.*" I lift a brow to drive my point home. "But since we're here and your mom has agreed to stay, I'll let it slide."

"Thanks, Dad."

Yeah.

"But if things go sideways and Mom leaves, you're still going to cooperate. Hear me?"

"Yes."

"Good." I grab Michael's arm, avoiding Snaps's nibble at my fingertips, and pull him back gently. "Hey. Wait."

He stops on the top step of Dad's cabin and looks at me over his shoulder.

"You and Mads didn't say anything to Pops about . . . anything, did you?"

"No." The corner of his lip pulls into a half smile. "Maddie still thinks everything can be okay."

"What about you?"

Michael rubs Snaps's head, holding the puppy close to his chest. Despite his broad shoulders and prominent Adam's apple, he looks like a kid. My kid. My little boy who shouldn't be old enough to be having this conversation with me.

"Well, I still think everything could be okay too," he says, looking me dead in the eye. "But I also think that if you can't work it out with Mom . . ." He shakes his head. "Look, your life isn't my business—"

I raise a brow. *Oh, the irony.*

"I know, I know." He chuckles. "But whatever you guys decide to do isn't my business. Or Maddie's. But I just want to see a smile on Mom's face again. You know? A real one, not one of those fake things she puts on to convince us everything is fine. She's a really bad liar."

My throat squeezes as my son makes me feel as small as a child. At the same time, my heart grows so big that it might explode.

"I do know," I say, patting him on the shoulder. "And I want that too."

My God, do I want that too.

He nods, nuzzling Snaps again, and moves across the porch.

"I wondered how long it'd take you to come over here to chew my ass," Dad says from the other side of the screen door.

"What would I chew your ass about?" I hold the door open for Michael, then enter myself. "Are you, *I don't know*, implying that I would think you had a hand in getting us all up here?"

Dad smirks from his old, rust-colored recliner. "I'd hope not."

"Here." I take the cooler from Michael and toss it into Dad's lap. "Did you even need this?"

"I don't know. I might've. You never know when you're gonna need extra insulin."

I roll my eyes.

"It's hell gettin' old, ya know?" he says, rocking back in the chair.

"Wouldn't know anything about that. I'm still young," I say. "You want to open some windows? It's musty in here."

He runs a wrinkled hand through the air. "Ah, it smells all right to me. Don't you have other stuff to do than worry about my windows?"

I make my way into his kitchen, taking in the thin layer of dust on the cabinets and table. The drop cloths that covered the living room furniture are lying in a heap in front of the sink.

As I pass the doorframe, I notice how faded the lines are that Mom marked on the wood every summer to see how much I'd grown. I also can't help but notice her red apron hanging on the hook by the refrigerator. It looks like she could walk right back in, sling it over her neck, and whip up a batch of her famous fried chicken.

God, I miss her.

"We were only going to stay a few days," I say, working to open the window over the sink. "Did you bring enough clothes and medicine to stay two weeks?"

"Do you think this is my first rodeo?" Dad asks. "I swear to ya, Michael, I don't know how this man has made it this far in life."

Michael chuckles. "He struggles from time to time."

"Must've gotten that from your grandma's side of the family," Dad says.

Finally, the window raises. "Michael, open the window in the living room. Let's air this place out."

"Oh, for crying out loud, Jack. Leave things be," Dad fusses.

I look at him and sigh.

As much as Michael is me twenty-six years ago, Dad is me, thirty-five years from now.

The three of us share the same dark hair. Dad's is spattered with gray. We have the same widow's peak and the same slight bow to our legs that Dad has always said makes us run faster. Our work ethic is unmatched. And, most of all, we're hardheaded.

I sigh again.

"You can't just come in here and take over," Dad protests, mostly to be a pain in the ass. "This is my house. You wanna act like you own the place? Go over yonder to the place you actually own."

"Don't send him to my house, Harvey." Lauren's voice rings through the room like a breath of fresh air. "I thought maybe he'd bunk over here with you."

She walks in the room with the poise of a woman who isn't considering a divorce. Her face is bright, a smile painted across her pink lips.

"Hell no," Harvey says, sitting up. "But you can stay over here if you want."

Lauren kisses Dad on the cheek. "Nice job teaching the kids to be deviants—lying to their parents and all."

"Me?" Dad looks up at Lauren like she hung the moon. "That wasn't me. That was your son over there. The little rapscallion."

"Oh no, Pops. Don't blame this on me. This was you and Maddie."

We all laugh. Lauren, meanwhile, moves toward me with enough hesitation that I notice. I want to reach for her, pull her against my side, and assure her everything will be fine.

But I don't. I'm not a liar.

"I just looked at the food you all packed," she says, stopping a few feet from me. "It looks like a couple of teenagers picked the menu."

"Um, that's because we did," Michael says.

"What were you going to eat, Harvey? You can't survive on nuts and Twizzlers."

"I had it covered. I had someone bring me a charcuterie board and some groceries tonight."

Lauren points at Dad, making us laugh again. "I'll go to the Cupboard and see what they have, food wise. One of us might have to make a trip into town, though, for more supplies."

Dad leans back. "Not me. I'm here to relax. You two can do the runnin'."

"Gee, thanks," I say. "Can we do anything else for you while we're here?"

"Yeah. You can stop openin' all my damn windows. The mosquitoes will get in here as soon as the sun goes down, and I'll be itchin' all night."

"Not if you close them," I say.

He rolls his eyes, grumbling.

"I'll come over tomorrow and get this place cleaned up," Lauren says. "And I don't want to hear a word about it."

Dad smiles. "Okay."

I throw my hands up.

"What?" Dad asks, grinning.

"Nothing. Not a damn thing."

"I don't argue with her. She's prettier than you," he says.

I look at Lauren. She's watching me, her eyes sparkling.

My lips part into a small smile. "I can't deny that."

I don't know if it's the heat and I haven't noticed it yet, or if she blushes. Either way, she looks down and clears her throat.

"I'm going back over to get the kitchen in order and the beds made," she says. "Good thing you all brought fresh sheets and blankets. The ones in the closet here need washing."

Harvey taps the side of his head. "The kids and I made a list, and I packed my truck before Jack got there. I was prepared."

"Do you need help with your bed?" Lauren asks Dad.

"Yeah, if you can come over later and help me get the sheet on. I don't do the top sheet anymore. I'm too old to fool with that nonsense."

She smiles. "Okay. We'll eat in an hour or so." She motions for Michael to follow her. "Come on, kiddo. We need to have a chat on the way back to the cabin, and then you're going to help me."

"I wanted to go to the lake," he whines.

"I don't care. Let's go." She sweeps her hand toward the door. "Move it."

"This is not how I saw this going," Michael says as he exits the cabin.

"See you later, Harvey." Lauren turns to the door, pausing as she faces me. She opens her mouth like she's going to say something but seems to think twice about it. Instead, she nods and leaves, following our son.

The cabin is eerily quiet. I watch the door as if she might come back in. As soon as I realize I'm doing it, I pull my gaze away.

Dad is grinning like the cat that caught the canary.

"What?" I ask.

"You ever worry about her?"

My brows tug together. "What do you mean?"

He leans back in his chair and slowly rocks back and forth. "She's as pretty as a picture."

"Yeah."

"And smart as a whip. I assume you saw her piece on the television about her picture books?"

My feet shuffle against the hardwood. "Yeah."

I've watched Lauren's segment a hundred times. Her smile, her pride, the way she glows with excitement both cut me and energize me. I'm so happy for her. But as excited as I am for her, it also burns. *She never talks about it with me.*

She doesn't need me. She doesn't want me to be a part of her new life. It's almost as though I've been replaced—our memories have been replaced—by ones from total strangers.

"I'm so damn proud of her, Jack. She's a helluva wife, a helluva mother, and now one helluva businesswoman. Your mama would've told every damn person she knew about Lauren."

I smile as far as I can without opening the gates to my emotions. I don't want, nor do I need, to start thinking about what Mom would've thought about this mess with Lauren . . . or how embedded Lauren is into the fabric of our family.

Hell, she's the thread that holds us together.

I jam a thumb over my shoulder. "I'm gonna get over there and see if she needs my help."

Dad grins. "You do that."

I turn to go.

"And, Jack?"

"Yeah?"

A pause fills the air—*one, two, three* seconds that seem infinitely longer.

"She didn't have to come up here, you know," he says.

His words are as heavy as they are crisp.

I don't look at him for a hint to what he means. Whether he smiles or smirks or looks at me with a severity that makes a chill run down my spine, I'm not sure. But the words rattle around in my brain and taunt me.

"I know," I say.

With a wave over my shoulder, I step onto the porch.

I know she didn't have to come up here, Dad. But she did—for you and the kids.

Not for me.

But if there is one thing I'm known for, it's being determined. I just have to work out how to turn this around.

CHAPTER EIGHT

LAUREN

I toss my hand towel next to the sink.

The cooler Jack brought with various food items dries upside down beside the trash can. Thankfully, he had the foresight last night to visit a grocery store for at least some hamburgers and hot dogs. There's not enough real food to last long, but we made a decent supper out of it.

A cool breeze floats through the room, reminding me that the windows are still open. I shut and latch the one over the sink before making my way into the living room to shut that one too.

Frogs croak from the small pond just beyond the tree line. Their song slips through the screen door, bringing a sense of peace with it— peace I cling to with everything I have. As it grows later and later, the calm I've carried with me most of the night starts to wane.

Before long, it'll just be me and Jack. *What then?*

"Mom! Are you still up?" Maddie yells from the second floor.

"Yeah. What do you need?"

"Nothing. I just wanted to tell you good night and sweet dreams."

I grin. "Want me to come tuck you in?"

"No," she says, disgusted that I would assume her teenage self would need her mom to put her to bed. "I just wanted to say good night. Don't make me regret it."

I roll my eyes. "Good night, sweetheart. Good night, Michael. Love you guys."

"Night, Mama," he calls back. "Love you."

I pause, giving our voices a moment to fade away. It also gives me an opportunity to peek down the hallway toward the bedroom I share with Jack. The light is still on.

I'm not ready. I need to kill more time.

A heaviness settles in my chest, grounding me firmly in the cabin. It's anticipatory. *I know what's coming.*

We managed to share the same space this evening without having to truly interact. There were questions here and answers there—a smile or a laugh at a joke at Harvey's expense over burgers. *And it was fine.*

I hate *fine.*

So many times I've stood on the precipice of falling into old roles, of giving my husband a real smile when he saved Maddie from a mouse in the pantry and bursting with pride when he taught Michael how to grill a burger. Tonight was a reminder of the life we could have had. It was the life I dreamed of, the one I wanted so badly for so long.

The one I want now, even if it's already fallen through my fingers.

I clear my throat, shoving down a rise of emotions. I'm tired and nervous . . . and hungry. *I really wanted that last half of a burger that Michael grabbed just before I did.*

Instead of going to bed, I peruse the list I started earlier. A straight line follows the length of the page and lists all the things we need if we're going to make it here for fourteen days without dying of starvation.

Somehow, my heart thumps despite the tightness surrounding it. Each beat is harder than the one before it. Every pump of blood through my veins inches me closer to—

"Lo?"

I wheel around to find Jack standing in the mouth of the hallway. Hair damp from the shower and clad in only a pair of black boxer briefs, his puppy in his arms, he watches me expectantly.

"What?" I ask, taking in the way Snaps glares at me. I glare back at him. *I'm not backing down, you little husband thief.*

Jack moves confidently into the kitchen, his body putting on a show.

Seeing him in his skivvies should be routine. I've seen him that way a thousand times over the years—naked a thousand times more. So why is he suddenly catching my attention?

Because I haven't seen him like this in months? Maybe it's just that I haven't had any action in what feels like forever . . .

"Just wondering what you're doing out here," he says. Our shoulders nearly touch when he breezes by me as if we pass in the kitchen half-clothed all the time. "The kids went to bed an hour ago."

And there's reality, smashing me in the face.

I cross my arms over my chest. "I had to wash the rest of the dishes. Get your cooler emptied so it doesn't reek from stagnant water. Sweep all the dirt we tracked in today. Inventory the food. Wipe the counters. Change a light bulb in the laundry area because I almost face-planted over a stack of blankets the kids ripped off the beds and deposited in the middle of the floor."

He doesn't look at me. Instead, he focuses on offering his puppy a drink.

"Oh, your dog shit in the laundry room. I cleaned it up too," I say.

He rubs his knuckles on the back of Snaps's head. "You can't shit in the house, Snapsy. Come on, boy."

I roll my eyes so hard it hurts. Jack notices my reaction and sighs.

"He's a puppy. Cut him some slack," he says.

As if he understands English, Snaps barks one quick sound of agreement.

Really? "Snaps is another living thing that I don't have the energy to maintain. Cut me some slack."

"No one asked you to do anything for him."

"What am I supposed to do when I nearly step in dog shit? Just leave it until you find yourself in the laundry room?" I snort, my frustration evident in the sound. "That would take a tornado ripping through Story Brook. The only way I can see you in there is if you're running for cover and it's the safest room in the house."

We face each other head-on, waiting for the other to blink.

"I'm going to bed," I say finally, heading down the hallway before Jack can respond.

My jaw clenches as a nasty exhale streams out of my nostrils. *Of course he doesn't understand. Why would he?*

Soft light casts a glow around the small main bedroom. On either side of the bed are two faux-Tiffany lamps that were Jack's mom's. They've always made me laugh. Who has fancy lamps in a rustic cabin from the early 1900s?

Us, I guess.

The bedspread, a thin blue-and-white design that I picked up at an end-of-the-summer sale years ago, is folded back. I bring it every year. The suitcase that Maddie brought for me sits on a chair. Beside it is the overnight bag that I packed when I thought I was just spending the night.

Standing next to the small closet that barely holds our clothes, I take in the sight in front of me. *I notice every little thing.*

The dent from Jack's head on the pillow next to mine. A bottle of his cologne next to my sunglasses on the dresser. Our shoes lying together on the floor.

Everything's just like it's been for the last two decades . . . except it's not.

"I'll clean up after the dog," Jack says.

I jump, making room for him and Snaps to enter the room. My heart pounds as I watch him set the dog down on the bed. Snaps prances across the blankets as if he owns the place.

"Please don't let this be a point of contention between us." Jack turns to face me, the puppy nipping at his fingertips. "If he makes a mess, just tell me. I'll get it or get one of the kids to."

"Sure."

He waits as if he expects that I'll say something more. Instead, I make my way across the small room and dig around in my bag until I find the T-shirt—his T-shirt—that's barely long enough to cover my ass that I brought to sleep in.

When I expected it just to be me in bed.

I wad it into a ball, my cheeks flushing, and march toward the bathroom.

Jack

The bathroom door clicks closed.

"Fuck," I say, sitting on the bed. Snaps jumps on my arm and barks. "Your opinion isn't needed. You don't even know her."

He tilts his head and whines before barking again.

I groan. Shooing Snaps to move, I climb onto my side of the bed. The sheets smell like Lauren's house—*my house.* They're faintly scented with laundry beads from the container with the purple cap. Lauren doesn't like the ones with a pink or blue cap. Only the purple.

My heart pounds as I try not to look like I'm obviously waiting on my wife, but that's hard with nothing to do. There's no TV. I didn't bring a book. I don't have anything from the shop to keep me busy either.

As the water shuts off on the other side of the wall, I swipe at my phone on the bedside table. There's enough wireless internet to download one book—the last title purchased on our account.

"Lay still," I say to Snaps as he walks in a circle at the bottom of the bed. "I should've crated you at night."

He stops and tilts his head at me.

"Don't look at me like that," I say. "I'm trying to figure out how to get her to like me again. I can't worry about making her like you too. Help a guy out, will ya?"

He drops to the bed just beyond my feet.

The bathroom door opens, projecting a squeal down the hall. I flip the page on my reading app and try to appear engrossed in a story about a woman named Coty. But as Lauren walks by, I sneak a look over the top of my phone.

Motherfucker.

Her hair is dry, hanging to the middle of her back. A dewiness kisses her skin. Her cheeks are pink from the scalding-hot water that I'm sure she used in the shower, and her other cheeks—the ones on her ass—play hide-and-go-seek from under one of my old Metallica T-shirts.

Is she screwing with me?

I adjust myself as discreetly as I can.

"When did you start sleeping like that?" I ask, my throat burning.

Her hand stills over her bag before she resumes motion. "Like what?"

"You usually sleep in pants and a top of some sort. You're just doing the top now?"

She turns toward me, her nipples hard against the thin fabric of the shirt. She starts to put her hair in a ponytail but stops when she realizes her shirt is going to ride up to her hips. Her eyes go wide.

I can't help it. I smirk.

"You know," she says, backing away from the bed, "I think I'll sleep on the couch."

What? I scramble to sit up. "You are not."

She blows out an exasperated breath.

"I'm sorry," I say. "Should I not comment on how hot you look? You're still my wife, Lo. It's not like I'm a guy catcalling you from the street."

She lifts a brow. "You didn't say I looked hot."

"Yeah, I did."

"*No, you didn't.* You asked when I started sleeping like this."

"Semantics," I say.

She hums in disagreement.

"Fine," I say, knowing I'm poking the bear but too ignorant to stop. "You're fucking hot."

Her face bleeds from pink to red. *"Stop it."*

"Stop what? Telling you the truth?"

"Why tell me now?" She looks at me, puzzled. "Why say that? Are you trying to make this more awkward than it needs to be?"

Snaps's ears perk up, and he raises his head.

I set my phone on my lap, next to my hardened cock. Her eyes follow the movement, widening slightly once they land on me.

I probably shouldn't draw attention to my current state of arousal, but *fuck it.* It's always walking on eggshells with this woman, whether it be that I screwed something up on her schedule or got buried too deep at work to remember dinner. I shouldn't say she's beautiful, because that would mean I'm just trying to get sex, or accidentally touch her when we're getting ready for bed, because that would denote that I haven't considered how many times the kids have touched her already that day.

"Get in bed," I say, as if she's going to listen to me. "Here." Grabbing the extra pillows, I build a little wall between us. "You won't even know I'm here."

A shadow drifts across her face. Slowly, as if she's climbing into a lion's den, she takes her place on the bed. Before she lies down, she reaches over and turns off her light. Then she lies with her back to me.

"Want me to turn mine off?" I ask.

"I don't care."

I sigh and pick up my phone again. Swiping every minute or so—the amount of time I think it would take to read a page—I let my mind wander.

What would she do if I reached across the wall of pillows and touched her? Dismantled the pillow wall altogether and pulled her close to me? Kissed her on that spot behind her ear that always makes her smile?

My chest aches in a way that it really hasn't in a long time. It's hurt, sure, but not like this. Not with the distinct pain of having Lauren right there . . . but not there at all.

"Jack?" Her voice is soft. "Can I ask you something?"

I place the phone on the table beside me. "Sure."

"You really didn't know Maddie and I were coming?"

"No."

She pauses. "Would you have come if you knew?"

I look at her over the pile of pillows. Her hair is splayed against the sheets. Her hands are tucked under her head and her legs are curled up beneath her. She's tugged the blankets so they cover her bottom half, and I want to remove them—to tell her she doesn't have to cover herself from me. *That she shouldn't.*

"Jack?" she asks again.

"I don't know if I would've or not."

I say it before I can think it over and regret it instantly.

It's true, though. Maybe I wouldn't have come. After all, I didn't know about the divorce then. I might've thought she just didn't want to be with me and stayed home. *God knows that's happened more than once.*

Whether I would've or not, I would've wanted to. I've been looking forward to this trip for months. It's the only time of year when the stress of normal life subsides and we can just be *us*. There are no schedules or appointments, no lawn that needs mowing or outstanding chores to catch up on.

Lauren used to say that she wanted me home more—and I understood. I was in the beginning stages of building my business into something that could support us long term, and I wasn't always able to walk away from work.

I had to be the man she deserved. A man who could take care of his family, like Dad took care of Mom and me.

But as fate would have it, as the shop found its sea legs and I didn't have to be there so much . . . Lauren didn't want me home. She was happier without me hanging around. Because of that, I was happier too.

It's pure hell being around a woman you love so fucking much and knowing you're making her miserable.

Despite it all, I've never once considered leaving Lauren. I've never considered that she would leave me. I can't fathom a life without her—I won't. Maybe we need to make some changes—maybe *I* need to do something different—but *we will* stay together.

We have to.

She's the best thing that's ever happened to me.

"Good night, Jack," Lauren whispers.

I turn off my light and slip under the sheets. Snaps curls up against my toes.

"Night, Lo."

CHAPTER NINE

LAUREN

L et's add this dish soap, and I think I'm done," I say, sliding a bottle of blue liquid into the heap on the counter.

Mrs. Shaw laughs, her eyeglasses bouncing on the cord around her neck. "Did you leave anything for anyone else?"

"Yeah, there are a couple of jars of honey back there," I say, laughing too.

Instead of tallying up my bill, she rests her wrinkly forearms on the counter and smiles.

The Cupboard is bright and airy. This has always surprised me about the store, considering that it's small and built out of dark wood, just like the cabins. I note the sweetness in the air, something Mrs. Shaw told me years ago was from her late husband spilling a bucket of freshly tapped maple syrup back in the fifties. The smell started that day and never left.

"How have you been, Lauren? I saw Michael zip by here on the way to the lake this morning. My goodness, how that boy has grown. I almost didn't recognize him."

"Tell me about it. I wish he'd stop."

"Oh no, you don't."

"Yeah, I kind of do," I say, frowning. "He'll be a senior this year and then off to college. I'm not ready for that."

She shoves away from the counter. "I remember when my daughters were about the ages of Michael and Maddie, and I was *so* upset about it. Just beside myself. What would I do with my time? I'd been a stay-at-home mom all my life—of course, there weren't the opportunities for women back then like there are now. I couldn't have started my own company and ruled the world like you."

My cheeks flush.

"Story Books," she says, grinning widely. "Did that name have something to do with the cabins up here? Story Books, Story Brook—I couldn't help but wonder."

A wash of warmth floods my veins. "I did my very first scrapbook up here the summer before Michael was born. My parents died when I was eighteen."

She nods.

"And, well, my mom didn't save much from my childhood. There's nothing for me to look back on and remember or use to jog my memory. I didn't want that for my children. I wanted them to have this history of their parents someday to keep." I shrug. "I made a little note in the first one all the way back then that said, 'Story Book Number One.' It just somehow stuck, I guess."

"I think it's perfect." She organizes my items in front of her. "I saw you on the television, and I have to say, you were the most interesting one on there. I liked the woman that makes wreaths—well, I liked her wreaths. She didn't seem too excited about it."

"She was probably just nervous. We were linked via video, which I thought would help my nerves. Being in an actual studio in New York City would've been worse, I think. But they just gave us two weeks' notice. I got a call asking if I would be up for a segment about businesses run from home that got started on social media. I didn't know what to expect, and I bet the wreath woman didn't either."

She smiles. "You're always so sweet."

"I bet my husband would disagree."

Mrs. Shaw plops a notepad on the counter and finds a pencil. I mosey around the store as she tabulates my bill the old-fashioned way.

The thought of Jack takes my spirits down a notch.

I woke up disjointed this morning from a whole three hours of sleep. Jack's breathing was steady, and his legs didn't twitch all night long. The only time he moved was when Snaps burrowed around at the end of the bed. I was terrified I was going to accidentally kick the puppy and send him flying across the room. *Why didn't Jack crate train him? Why did he get a dog to start with? I'm not going to want to sleep with a dog in my bed.*

Apart from Snaps, I was just so uneasy. I didn't want to roll over and confirm Jack was awake because . . . what if he was? *What then? What would we talk about? Would we talk or just lie there awake awkwardly?*

Instead, I lay on my side facing the wall. The darkness was too deep to see anything and the silence too intense to do anything but breathe. It was odd, yet strangely comfortable, being next to him for eight hours without saying a word, counting the years we've shared this particular bed. Smiling at the memories. Getting teary over them all the same.

This is the life I wanted. Jack beside me. Our two beautiful children asleep upstairs. A peace outside and inside—of both the cabin and me.

"How is Jack?" she asks. "I feel like I just saw him. Michael is the spitting image of his daddy at that age. Has Harvey shown you pictures of Jack when he was a teenager?"

"Yes, I've seen a bunch of them. Harvey gave me a trunkful of pictures last winter. The kids and I had fun going through them and catching up on Jack's shenanigans through the years."

She laughs. "He was a wild one. Such a good boy, though. His mother, Myra, used to bring Jack up here all the time when he was growing up. She used to say that this was the only place she could bring him where she knew he couldn't get into too much trouble."

I smile, picking up a cantaloupe and sniffing the blossom end of the fruit.

"Myra and Jack were here all the time," she says. "Harvey would come up now and then. He worked so much that Myra was mostly a single mother all summer. She was such a nice woman. She passed the summer before you started coming with Jack."

"I wish I could've known her."

"She would've loved you. You remind me a lot of her. Determined. Fierce. You both give as good as you get. I think that's why those Reed men love you both so much—you don't take their nonsense lying down."

I set the fruit down and dust my hands off. "They do have nonsense about them."

She laughs. "That they do, honey. That they do."

A smile splits her cheeks as she inspects a jar of honey for a price tag. She nearly glows as she marks something down on her notepad.

"Mrs. Shaw, may I ask you something?"

"Sure, honey. What is it?"

I stand by the counter and lean against it. "How long ago did your husband pass away?"

She sets her pencil down. "Fifteen years ago. He was taken way too young. Not a day goes by that I don't think about Frank."

"How long were you married?"

"A long damn time." She laughs, holding a hand on her round stomach. "My Frank was a treat of a man, I'll tell you. A treat. You know how women are always going on and on about those . . . what do they call them? Alpha men?"

I giggle. "Yes."

"I know you know what I'm talking about. I've seen your husband," she says, tossing me a wink. "Well, my Frank was nothing like that at all. There wasn't an alpha bone in his body. He was a . . . I guess you'd call him a beta male." She laughs again. "He was as soft spoken and passive as they come. The sweetest damn man you'd ever meet."

"That sounds nice."

"Oh, it was." She goes back to her notepad. "Not a day went by without him telling me he loved me. I miss that. I still wake up some days and expect to have a little note beside my head from him. And when reality hits that I'll never get another note for as long as I live, some days that's really hard to get over."

I watch a wave of emotions pass through her features until the nonchalant Mrs. Shaw I know resurfaces.

She busies herself getting all my items into bags. I don't try to help, because she'll smack my hands and tell me to go away. We've done this before. Instead, I watch her work and wonder what her life was like with Frank—and what it's like without him.

"I'm going into town today to get some hamburger and lunch meat," I say. "Would you like me to bring anything back?"

"Do you have to get anything else?"

"Nope. Just meat. It's a long story."

She grins. "My granddaughter, Ava, is going to town this afternoon. Why don't you just let me know what you want, and I'll have her bring it back for you."

"How is Ava?"

"Too cute for her own good."

I laugh.

"She's going to the butcher shop," Mrs. Shaw says. "We just run a tab there, and I go pay it at the end of the month. She can bring me the receipt, and you can just pay me tomorrow."

"Are you sure?"

"Absolutely." She hands me her notepad. "Just jot down what you want."

I make quick work of listing what we will need to get through the next week. Then I take my bill and hand her my credit card.

"What are you going to do today?" she asks, fighting with the credit card machine. "It's a beautiful day."

"I'm going to clean Harvey's cabin first. Then I might go down to the lake. I'm not sure." *I'm totally sure. I'll be avoiding Jack.*

"Oh, is Harvey here too?"

Her voice raises as high as her brows. It makes me giggle.

"Now, Mrs. Shaw. Do I sense a little interest there?"

She pats the side of her head. "I might have to spruce myself up a little if he's around. That's all I'm saying."

"I thought you were into beta males. You know Harvey is . . . not that."

"I was into marrying a beta male, honey. Things change as you get older—tastes, experiences, desired outcomes."

This is not the conversation I expected to have today—least of all with Mrs. Shaw and her corncob-printed sundress. *What is happening to my life?*

"I'm not looking for someone to spend sixty years with. Heck, I won't be *alive* in sixty years," she says, her eyes twinkling. "You get to be my age, Lauren, and you realize the preciousness of time. You just go after what you want because there's not a day to waste."

I pick up the cantaloupe again and weigh it in my palm.

Her words settle on my soul. I might not be in the twilight of my life just yet, but I understand exactly what she means.

"What's going on, honey?" she asks.

"Nothing." I set the fruit on top of the others. "I was just thinking about how I get what you're saying about appreciating time. That's been a big thing for me recently."

She places a bundle of tomatoes in the last bag and watches me curiously. But instead of elaborating, I wander around the front of the store.

My face is hot and my heart beats hard. The only person I've talked about this with is Billie. It's a relief to open the topic with Mrs. Shaw, but it also feels like I'm betraying my family.

"Do you want to know something funny?" she asks.

"Sure."

"Ava and I pulled out a bunch of old VHS tapes from years ago. She'd never seen one before and thought it was the neatest thing she ever did see." She chuckles. "Anyway, we sat down and watched some of them—old birthdays and family reunions, that sort of thing. And it made me think about how much I've changed over the years. I was this little chaste thing when I married Frank, when I was barely eighteen. Then, in my twenties, I started having babies. I was really a baby myself. Oh, those twenties were so hard."

"I can relate."

"I'm sure you can." She smiles. "But then came my thirties—my sexual awakening. The kids were out of diapers and could wake up and not run into the road anymore, and I had a minute to take a breath. Then came my forties. That was probably my favorite decade. The hardest in some ways because the kids moved out, and it was just Frank and me at home, really for the first time since we'd been married. It was scary having all that time on my hands but also powerful. And that's what I found in my fifties. *My power.* And, also, my purpose."

"Can I borrow some of that knowledge? Please?"

She hands me my card. "You'll find yours. I promise. And one day, you'll be my age and you'll look back on all the decades of your life—the easy ones, the hard ones, too—and you'll realize it was just a beautiful journey. You weren't meant to be the young, beautiful version of yourself with purpose and power at the same time. Can you imagine that mess?"

I laugh.

"Really, Lauren, you're the same person the whole time. Just the same person with different experiences. You weren't born to stay static. That was never the plan."

I slide my card in my pocket and lift the bags off the counter. A thought prickles the back of my brain.

"Did Frank change like that, Mrs. Shaw?"

Her smile softens. "Of course he did, honey. He was a human being."

I regrip the bags, the paper handles slipping against my sweaty palms.

"Frank and I had our biggest challenges when one of us was growing or changing. They were some of the watershed moments of our marriage."

"How did you get through them?"

She chuckles. "Sometimes by the skin of our teeth."

The door swings open. A man who bought a cabin by the lake a few years ago comes in. After a quick wave to us, he heads for the firewood bundles.

"Honestly, Lauren, marriage is hard. Well, I'm sure you know that. It's the hardest thing you can do. The thing that got us through them was simple—we *wanted* to get through them. It's amazing how far that one little thing goes."

Her words roll around my brain. "That makes sense."

"Mrs. Shaw—how much are these again? I don't see a sign," the man says from the back of the store.

"Go. I'll see you soon," I say.

"I'll send Ava up with your meat as soon as she gets back."

"Thank you."

"No problem, honey," she says as she rounds the corner of the counter.

I push open the door and make my way into the warm summer sun. The two bags are heavy, but not nearly as heavy as the thoughts in my mind.

Mrs. Shaw's perspective on marriage, on life—it's so different from Billie's. Because Mrs. Shaw's words truly resonate with the deepest parts of my soul. I've clung to my marriage because I made vows and promises that I would.

But it feels like it's been a one-sided endeavor most of the time. *What about the vows and promises Jack made too?*

"The thing that got us through them was simple—we wanted *to get through them. It's amazing how far that one little thing goes."*

Is it really that simple?

Is that the little thing that's missing from our marriage?

CHAPTER TEN

JACK

The rag swipes down the hinges, soaking up the excess lubricant. "Let's give it a try, Snaps," I say.

The door opens and closes without a squeak. The puppy cocks his head to the side before barking at the screen. I pat him on the head as I stand.

"That's better, isn't it?" I ask.

Snaps must agree because he bolts down the stairs and toward Dad's cabin. I glance over to see Dad sitting in his rocker on the porch.

"I got him," he yells, fanning the air in front of his face like he's hot.

"How's that cigar, Pops?"

"Mind your business."

"That's gonna kill you."

"Probably."

I shake my head and go back inside.

The cabin is lit up with the early-afternoon sunlight. The white curtains with thin brown stripes flutter in the open windows. Scents of bleach and laundry soap fill the air, and if I allowed myself to, I could believe that things are perfectly normal.

That is, if I didn't focus on the fact that Lauren left before I woke up.

My head is surprisingly clear, considering last night's sleeplessness. I lay there knowing damn good and well that Lauren was awake too. More than once, I started to reach for her or to say something in the darkness of the night. But every time—I stopped myself.

A weight sits on my chest. It's saddled with guilt and anger, humiliation and regret.

The silence last night gave me ample time to think. To reflect. To absorb the reality of my situation.

I haven't had time to really internalize the kids' revelation. *Their mom plans to file for divorce. She's really done.*

How did I not see this coming? Why was I so willing to let things go the way they were? Did I really think staying away from her, avoiding the house, rescuing a puppy—which, in retrospect, may or may not have been the smartest thing I've ever done—would be okay? *We didn't even discuss it. I didn't mention it, not even vaguely. But then again, I don't mention much to her these days.*

Having her beside me and not being able to touch her—being afraid to even speak to her—was an eye-opener. *What is it about confined spaces that brings truth to light?* Maybe it's because there's nowhere to go. There are no distractions available to avoid reality. There's no running from what's real.

And last night, what was real was that I'm now losing my wife. If I've not already lost her.

My heart sinks as my blood pressure soars. I must get a plan together. But where do I start?

"Hey, Daddy," Maddie says, the door slamming shut behind her. "Um, what are you doing?"

"I'm standing in the kitchen. What are you doing?"

"You look like you're about ready to pass out," she says warily.

"I'm fine. What's going on?"

She waits a long moment before switching back to her usual self. "I came to get my phone. Daniel is supposed to call me in about an hour, and I don't want to miss it."

I take in her blonde hair with red streaks, thanks to the sun. The freckles across the bridge of her nose. The tan lines peeking out from beneath her tank top strap. *She looks just like her mom.*

"Where have you been this morning?" I ask.

"The Fritzes got here yesterday, so I've been hanging out with Hannah and Hillary. We're going down to the beach after lunch, I think. Their mom is making these little mini-sandwich things. They're gonna be delish."

"Awesome."

She rolls her eyes. "Where's Mom?"

"I don't know."

"Where's Michael?"

"I don't know."

She sighs. "What *do* you know?"

"I know my daughter is getting a little mouthy for her age. I know that for a fact."

Maddie giggles and wraps her arms around my waist. "I love you, Daddy. But I need you to work faster."

"'Work faster'?" I look down at her. "I'm not following you."

"We've been here a whole day, and you and Mom are still on opposite ends of the planet. *Fix it.*" She pats my back before pulling away. "Now, I have to find my phone before Daniel calls."

"Hey."

"Yeah?"

I take in my daughter's sweet innocence. Despite her freckles and baby face, she's growing up. Daniel will likely be the first of many boys trying to capture her heart, and as much as I hate it—she's my baby girl—I need to make sure she's strong.

"Maybe you shouldn't worry so much about Daniel, you know? Enjoy the family vacation you went to such drastic lengths to make happen."

She places both palms on her chest. "But I'm in love, Daddy."

"You are not in love."

I say it before I think about it—a knee-jerk reaction to Maddie's statement. And as her eyes go wide and the offense she's taken to my statement becomes obvious on her face, I regret it. *This isn't helping, Jack, you fool.*

"*I am.* I love Daniel. He's my soulmate. And when we get back home, I want you to meet him, okay? I'll have him meet us at the shop, and you can get to know him."

That's the last fucking thing I want to do. All I can think about is a snot-nosed kid who's thinking with his dick and not his head. I don't want that dick anywhere near my beautiful daughter.

But there will be boys, Jack. Don't be the bad guy here.

"You know what?" I ask. "Let's do that. Bring him to the shop."

She looks at me warily.

"If you're in love with this guy, I want to know what he's all about," I say. *And show him all my tools and how good I am with them.*

"Really?"

"Really."

Her smile stretches across her cheeks. "Thanks, Daddy. You're the best."

I blow out a breath as she skips up the stairs toward her room.

"Fucking Daniel," I say, pulling a bottle of water out of the fridge.

How do I handle this boyfriend shit? Do I just lock Maddie up in her room and never let her out? Because boys are going to find her if she breathes the same air as them. She's too cute and funny. *Just like Lauren.*

I take a long swig of the water, letting it cool me down.

Jealousy at the thought of another man's car being at my house the other day, even though it was Billie's, floods me again. *I have to get control of this situation now.*

Maddie's sandals smack against the stairs again. I turn around to see her flying out the door. I also see Lauren through the screen door. She's not expecting me; the surprise on her face proves that to be true.

"Hey," I say, my throat dry despite the water I just drank.

"I just went to the Cupboard." She sets two bags on the table. "Mrs. Shaw is having her granddaughter bring us some meat later."

"Okay."

She pulls out a variety of items and puts them away.

"Want some help?" I ask.

"I have it. Thanks." She looks at me sideways. "Where did she just run off to?"

"The Fritzes'. Tina is making some kind of mini sandwiches for lunch, and it's very exciting."

Lauren grins. *There's my girl.*

"But she's also waiting on a call from Daniel." I sigh in frustration. "I hate that kid."

"You don't even know him."

"Don't have to know him. I hate him."

She wraps her hands around the top of the chair. "You don't hate him, Jack. Give the kid a chance. He's actually a pretty sweet—"

"You've met him?"

"Of course I've met him. He's come over after school a few times. Stayed for dinner. He's chatted with me while I've waited on Maddie to come out of cheer practice."

"Why was he there?"

She laughs. "Because he plays basketball. There's not some big conspiracy here."

It sure as hell feels like it. I take a deep breath, refusing to step away from my point. "I don't see why you're encouraging this. He'll just break her heart . . . *or worse.*"

She holds my gaze, not even pretending not to stare. "What's worse than breaking someone's heart?"

The room heats. It suddenly feels much, *much* smaller.

I see where she's going with this—subtly poking me over our current situation. But if she thinks she's the only one who's been hurt over the last year or so, she's wrong.

"What's worse than heartbreak?" I ask. "Apathy."

"Maybe the apathy is a by-product of the heartbreak."

"Maybe the heartbreak was unintentional."

"Maybe that doesn't matter anymore."

My brows pull together. "What do you mean it doesn't matter? Of course it matters."

"But does it, Jack?"

Fuck this. I'm taking the blanket off the baby. "I didn't know you were filing for divorce before now."

Her eyes widen. "So, that's it—it only matters because you know I'm going to file?"

You were *going to file.* I run a hand down my face. *Breathe, Jack. Stay calm.* "I didn't realize how bad things were."

"Whose fault is that?"

"Mine."

"Yes, it's yours. Because I tried to tell you. I tried to tell you so many times. I begged you to come home, to help me, to—"

"Lauren, *I know.*"

I haven't been home for dinners, but I've been looking after my family. I've been depositing checks into our bank account, and as far as Lauren is concerned, that's not enough. *I know.* But I also know divorce is so . . . *final.*

Her eyes cloud with unshed tears, and the sight of them is a knife in my heart. I reach for her, but she takes a step away.

"Let's not do this," she says, wiping her nose with the back of her hand. "There's no reason to."

"I don't want to fight with you."

"Then let's not." A flurry of emotions flies through her beautiful blue eyes before she shoves away from the chair. "I need to help your dad get things cleaned up."

My heart leaps. I don't know what to say, but I don't want to leave it like this. There's so much to figure out, to talk about—to resolve. But we can't do that if she goes. "Lo, wait."

She shakes her head and leaves without looking back.

The door smacks shut behind her.

A burst of energy floods my veins. The sound of an invisible clock ticks in my head. I'm out of my league here.

The fact that I don't know how to fix this with my own damn wife says everything.

CHAPTER ELEVEN

Jack

My shoes dangle over the water.

Sitting on the often-forgotten dock tucked away on one of the lake inlets, I gaze at a small hill across from me. There was once a bench that sat there and a metal camp grill that I always found odd. A friend from another family who summered here when I was a little boy helped me start a fire in it when we were ten. He'd sneaked matches from his mom's kitchen, and I'd brought newspapers from mine. Together, we collected sticks and angled them into a cone shape. Then he struck the match.

We were so proud of ourselves. We felt like real men. Looking back on it, what an odd thing to think—that building a fire made you a man.

If only it were that simple.

A raw, angry knot sits in my stomach, refusing to budge. I can taste the bile it squeezes up my throat. My intestines churn with fiery acid.

I can't ignore the feeling building inside me, the urgency that continues to worsen. The feeling that I need to talk to someone is overwhelming.

It's ridiculous to begin with—what good would it do? Spread the dissension in my household outside its walls? No one needs that to happen. Problems are best resolved at home.

Yet this problem was created there too. Or, at least, it began there. *No, it really began with me. It has to end with me too.*

I pick up a rock and toss it into the water.

As the day wore on, as the afternoon slipped into the evening and Lauren still hadn't come back to the cabin, the weight of the situation became more and more unbearable. And the more I thought about it, the more confusing it became. The facts surrounding my marriage are cloudy, hazy—nothing makes sense.

And I have no one to talk to about it.

The guys from work will take my side. They'll agree that I was working my ass off for Lauren, and they'll say, *"Fuck her if she doesn't see that."* I can't talk to Dad about this for about fourteen thousand reasons. And we've already said enough around Michael and Maddie. *God knows they don't need to be involved any more than they already are.*

I don't have anyone. It dawns on me that I don't have any true friends. The people I work with, and for, are more business associates and employees than pals. I used to have a core group of buddies who would meet up for a drink, or we'd go camping over the weekend. But now that I think about it, they're gone too.

A deep emptiness settles further in my soul.

"What am I going to do?" I ask the bird staring at me from the water's edge. "Do you have any advice?"

It lifts off the bank and flies away.

"Nice."

I plant my hands behind me and lean back, tilting my face to the sinking sun.

Maddie's comment about her mother not being hard to understand has crept on the edges of my mind ever since she said it in the truck. *"She's not hard to understand, you know."*

Lauren used to be easy to understand. I loved her and she loved me back. It was not only easy; it was simple—the simplest exchange I've ever experienced. That's what made us so good together. It was uncomplicated.

It was just me and her.

"Mom is pretty self-sufficient. It's not like she's sitting around waiting on someone to take care of her, you know?"

I roll my tongue around my lips.

When I think about it, *really think about it*, Maddie is right. Lauren has always been capable, but now it's more than that. It truly is self-sufficiency. I can't think of a thing she doesn't do herself. There's not one thing she really needs me for these days.

My throat tightens.

No one needs me anymore. Everyone in my life—Lauren, the kids, Dad, my friends—they've all moved on because *I* checked out. *Me.*

I have no one to blame but myself.

My stomach drops. The weight of the acid churning inside it splashes over, singeing my veins.

Lauren is this way—self-sufficient and capable, angry and bitter—because I made her this way.

"Damn it," I groan, shaking my head to clear the cobwebs that I only now see.

I get to my feet as a stream of situations and conversations roll through my mind.

"You didn't say I looked hot."

"Yeah, I did."

"No, you didn't. You asked when I started sleeping like this."

I wipe a hand down my face.

"I said she was hot, but that's not what she heard. She heard me say she was acting different," I say to no one in particular. "But it wasn't *her* acting different. *I* was acting different."

Sweat trickles down my back as I rack my brain for the last time I told her, prior to this, that she was beautiful. I come up empty.

My mind reels, searching desperately for something to hold on to.

"When was the last time I just did something nice for her? When was the last time I told her I was proud of her? When was the last time

I made her feel like I love her?" I grit my teeth so hard that I hear them rub together. *What have I been doing?*

Every conversation we've had where, instead of listening, I was defending myself—sure as shit that I was right—plays through my memory. The justifications for being gone. The excuses for missing dinner and date nights. All the reasons I gave, with only half a thought about why I was on the periphery of her life.

I've been filling up buckets with holes in the bottom.

"I've been depositing money in our account and nothing into our life—my family's life. *Fuck*," I yell, sending a flock of birds into the air.

Everything looked fine because I wanted it to be fine. It was never okay.

Frantic, I grab my phone from my pocket and pray that I see a few bars of service. There they are—one, sometimes two, little promises of connection.

I don't want to make this call, but I have no other choice. I need a sounding board, and I have only one person I can count on to make sure I don't fuck this up.

It rings four times before she picks up.

"Hello?" Billie asks.

"Hey, Bills. It's Jack."

"Is everything okay?"

Groaning, I pace a small circle on the dock. "That's a loaded question."

"All right. Well, is everything okay with Lauren and the kids?"

"Yes. Thanks for caring about me too."

"Shut up."

I sigh, tugging at my hair. "This will come as no surprise to you, I'm sure, but I've just about fucked up my marriage."

She hums.

"I'm panicking, Billie. I don't want to lose her."

Her chuckle is uneasy.

"It's my fault," I say. "I know I've been a shit partner and not the greatest dad either." *Or son, but let's stay on track and deal with that one later.* "I understand the problem. I don't fully understand the answers, and I have, like, two weeks, I feel like, to convince my wife to give this another try."

"See," she says, "I'm on a precipice here. Do I listen and offer my assistance? Or do I hang up because this sounds a lot like consorting with the enemy?"

I groan.

"I don't know whether to be happy that you're coming to your senses or sad that you're this out of touch," she says.

"Be both. I am."

She takes a long pause. "But why, Jack? Before I say anything to you, answer this—*why?* You and I might be friends, but I'm always on Lauren's side. Remember that."

Her loyalty to Lauren makes me smile. *God, I'm glad Lo has her.*

"I have been a shitty husband. I haven't been there for her. I've focused on creating this life for her but then removed myself from it. I didn't mean to. I swear, I didn't. I don't even know how it happened, but here we are, and now I have to fix it." My shoulders fall, and I blow out a breath. "I love her so fucking much, Billie. I can't lose her. I'll do anything."

A long pause fills the line. Each passing moment builds my trepidation. Each level of anxiousness that I arrive at only makes me more frustrated.

I switch the phone between my hands.

"I'm not walking away from this," I say, my voice growing louder. "I'm fighting for her—*for us*—and I'm out of my depth here, Bills. All I want to do is fix things, be the husband Lauren needs, but I'm so fucking out of touch with reality that I'm not sure I even know what that is."

"Then how do you know you want to do it?"

I look at the sky and smile sadly. "Because I'll do anything."

Billie sighs, but I can almost hear her smile. "I've never been happier to hear a man admit he was wrong."

I watch the deer disappear back into the forest. I wonder if they can see the forest for the trees.

"You got a fucking puppy that you keep at the shop. So that really seems like it's your home now, doesn't it?"

My throat dries. "I need to prove to Lauren that she's my whole life. That I'm present, that she's my first priority. That she's beautiful and sexy and intelligent—that . . ." I take a deep breath. "That I'm nothing without her."

"Okay. Then here's the plan . . ."

CHAPTER TWELVE

LAUREN

"What's for dinner?" Michael asks, coming into the kitchen. "I don't smell anything."

I glance at the clock. "I haven't started anything yet. I got distracted."

He sits beside me and slides a box across the table.

While Jack and the kids went to the lake, I stayed behind. I planned on cleaning off the back porch and getting the grill ready for the summer. Instead, I found myself with a glass of sweet tea and a romance novel. *Not a bad way to spend an afternoon.*

The cabin is full of life. The kids come and go—sometimes with their friends and sometimes not. Harvey ambled in a little while ago and made himself at home in the living room. Jack grabbed a shower after returning from the lake, finding it necessary to fix a broken shelf in the pantry sans shirt.

It's a peculiar move for him—both the fixing of the shelf without being asked and the forgoing of a shirt in the middle of the day for no apparent reason. *It's not just the box that's distracting.*

"What is all of this stuff?" Michael asks, pulling my attention away from his father.

"I found all of this in the closet upstairs between your room and Maddie's," I say. "I was looking for the extra mop for Pops's floors and discovered this instead."

I set a stack of pictures on the table and watch as my son digs through a box of keepsakes from cabin summers years ago. The smile on his lips—reverent and joyful—is akin to the one in my heart.

"Look at this," he says, holding up a hummingbird feeder. "Mads and I made these the summer I wanted to be a conservation officer. Remember that?"

"Yes, I do. That was the summer a bat got in the cabin, and you were more worried about its safety than about us."

He chuckles. "You were such a baby about it."

"They suck blood, Michael. I'm not sure what else you want me to say about that."

"Ooh, Pops—check you out." Michael holds a picture of Harvey in a pair of shorts that barely cover his crotch. "This is quite a fashion statement."

"It's a good thing I can't see that far," he says.

I make a show of looking at the photo. "Nice legs, Pops."

He lifts a leg and tugs at his pants. "I still got 'em, if you wanna see."

"You trying to pick up my woman, Dad?" Jack walks by me, winking as he passes. "I thought we talked about that."

My chest squeezes.

And this is the problem with a broken heart. It always remembers how to repair itself—and it doesn't care if cracks remain.

A knock raps against the door. Jack swings it open, and a pretty blonde walks in with two bags and a picnic basket.

Michael is on his feet in two seconds. "Here, let me help you."

Her cheeks flush as she hands him the bags. "Thanks, Mike."

Mike? I look at Jack. Smirking, he shrugs.

"Mom, Dad—you remember Ava Shaw, right?" Michael asks.

"Yes, of course. Hi, Ava," I say, returning her smile. "Thank you for picking up a few things for us in town."

"It was no problem, Mrs. Reed. My grandma sent you this picnic basket too. She said something about picnics helping you through watersheds—or something like that. It made no sense to me."

I take the proffered basket and grin.

"Frank and I had our biggest challenges when one of us was growing or changing. They were some of the watershed moments of our marriage." Oh, Mrs. Shaw.

"I'll be sure to tell her thank you tomorrow," I say, noticing how close to Ava my son is standing.

Ava turns to Pops. "Harvey, my grandma is frying pork chops and making scalloped potatoes tonight. She wanted me to invite you to come have supper with us." She looks up at Michael and flutters her lashes. "And you, too, if you want."

"Yeah," Michael says. "I love pork chops."

I cover my mouth with my hand to keep from chuckling. *The kid hates pork chops.*

Pops is on his feet faster than I've seen him in a long time. "I was just thinking that a plate of scalloped potatoes sounded good. I'll follow you kids out."

Ava smiles at Jack and then returns her attention to me. "I go to town a couple of times a week for piano lessons. So if you need anything, just let me know."

"I will. Thank you."

Michael races to the door, holding it open for her and Pops. He exchanges a look with his father before he sets off after Mrs. Shaw's granddaughter.

"What was that all about?" I ask, staring at the doorway.

"I think you know what that was all about." He saunters toward me. "What's in the basket?"

The look in his eye makes me flush, and I head to the refrigerator to make a glass of tea instead of standing close to him.

"Lasagna," he says. "Garlic bread and a bottle of wine."

I look over my shoulder as Jack sets the wine next to a baking dish. The room is scented with garlic and tomatoes, making my stomach rumble.

The door flies open, catching us off guard. Maddie sticks her beaming face around the frame. "I'm going to Ava Shaw's for dinner, okay? Bye!"

The door slams before we can answer her.

My heart races as Jack's attention lands squarely on me. There's nowhere else to divert it, no one else around to include in our conversation. It's not even bedtime, when I could feign sleep.

This is precisely what I don't want.

There's no way for this to end well. Either we end up in a heated conversation about something inconsequential—where we'd then have to contend with animosity between us for the next two weeks—or we manage to be civil. Where would that get me?

I've fought too hard to get here—to the stage of apathy that Jack has deemed worse than heartbreak. I'm finally to the point where I've accepted my marriage for what it is . . . and what it isn't. And life is easier when those lines aren't blurred.

Why bother blurring them now? *It's one dinner, Lo. You are totally overthinking this.*

"I guess it's just me and you," he says. "This is still warm. Want to eat now?"

I face the window and close my eyes for a moment.

"We could go sit out back," he says. "Maybe I could clean out the firepit, and we could pull up some lawn chairs."

A smile ghosts my lips as I open my eyes again.

"Or we could just pack this back up and drive out to where I proposed." His voice is a touch shakier than before. "I don't think the mosquitoes are as bad as they were that night."

My heartstrings pull just enough to loosen the guard around my heart a little bit more.

"And ticks," I say, still not facing him. "That year was so bad for the tiny ones. I wore my brand-new engagement ring into the dollar store and bought lint rollers to try to get them off us."

His chuckle caresses me from the other side of the room.

"That was one of the happiest days of my life," I say, the words fading into the evening.

Jack moves quietly across the kitchen before coming to a stop behind me. His presence is that powerful, that familiar, that I don't have to turn around to see if I'm right. My body instinctively leans toward him, and it's all I can do to fight it.

"That was one of the luckiest days of my life," he says softly.

"Not the happiest?"

"I think I was too awestruck that you actually said yes to be happy." My chest bounces with a suppressed laugh.

"Lauren Madeline McKenzie, I can honestly say you weren't looking your best the night we met," Jack says.

I laugh and hold tight because this is going somewhere. Something is on his mind, and it has been all weekend. The impromptu trip to the cabin. His inability to sit still. The odd suggestion of a picnic and the coincidence that Mrs. Shaw had a picnic basket ready at the Cupboard.

His face smoothens and then grows serious. A bubble of anxiety mixed with excitement grows in my stomach.

"Jack—"

He places a finger against my lips. "But even then, with your alcohol-poisoning fears and vomit breath, I knew you were the one." His shy smile melts my heart. "I loved you then, but I love you even more now."

My heart pounds. Is he . . .

"Marry me, Lo."

I gasp. "Jack . . ."

He chuckles nervously. "Is that a yes?"

"That's a . . ." I blink back tears and fling myself into his strong arms. "I would be honored to marry you."

"The happiest day," he says, brushing a strand of hair off my shoulder, "is the day you followed through with it and married me."

Tears cloud my eyes. The emotion in his voice—the genuineness, the hope, maybe—stirs a barrel of similar feelings in my heart.

"Why are you doing this?" I ask, not pulling away as his knuckles slide down my arm.

"What exactly do you think I'm doing?"

I exhale and pivot on my heel.

The depths of his brown eyes knock me off-balance. There isn't a shield separating us. No levity can be found. It's just Jack. *My Jack.*

"What do I need to do to fix this, Lo? Tell me."

I sigh, walking around him in a wide circle. My head and heart collide. They both want what's best for me. The problem is that they don't agree.

"Don't walk away from me," he says, frustration thick in his tone. "Talk to me."

"Why? Because you decided that right now is convenient for you?"

I stop at the far end of the table and face him. It's enough space to give me room to think.

His lips part for what I'm sure is going to be a sarcastic reply, but he stops himself. Then he restarts. "That's fair."

I look at him, mouth gaping. My brain spins at this unexpected twist of events.

"Lauren, I'm sorry."

Blood pushes through my veins at warp speed. "Sorry for what?"

"When it all boils down, I'm sorry for putting you in a position where you think the only way you can be happy is to be without me."

I steady myself against the chair in front of me.

"I had no idea you were thinking about divorce," he says. "And it's bullshit that it took that to make me realize what was going on. That's probably a symptom of the problem. But, Lo, there has to be a way for us to work on this. To fix it. *Please.*"

The evening orchestra of insects and frogs has begun to play outside the window. Their soft rhythm amplifies the tension in the room.

"You can't want this," he says. "You can't want to walk away from the life we've built."

"That's not the choice I'm making."

His brows raise.

"I'm not making a choice about whether to walk away from our family or not," I say. "I'm choosing to *have a life*. To not feel like an after-thought, like . . . an actress in the background of your life that gets to come onstage every now and then and say a line before exiting stage left."

The words topple from my lips. Jack, for his part, stands silently. Whether he listens to what I'm saying, I'm not sure. He might be using the time to construct his next argument instead of hearing mine. *That would be par for the course.* But to his credit, he doesn't try to interject. So I keep going.

"Think about it," I say, releasing the chair. "What have you done in the last twenty years?" I pause, waiting on a response that doesn't come. "Okay, I'll help you. You've started a business that you've wanted to start since you were a teenager. Every day, you get up and go work on your passion. Yes, you make money and take care of your family—I'm not taking anything away from that. But you get to do it while working on cars. *You chose that.*"

He nods carefully.

I pace the kitchen. "You coached Michael in wrestling for a few years, but now you don't have time. You have a ton of people that you go out with for lunch because you have to. How often do you go to lunch because you feel like it? How often do you hop in the truck with one of your buddies to go check out a car and talk and catch up on the way? When was the last time you thought about calling me and seeing if I'm free for lunch?"

His face falls.

"You dictate your own schedule, and it rarely, if ever, coincides with mine. Oh—you're on the town business board, which you love, and I'm happy for you. Your life is rich with choices and options and opportunities and friends and fulfillment. It overflows with shit that you get to decide, that fulfills *you*." I gasp a breath. *I can't believe these words are finding air.* "But those options? Those all-consuming things? They don't include me. And they haven't for a long damn time."

He runs a hand down his face, his eyes wide. I should stop. I've said enough things that I'll probably regret later, but I can't. The words keep coming.

"You have the privilege of doing those things—why? Because everything else in your life is taken care of. All of that tedious, tasky stuff like bills and laundry and science projects and fighting with the insurance company over Maddie's braces—guess who gets the pleasure of doing that?"

His chest rises and falls, but he doesn't speak.

"Me," I say, pointing at myself. I stop next to the pantry. "You have the luxury of creating a life because I've taken all the pressure off you otherwise."

Jack's eyes widen.

"I'm not complaining about being a mother. I realize that I had the luxury of staying home with the kids because you took the financial pressure off of me. I get that. *I appreciate that.* But when did becoming a mother mean I had to give up everything else? When did it become an exclusive choice: 'Be a mother, but that's all you can be'?"

I pause, heaving a breath and giving him a chance to respond. He doesn't.

"I have given *my life* to you and the kids, Jack. And I don't even care that no one sees it. I don't want a 'Thank you' or an 'Attagirl.' It's truly my pleasure. But when did you forget about us, Jack? When did it stop occurring to you to want time with me? Because it's as though somewhere along the line, I became an accessory to your life. Not your partner, your best friend. An invisible person that keeps you going behind the scenes. And I just can't . . . I want . . . what I want, *what I need*, is for someone to just . . . *see me.*"

Tears fog my eyes again. I bite my cheek in a futile attempt at stopping them from falling.

We've never gotten here—never gotten to the true crux of the matter. We've had pieces of this conversation, scattered over the course of many years. Spewed with anger. Spat with bitterness and snide remarks.

But we always end up bickering, cutting one another off, and rolling our eyes before we ever get to the point.

I gasp a breath, the air filling my lungs more easily than it has in a long time. My heart beats unencumbered. With the truth now hanging between us—reality raw and true—I'm able to stand a little taller . . . and freer.

"Lo . . ."

"Michael and Maddie will be graduating soon and moving out. If we stay in this same pattern where our lives continue on as it is . . . what's left for me? *Of me?* Story Books, I hope. But who knows if I can make a long-term run at professional scrapbooking." I laugh, wiping my nose with the back of my hand like a lady. "But what else is there? More nights alone? More tears in the shower? Another meal standing at the island watching videos on my phone, so I forget how lonely—how forgotten—I am?"

"You are not forgotten."

"Really?" I smile sadly. "Did you realize I stopped calling you at night six months ago?"

His Adam's apple bobs.

"When was the last time we had our Wednesday lunch date?" I ask.

His shoulders drop.

"I was on national TV, Jack, and you didn't mention it." My voice breaks, hiccuping the hurt. "You forget I'm there. You can say you don't, but you do."

He reaches for me, but the wildness in his eyes makes me pull away.

"I love you," I say, tears falling freely. "But I feel so broken. I can't break myself to build you anymore."

"Lauren . . ."

I don't hear the rest of the sentence. The screen door slamming behind me echoes loudly into the night.

And Jack doesn't follow me.

CHAPTER THIRTEEN

LAUREN

Here you go, Snaps," Maddie says, pouring water from her bottle into a collapsible bowl. "It's hot out here, buddy."

The puppy plops a foot in the bowl before drinking, his little tail shaking happily. His fur presses against his body from a swim in the lake with Maddie. I'm not sure that I've ever seen a happier puppy.

Water laps against the side of the boat. The sun glows overhead in a hazy, muted kind of way that is amazing against my skin. I stretch out on the bench and get repositioned on my towel.

We left the cabin after breakfast and headed for Story Brook Lake. Michael put up a small fight, wanting to spend his day with Ava instead. But once Pops alerted him to the fact that Ava would be in town at piano lessons—something he'd heard from Mrs. Shaw—Michael capitulated.

"It's been a nice day, huh?" Maddie asks, situating herself on the bench across from me.

I grin. "It really has."

"It's better with the boys in the other boat." Snaps curls at her feet. "I'm always afraid they're going to stick me with a lure when they're casting."

"That happened to your dad once."

"It did?"

I nod, tugging my hat over my eyes. "Well, your dad did the sticking. Pops got stuck."

Maddie laughs. "Makes perfect sense. I mean, have you seen Dad fish? His patience doesn't translate well to the sport."

Chuckling, I rest my hands on my stomach and breathe in the fresh, sunblock-scented air.

I woke up this morning with a lightness I wasn't expecting. When I came back to the cabin last night, Jack was waiting at the table. There wasn't time to talk, thankfully, because the kids returned soon after I did. I wasn't sure what I was going to say anyway.

They convinced us to play euchre—me and Michael against Jack and Maddie. After four games, a bottle of wine, and reheated lasagna, I wasn't any closer to knowing how to follow up on our earlier conversation. Nor was I closer to wanting to hear his rebuttal. And when we went to bed with a welcome buzz fueled by alcohol, carbohydrates, and laughter, I fell asleep as soon as my head hit the pillow.

"Hey, Mads," Michael calls from the other boat. "Come here and see this."

Maddie scoops up the puppy and carefully climbs into her brother's boat.

"Jack, can you grab me a drink?" Pops asks. "This heat is starting to get to me."

"Do you need to go back, Pops?" Maddie asks.

"It probably wouldn't hurt anything to head on back. You kids can stay out here, if ya want."

The boat rocks with Jack's weight. I close my eyes just in case I can catch a glimpse of him under the brim of my hat.

"You want a drink, Lo?" Ice rattles in the cooler. "Michael, catch this for Pops."

A spray of ice-cold water drips across my body as the bottle flies above me. Water droplets sit on my skin, quickly drying in the heat.

"Sorry about that," Jack says, making it clear he's not at all sorry.

I ignore him.

I've had a lot of time today on the water to think about last night. Vocalizing my feelings to Jack—*and having him listen*—freed me in a surprising way. The vault of bullshit I've harbored inside me for years was emptied. The crap is still there, lying around my soul like rubbish. None of it was picked up, so to speak. But at least it's not stacked so high that it's choking me out.

My thoughts, my marriage—it's all more manageable today. It's clearer. It's as if those words I spewed at Jack relieved me of some of my burdens. I can now see other things.

My overfunctioning in this relationship, my need to control details of our lives, is a big component in our disfunction too. The link between me doing everything and Jack doing even less is strong . . . and that's a hard marble to digest.

I've been making it impossible for Jack to do many of the things I'm asking him to do.

That's been eating at me all day.

The peace is broken by the other boat's engine coming to life. I sit up to make sure the kids are seated. Jack is bent over our boat's engine, fiddling with it.

"What's wrong, Dad?" Michael asks as Maddie unties our boat from theirs.

"I don't know. I think we're out of fuel," Jack says.

You've got to be kidding me. "What do you mean 'we're out of fuel'?"

Jack turns around, wiping his brow. "I mean, I don't think there's fuel to start the engine."

"Whose job was it to check that?" I ask, ignoring the sweat droplets trickling down his chiseled abdomen.

Slowly, Jack turns his attention to the other boat. So I do too.

Michael grins sheepishly as they drift farther away. "Um, I might've forgotten to do that."

"Michael," I say, watching Maddie use Snaps's paw to wave goodbye. "Come back here so we can get on your boat."

"And then what, sugarplum?" Pops asks. "We sink and none of us get back?"

"You won't sink with us on there, Dad," Jack says.

Pops shrugs. "I don't make the rules. There's a sticker on this thing somewhere that gives a weight limit, and we'll exceed that if you two get on here."

I get to my feet. "This is not funny."

"We'll bring you a gas can," Michael says. "It won't take that long."

"We're at the farthest inlet from the boathouse," Jack says, a hand on his hip. It draws attention to the muscle that runs along his side. "It'll take you at least an hour to get there, find gas, and then get back out here."

Pops snickers. "An hour at least. Hell, it might be three if that little blonde is done with her piano lessons and is sitting on the beach, waiting for Michael."

"You'll be fine," Maddie says. "And if we get sidetracked coming back, you could always just sleep on the boat."

"Or hike back. The cabin ain't but a couple of miles up that trail over there." Pops points at the dirt lane barely noticeable through the pine trees.

"If you don't come back with a gas can, you're both grounded," I say.

My words get lost in the roar of their engine as they speed away, laughing.

I plop down on the bench and sigh. *Now what?*

"Your kids are starting to get on my nerves," I say.

Jack laughs. "My kids, huh? This is definitely *your kids* shit."

My gaze follows him as he moves effortlessly across the boat. He sits across from me, his cologne amplified by the heat. His arms stretch along the edge of the boat, and he smiles.

"You're not worried that we're stranded here?" I ask.

"Not really."

"You don't really think they'd let us sit out here all night, do you?"

He smirks. "Lo, I'm not really sure about anything when it comes to those two working in conjunction with my father."

I settle back, resting against the side of the boat.

We sit quietly for a few minutes, riding along with the waves. Tall pine trees loom overhead. They provide a bit of shade as we float into the shadows.

"I'm not really sure what I'm supposed to do here," Jack says.

"What do you mean?"

"I mean, we're sitting on this boat staring at each other, and I don't know if I'm supposed to make small talk like you're a stranger or talk to you like you're my wife."

"What's the difference?"

He cocks a brow toward the sky.

"We've been married strangers for a long time," I say. "This should come naturally to us at this point."

"The fact that it's not natural means something, does it not?"

I shrug. *I don't know.*

The truth is that when we're all together, playing euchre or hanging out on the boat with eighties hits—the only music we all can agree on—rocking through the speakers, I remember what it used to be like with us.

The heat in Jack's eyes across the bow of the boat. How his fingertips would graze the small of my back like he couldn't manage not to touch me. The inside jokes we'd laugh about despite everyone else thinking we were goofy.

I felt so safe with Jack for so long. I was happy—blissfully so—with him for so many years. And then . . . then I just wasn't.

"I had no idea you were thinking about divorce. And it's bullshit that it took that to make me realize what was going on. That's probably a symptom of the problem. But, Lo, there has to be a way for us to work on this. To fix it. Please."

My breath stalls in my chest as his words ring in my mind. I can't shake them. I almost can't move on from them.

I expected a reaction from him—a guilt trip or a charge of overreaction. I hadn't considered that he would want to resurrect something he's simply let go.

He says he doesn't want a divorce, but is that really true? Is he panicking because he hasn't had enough time to sit with the idea of ending things? Or does he mean it when he says this isn't over?

Could things go back to the way they used to be?

I wonder, *I'm scared*, that it's the same phenomenon that occurs when a nasty person dies. No one goes to their funeral and talks about the awful parts of their life. No one says, "Uncle Joe was an asshole who cheated on Aunt Nancy and gambled away all their money." It's never that. It's always tears and tales of all the good things that person did—even if they have to practically make them up.

Is that what it would be if I gave in? Would I get a couple of good days with my family, if I'm lucky, and then go right back to the life I've been desperate to change? Am I effectively in the funeral stage of my marriage, remembering all the good parts before I bury it forever?

"Fine," he says, running his hands down the length of his crimson board shorts. "I'll pick. You are hot as hell, Lauren Reed."

His tone is thick with intent, and his gaze settles so heavily on mine that I can barely breathe.

"If I wasn't already married to you, I'd be figuring out how to be," he says. "And since I already am, I'm figuring out how to stay that way."

I look across the water, my cheeks matching the hue of his trunks.

He gives me a moment to let that sink in to my brain before he moves on—thankfully, in a different direction.

"You know they're not coming back, right?" he asks.

"Yeah." I sigh. "What do we do?"

"Well, Dad was right. That trail over there will practically take us to the back door of the cabin."

I turn to him. "I'm not really feeling a two-mile hike in this heat."

"Wanna camp out here with me, then?" He grins. "There's not a ton of room for you to fake sleep. Keep that in mind."

"Says the man that pretends to be asleep every night we've been here."

"I've been reading the room."

"Sure," I say, nodding sarcastically.

"When you roll onto your side and basically play dead, I take the hint. It's called 'giving you space.'"

"You're really good at that."

"What? You don't like it?" he asks.

"I think I've made that abundantly clear."

His lips twitch into a smirk. "Noted."

A fire heats in my belly, and I squirm in my seat.

"What else don't you like?" he asks. "What else do I do that bothers you?"

I snort.

"Come on," he says, goading me. "We have time. Give me a list. Get it all off your chest."

I consider blowing him off. I also weigh the option of diving from the boat and swimming to shore. But the intensity in his eyes and his repeated requests to fix our marriage break me down. Not that I think he'll follow through with it, but more to make him stop playing this game with me.

"Okay," I say, grabbing a water bottle from the cooler and sitting back down. "I'll humor you."

He smiles.

"What does Jack Reed do that bothers me?" I say before taking a long drink. "Where do I start?"

"God, you're beautiful."

"That." I point at him. "That bothers me."

His brows pull together. "That I give you a compliment?"

"That you're insinuating that I'm that easily won over. That I'm so pathetic that you can tell me I'm pretty and I'll forget all about the rest."

"*Okay.* Continue," he says, like he's not sure if I've had heatstroke.

"It bothers me that you don't see me as a whole person with hopes and dreams of my own."

"And?"

"And I hate when you tell me not to handle things because you'll do it, and then you don't."

"Like what?" he asks.

I stretch my arms out along the side of the boat. This amuses him for some reason, and he mirrors my position.

"Like when you tell me not to hang the mirror in the foyer," I say.

"Are you serious?"

"Yes, I'm serious."

He laughs. "Lauren, it's a fucking mirror."

"That I have to see every fucking day. It matters to me."

"You and ladders have proven, *repeatedly*, that you aren't friends. I apologize for wanting to save your life."

"I didn't ask you to save my life. I asked you to hang a mirror. *A year ago.* When you don't do it, I have to because it can't sit there leaned up against the wall forever. It'll get broken."

He nods, holding up a palm. "Okay. What else?"

"You know what I really hate?" I ask, my face heating. "I hate when you *are* home and the shop calls and you just get up and go. There's not even a flinch of thought about it. *The shop always wins.* It doesn't matter if we're doing something as a family or at a wrestling meet. You just . . . go."

"But, Lo—it's my business."

"Yes, *but we are your family.*" I force a swallow past the lump in my throat. "I'm not saying you never have to get up and go because, believe it or not, I am rational. I understand things are important and you're the boss. But you've trained your team, Jack. They've stopped even trying to do things because they know you'll come running. That pisses me off—not just for me and Maddie and Michael, but for you too."

His temple pulses. *Have I pushed too far?*

"Okay, got it," he says. "What else?"

I stare at him for a long moment. *What else? He really wants me to keep going?* But the longer I sit quietly, the longer he waits me out.

Fine. "Mow the field beside the house."

"I did mow the field beside the house."

I laugh. "Yeah. You did. Two years ago. Want to know how I know? Because last year, I paid to have someone do it because the kids couldn't even play basketball on the driveway because of the bugs. And last month, the guy I hired last year came back to see if I wanted him to do it again—which I did, by the way. Did you even notice? Or did you assume, I don't know, that I was doing it?"

He sighs, his jaw flexing. *Guess what, Jack? I don't like this either.*

A rise of emotion lifts from my chest—the burn of anger, the fog of sadness, and the bitterness of regret. It's all I can do to hold it together—to stay calm. To show him the things that have gotten me to this point. But the mountain of grudges I want to get off my chest feels insurmountable, and the pain of it all grows by the second.

"Okay," he says, finally. "I'll put a reminder in my phone to mow—"

"I hate that you never want to have sex with me."

The words are in the air before I know I'm going to say them. It's as if they've been sneaking behind the other frustrations until they could find an opening to burst into the scene.

And in the scene they are.

Jack's eyes widen, and his jaw falls open. I pull my arms down and shift on the bench.

"You think . . . ," he says, pausing to gather himself. "You think that I don't want to have sex with you?"

The words are padded with disbelief. They're laced with shock. He says them like he's still trying to process them . . . and failing.

"What else am I supposed to think?" I ask, my cheeks warm to the touch.

He runs a hand down his face. *"Wow."*

"It doesn't matter what I do," I say. "I don't get your attention."

"When I give you my attention, you get pissed."

It's my jaw that drops this time. "What are *you* talking about?"

"I come up behind you while you're cooking, and you complain about your day. I ask you to ride with me to look at a car, and you act like it's the last thing you want to do. I climb in bed and reach for you, and you pull away and rattle off a list of all the shit you want me to do—and none of that is having sex."

"I . . ." *He's right. I do that.* I force a swallow that almost gags me. *Why can't he just hear me?* "I'm bitter. That's the ugly truth of it. It feels like just another thing I get to do for you."

His eyes widen.

"That sounds terrible, I know. But it *feels* terrible too," I say, blinking back red-hot tears. "I have no outlet. There's all of this stuff building inside me, and I have no one to talk to about it. It feels like no one cares. So when you do try to have sex with me and haven't bothered to even talk to me, let alone ask how my day was or take out the trash that's running over onto the floor, it feels like you're just asking me to use my body—the last thing that I have that's mine—for your benefit. And that's . . . hard."

"Wow." He blows out a breath, bowing his head. "I need to process that."

"I'm just frustrated," I say, my heart thumping. "It's hard to feel like you've skipped off to have a life and left me behind to clean up after you. I have value beyond my homemaking skills, you know."

The irritation gathered at the corners of his eyes is there, but it's softened. The blaze in his eyes has calmed a touch. I'm too seasoned to hope he's actually listened to me. *But I wish I weren't.*

"Maybe if you didn't act like you didn't want me around, I'd put more emphasis on coming around," he says. "It's really hard to initiate sex when you know you're going to get turned down, Lo."

I look at the deck.

"And it hurts a lot fucking worse when you're getting turned down by the love of your life," he says. "That's why I haven't tried since Thanksgiving weekend."

I can't deny the pain in his voice, and I can't pretend that it's not warranted. If I'm being honest with myself, he's not wrong. And that makes *me* feel shitty.

The whole thing is complicated and screwed up and awful—and I just want it to end.

Jack stands, causing the boat to rock. "I'm going to hop in the lake and grab the rope. I'll swim over to that tree over there and get the boat secured. Then we can hike back to the cabin."

I nod, pulling my gaze to his.

Energy crackles between us. I hold my breath, unsure what's about to happen.

Will he grab me and kiss me senselessly? Maybe. Is he going to tell me that I'm right and we need to divorce? Possibly. He could tell me he's equally sick of this and to fuck off—I don't know.

My heart pounds, and my breathing quickens. A frantic blast of panic races up my spine.

"Jack—"

Splash! He dives into the water, grabs the rope, and swims toward shore.

He doesn't look back.

CHAPTER FOURTEEN

LAUREN

Y ou have to get your kids under control—*ouch!*" I yelp, jerking my arm away from a thornbush. My flip-flops, the absolute worst footwear decision I might've ever made, slip on the dirt, and I slide. "They went too far with this."

Jack stands a few feet up the trail, grinning. "Come on. You're doing great."

"Stop." I check out the scratches on my arm. "Don't pander to me."

"Fine. We could've been back half an hour ago if you would stop getting into every prickly piece of vegetation you can find. So can you just stay on the trail and move it?"

I narrow my eyes at him. "Pander to me."

He laughs, offering me a hand. I slap my palm in his begrudgingly and let him help me up the slope.

The air is thicker in the forest. Somehow, it's more humid. Bugs are everywhere, swooping toward my face and landing on my bare legs. I'm not sure if they're drawn more to my dripping sweat or the specks of blood pricked by the plants. Either way, they love me.

I do not love them.

"Maybe one of our kids can be an insectologist and figure out how to rid the world of gnats," I say, batting my hand in front of my face and blowing. "We can go to Mars, but we are still battling gnats. Make it make sense."

Jack stops and lets go of my hand. I plant my palms on my knees and draw in a long breath, praying I don't inhale any winged protein.

"Bugs have a place in the ecosystem," he says, looking amused.

"Then I don't. We're mutually exclusive." I stand tall and peer up the hill. "How far are we away?"

His gaze follows mine. "Farther than you want it to be. I don't know why they rerouted that trail, but it probably added an extra mile back to the cabins."

"You're telling me we have a mile to go?"

He laughs and smacks me on the ass. "Get moving."

I groan and follow him.

We've been walking for what feels like forever, and although my legs are lead, my heart is heavier.

"And it hurts a lot fucking worse when you're getting turned down by the love of your life."

Jack slows and I walk beside him, sneaking a peek at his profile. I notice the downturn of his lips and take in the lines around his eyes. He's in thought too. *I wonder if he's thinking about me.*

I hate that I made him feel that way, because I know how much it stings. That's how he's made me feel.

Is it possible that Jack didn't mean to hurt me, just like I didn't mean to hurt him? Are we both victims, in a sense, of our situation? Did one wrong turn into two, and before we knew it, we'd made so many wrong turns that we were now on different streets?

The possibility makes my chest burn. *What do I do with that? Does it change anything? Aren't we still in the same place we were before—now we just have a better idea of how we got here?*

"When did you start sleeping in my shirts?" he asks.

I shrug. "I don't know. Around Christmas, maybe. I started getting hot flashes and couldn't stand wearing much to bed. But you know I have that fear of the house burning in the middle of the night, so I have to wear something to bed in case firefighters bust into my room."

The corner of his lip twitches.

"Do you care that I sleep in your shirts?" I ask.

"Not at all. I like it, actually."

I tuck my chin against my chest to hide my grin.

"How is Story Books going?" he asks, slowing his pace even more.

My grin grows wider, and I give up. I look at him, my heart turning over like an hourglass. Only this time, it's slowly filling instead of consistently running out.

"It's going really well," I say, stepping over a fallen tree. "I have work booked through the end of the year already, and I've probably turned away three times as many projects as I've taken on."

He nods. "Wow."

"Yeah. It's wild, really. To think that Maddie's silly videos made this all happen for me is mind blowing."

"She didn't make that happen for you, Lo. *You* made it happen."

The bridge of my nose burns like it does when I stumble upon a video about someone being nice to someone else or a special reunion between a mother and her child. *Or a husband and wife.*

"I'm really happy for you," he says softly. "And I have so much respect for you."

My throat constricts, and my eyes blur.

"I started the shop, and it's all I had to do, you know," he says. "I could pour twenty-four hours a day there if I needed to. Then I could go home, and my kids were healthy and happy because you were there taking care of everything else." He chuckles. "But you manage to do *everything else* and start a business that will wind up being more profitable than mine."

Using the edge of my shirt, I dab my eyes.

The flood of emotions pouring into my heart is more than I can weather. Hearing my husband tell me he respects me, and that he recognizes what I'm doing, is everything. It's more than everything. It begins to fill a hole in my soul that was gaping a lot more than I realized.

"I'm proud of you, Lauren. I can't wait to watch you kick ass."

"Damn you, Jack," I say, laughing through my tears.

"What?" He holds a tree branch back until I pass. "Why 'damn me'?"

"Because it's easier when you're a dick, and I can just be mad at you."

"Oh, so now you're mad because I'm *not* a dick? I'm never going to be able to win with you, am I?" he asks, smiling. "You're impossible."

"I'm—*shit!*"

The toe of my flip-flop gets tangled in the root of a tree sticking up from the dirt. The rubber bends enough to trip me. I launch forward, spiraling through the air, until I land on my hands and knees in the hard, rocky dirt.

"What the hell?" Jack kneels down beside me, helping me turn over onto my butt. "Are you okay?"

I whine, reaching for my ankle. A shot of pain blasts up my calf, and I can feel my foot starting to swell.

Jack presses the side of my foot. I jerk it back and yelp.

"Does that hurt?" he asks.

"No. It feels great." I pull it farther away from him. "Don't touch it."

"How will I know if it's broken if I don't touch it?"

"What are you, a doctor now?"

He laughs, shaking his head.

"This freaking hurts," I say, wincing as a zip of fire makes its way through my foot. "Ouch!"

"What do you want to do?"

I close my eyes and fake cry.

"That's not going to help," he says.

I look at him. "You asked what I want to do. In lieu of better solutions, crying is my choice."

He rolls his eyes and offers me his hand. I take it and let him help me to my feet. He finds my flip-flops and slides them on for me.

"Can you stand on it?" he asks.

I put it down gently. My foot throbs, but the pain isn't as intense as I feared.

"Can you walk?" he asks.

I take a step forward. It's more of a hobble than a walk, but it's forward progress.

"Yeah," I say, sucking in a breath as a bolt of heat knocks me off-balance. "I can make it." I take a few more half steps while Jack watches, unamused.

"It will take you all night to get back," he says.

I stop in the middle of the path. "What choice do I have? Want me to crawl? That'd be great for my knees."

He smirks. "If you want to do something on your knees, I can give you a better alternative."

My stomach tightens at the heat in his eyes.

He holds my gaze for a long moment before walking in front of me. "Climb on."

"What?"

"Climb on my back. I'll carry you to the cabin."

I laugh. "You're not giving me a piggyback ride for a mile."

He sighs. "What do you want to do? Hobble?"

"I'll walk. Slowly," I say, thinking it through. "But I can walk."

"Look, you have two choices. One, you can climb on my back. Two, I'll pick you up and throw you over my shoulder."

The knot in my lower belly grows even tighter. *Am I this deprived?* He grins as if he knows what I'm thinking. *Yes, yes I am.*

"The closer to dusk it gets, the more bugs are going to come out," he says, hitting me where it hurts. "I'm also so thirsty that I might hold you down and drink your spit."

"Ew!" I say, laughing.

He laughs too. "Now hop on, or else."

A part of me wants to see what the second option would get me because something tells me that if I push it that far, there will be more involved than being thrown over his shoulder. And despite the pain gathering in my ankle, it might be worth it.

"Let's go," he says, turning his back to me.

"Fine," I say, gripping his shoulders before hopping on his back.

He gets me situated and marches off like some kind of trained special forces soldier.

I drape my arms over his shoulders so I don't find myself pawing at his muscles. The feeling of him between my legs brings back a load of memories that I'd either forgotten or buried.

Good lord, we couldn't keep our hands off each other. The intensity of my orgasms on our honeymoon—I thought I would split in two. The night Jack went down on me and I moaned so loud that the people in the apartment next door started pounding on the walls. *Because I was in heaven.*

Driving around old country roads, listening to a song that made us both so horny that we had to stop. We fucked on the hood of his car next to a herd of cattle under the moonlight. And I saw stars—not just the ones in the brilliant night sky.

The week we bought our first home, I was so worried that Harvey would come over and find a bra or thong lying somewhere, because Jack and I would tear each other's clothes off as soon as we walked in the door after work. Multiple times. Multiple positions. Multiple locations . . . *every night.*

Stop. Stop thinking about this. Switch gears.

"How is the shop doing?" I ask. *I haven't asked him about this either.*

He presses his fingers against my thighs. "Good. I just found a machine that will let us dyno-tune cars. It should bring us a lot of new customers. I'm pretty excited about it."

"That's great, Jack."

He stops and adjusts my position before starting again.

"I really hope you'll come by one day and let me show you around," he says. "I know it's not your thing, but you've helped build it. It would mean a lot to me."

My heart softens. This. This is what I've missed. Jack's invitation into his life. "I'd love to."

"Really?"

I don't know why I'm smiling, but I am. I also don't know why I agreed to go to the shop or why I said I'd love to . . . but I would.

When Jack first started the shop, I used to go by all the time. Seeing him excited and proud of his work made me excited and proud of him too. But at some point, that changed. *Maybe it just changed for me.*

"I mean, I'll have no idea what I'm looking at and I won't understand anything you're talking about. But, yeah. I'll come by and see your dinosaur thing," I say.

He laughs. "Dyno-tune, not dinosaur."

"Whatever," I say, laughing too. "But if you want to see something that makes less sense than a dinosaur machine, come by my brand-new office that used to be the guest room and see this scrapbook I'm doing for a lady from Boston. She sent me thirteen feathers, a cigar box of pine needles from somewhere in Arizona, and a piece of what I'm hoping is a balloon—among other things."

"What?"

"I can't make this up. People are so weird."

"That they are."

We walk along the path, Jack twisting to keep sticker bushes from brushing against my legs. The forest begins to darken. The sunlight streaming through the leaves dims. A heaviness settles into my heart, and I blow out a long, deep breath.

"Hey, Jack?"

"Yeah."

I force a swallow. "I'm sorry for not asking about the shop and how things are going there. I guess I've kind of checked out of your life too."

His pace slows. "Thanks, Lo."

I settle against him and sigh.

The cabin comes into view just beyond the top of the incline. Jack plods up the path, through the small backyard, and around the side of the house. We make our way up the stairs with ease.

"That last mile went a whole lot faster with you doing all the work," I say.

"You always preferred me to do all the work."

I smack his shoulder, making him chuckle.

"It wasn't a mile," he says, squeezing my thighs again. "Maybe a half. Or maybe it *was* a mile, and I was distracted with your legs wrapped around me."

Grinning, I pull the screen door open, and we step inside the living room.

"Home sweet home," he says as he carries me to the couch.

I slide off his back, soaking in every last bit of contact with his body. Once I'm off, he turns to face me.

He searches my eyes, the deep browns speckled with a host of gold flecks. I hold my breath, unsure if he's going to smile, kiss me, or switch back to disagreeable Jack.

He leans forward, lowering his head slowly toward mine. I hiccup a quick breath as my heart smacks against my ribs.

"I'm sure you want a shower, but let's get you on the couch and that foot elevated first, okay?" he says, reaching beside me and grabbing a pillow. "I'll get you some ice."

I blow out a breath and release the hope I had inadvertently gathered.

"Okay," I say, lying on the couch. I prop my foot on the pile of pillows Jack's put together. "How's that?"

"Perfect."

And with that, he heads to the kitchen, leaving me with a throb in my foot and an ache in my chest. Because for the first time in a long time, I think I want to kiss my husband.

CHAPTER FIFTEEN

JACK

I run a hand through my hair and give my reflection a final glance. "Not bad, Reed. Not bad."

The bathroom is scented with Lauren's bodywash. She's used the same brand the entire time I've known her, because she remembers her grandmother promising her that if she used it, she wouldn't get wrinkles.

The thought makes me smile.

I go back to the bedroom and slide on a pair of shorts and shirt. Lauren's towel is on the edge of the bed. She insisted on a shower, but I hurried her through it and got her back on the couch with a drink and a book—and her ankle propped up on the pillow tower.

My heart beats steadily, encouraged from our interaction today. I wasn't sure how it was going to go when we boarded the boats. But thanks to those damn kids of ours, I couldn't have asked for a better ending.

I adjust my cock. *Well, aside from ending it with that.*

It's been entirely too long since I've slept with my wife. After a huge fight about it at Thanksgiving, I haven't even brought it up. When she doesn't want me, it kills a part of my soul.

But that doesn't mean I've stopped thinking about her or wanting her, and the anticipation of maybe getting to touch her again makes me feel like I did the night I met her.

Before I can get to the hallway, my phone buzzes on the dresser. Cursing the reception gods—*Why can't phones not work in the cabins at all this year, like they haven't the last four decades?*—I pick it up.

"Hello?" I ask.

"Hey, it's Tommy. We have a problem."

I sigh. "What's going on?"

"The city inspector is here. Someone filed a noise complaint."

"What for?"

"We've had a car on the dyno all morning. The thing is loud as hell, but there's nothing I can do about it."

Fuck. I squeeze my temple. "What's the inspector saying? Who is it, Hulburt or whatever his name is? The new guy?"

"Yeah, that's him. He's just asking questions about what we're doing and poking around, as they do."

I drop my hand. "Well, Hulburt is pretty reasonable. Explain to him that we're legal. Our place is zoned commercial, and we can do whatever we want during business hours."

"I told him that, and also that the people that moved into the place behind us—because you know they're the ones that called and complained—knew this was zoned commercial when they bought their house. That's on them. Our equipment is supposed to be here. That's what 'commercial' means." He pauses. "I think."

"That's what I would've told them."

"Well, maybe he would've been more apt to listen to you, because all I'm getting is a threat of a fine."

You've got to be kidding me. I groan.

I rustle through my things on top of the dresser, looking for my keys. It'll be a solid three hours to the shop, and I'll have to stop and get gas. *Fuck.*

The last thing I need is a fine to fight out with the city—not to mention that having a fine on our record, whether I get it removed or not, wouldn't make us look good. I don't want the reputation of being a troublemaker or the community to think I'm running a shady business.

"Jones is talking to Hulburt now," Tommy says. "I was starting to lose my cool."

That's two of us.

I find my keys under my hat and unplug my phone charger from the wall. But as I turn to the door, Lauren's cough travels down the hall.

My stomach clenches. I still.

This is where the rubber meets the road.

If I don't deal with this, it could cost me hours of my time—if not hundreds of dollars. It could also become a standing issue with the new neighbor. But if I leave . . .

My keys are heavy in my hand, and my shoes are sitting by the door. All I have to do is slide them on and take off.

Instead, my feet stay glued to the floor.

"Yes, but we are your family. I'm not saying you never have to get up and go because, believe it or not, I am rational. I understand things are important and you're the boss. But you've trained your team, Jack. They've stopped even trying to do things because they know you'll come running. That pisses me off—not just for me and Maddie and Michael, but for you too."

I was going to do exactly what she said I'd do. I didn't even think about it.

I toss my keys onto the dresser. They clatter against the wood. Relief flows through my body at the decision being made.

"Handle it, Tommy."

"What do you mean 'handle it'?"

"Handle it. Do your best. If he gives us a fine, I'll deal with it when I get back."

There's a long pause. "So . . . you're not coming back?"

"Nope. I'm here with my family. You're in charge back there. Figure it out, all right?"

"Cool," he says, not bothering to hide his surprise. "I got it. Go enjoy your family."

I grin. "Talk to you later."

"Later."

The line goes dead.

I hold the phone in my hand and force all thoughts of work out of my mind. *The shop will be fine without me. My family might not.* I toss my phone on the bed.

"Fuck it," I say, going down the hall.

Lauren's book is on her chest when I walk in the room. Her brows are pinched together.

"What's wrong?" I ask, heading to the fridge.

She clears her throat, starting to pull her leg from the pillows. I lift a brow and she freezes. I go back to the fridge.

"I wasn't eavesdropping," she says, settling against the sofa again. "But the cabin is so quiet, you know, and your voice drifts through the place."

"Okay?" I slide out a package of hamburger meat and toss it on the counter. "What about it?"

"Are you going back to the shop?"

The question is straightforward—an inquiry about my intentions about work. But that's not all it is.

It's an inquiry as to whether I've been listening.

My chest constricts as I come to terms with her expectations. *She expects me to leave.*

I glance at her over my shoulder, and the tightness around my lungs leaves little room for air. *I'm sorry for doing this to you, Lo.*

Billie's advice rolls through my head. In typical Billie fashion, it made sense . . . mostly.

"I'll put it in Jack terms. Do you even have a marriage maintenance plan?"

I laugh at her. "A what?"

131

"You're a mechanic. How often do you recommend people have their cars checked for oil, brakes, whatever?"

"Once a year, at least. Or whenever something seems wrong."

"When is the last time you did that with Lauren?"

My laughter subsides.

"Look, Jack—this doesn't have to be complicated, and you don't need my help. Actually, I can't even help you. You just need to . . . prioritize your life. Your real life. The core of who you are as a person."

Shit.

"If she's the most important thing in your life, then treat her like it," she says. *"Because the fact of the matter is that she's going to believe you when you show her how you feel. Remember that."*

I turn on the tap and wash my hands. *I owe Billie when I get home.*

"There used to be a pitch-in dinner at the end of the lake season, as we called it back then," I say, turning off the tap. "One summer, I was probably eight or nine, it was . . . *magic* that year. The weather was perfect. The lake water was cool and clean. All the moms would meet at the Cupboard in the evenings and play cards and have drinks or whatever. The dads would play horseshoes or sit on picnic tables and smoke cigars. It was a big community vibe."

"That sounds nice."

I grin, drying off my hands. "It was." I toss the towel next to the sink and take out a platter and seasonings. "Anyway, that particular year, everyone was jacked for the last get-together before we all went our separate ways. Mrs. Shaw procured a couple of homemade ice cream makers, and there was just this buzz about the night."

Lauren sits up. Interest mixed with confusion—*Why am I telling her this and not answering her question?*—is written across her beautiful face.

I open the package of meat and begin making patties. I remember doing this with my mom for years.

"Mom worked all afternoon making this pretzel-strawberry salad that my dad loved. And she made cucumbers and onion in vinegar—don't ask me why I remember that." I chuckle. "We were getting ready to head to the Cupboard. Mom had her little basket full of Tupperware, and I had my flashlight in case a game of flashlight tag popped off."

Lauren grins.

"And Dad left. Someone called in from work, and he split. Now that I think about it, he must have given them the landline number for the Cupboard to reach him. Anyway, I'll never forget the look on Mom's face as he kissed her cheek and let the screen door slam behind him. She stood there for a long second and then turned to me and acted like nothing happened. But I knew."

Lauren sets her cup on the end table and sits upright. Her eyes are wide, but she doesn't say a word.

"And I know that I've done that to you," I say slowly. I put a perfectly round patty on the plate and start on another one. "I don't know how I got so fucked up, Lo. Yeah, I was justifying things by saying I was working—and that was true. But I don't know how, or when, work took top priority." I look up at her. "I'm sorry for that."

She holds my gaze but doesn't speak. Her pupils widen, and I can see my words filtering through her eyes.

"Wow, Jack," she says, blowing out a breath. "I wasn't expecting that."

"I know. And I'm sorry you weren't." I frown. "So, the answer is no. I won't be going to work tonight. Tommy can handle it, and if he can't, then I'll handle it when we get back to town."

The smile that crosses her lips lights up a part of my soul that I'd forgotten was even there. I haven't seen this look on her face in years. Her smile is directed *at me* for something I've done—some way I've made her happy.

My God, how I've missed it.

"Well, Jack," she says before clearing her throat. "I appreciate that."

"You're welcome."

"I think I should apologize to you too," she says carefully.

I make the final patty and then throw the container away. Then I head to the sink to wash my hands again.

She exhales heavily. "Things became so *about me*."

"Well, I'm glad one of us was looking out for you."

The tension that's always between us is there, but different. She's not ready to storm out or shout at me, nor is she on the brink of hurling passive-aggressive insults my way. And for my part, I'm not waiting to dismiss what she says.

It's a juxtaposition—a comfortable strain stretching between us.

It also might be progress, if we're careful.

"I'm sorry I haven't . . . tried more, I guess," she says. "I've given up on us lately. There were reasons why; I remember the day I threw in the towel. But maybe if I hadn't—"

"As long as you pick it back up, we're going to be fine."

She smiles sadly. "Jack, I want us to be fine. I really do. But even admitting that out loud scares the shit out of me, because what if we get home and it all goes right back to the way it was? Will I have to start this process all over again? I don't know that I can do that."

Her shoulders soften.

"I promise that you won't have to do that," I say softly. "We've both made mistakes—me many more than you—but we have another four, five decades to work on it. And I don't want to go through those without you."

The smile she gives me is one of the most genuine ones I can remember in a long time. "Can you—"

"Hey, guys," Michael says, blasting through the door. His smile is stretched from ear to ear. "I see you made it back."

Damn it, Michael.

"When we get home, you're grounded," Lauren says, although she's smiling too.

Michael laughs. "Cool. We'll sit around the table, all four of us, and eat cake. It'll be great."

I catch Lauren's gaze. *Maybe things will be okay.*

"Whoa, Mom—what happened to your foot? Are you okay?" Michael asks.

Lauren places her foot back on the pillows. "It's much better than it appears. Your father is making me prop it up."

Her small smile sends a fire blazing in my chest. *God, I love her.*

"Okay, so," Michael says, "Ava's family has invited me for dinner."

"Again?" Lauren asks. "Michael, you're going to wear out your welcome."

"They love me. They think I'm handsome and charming—and I help do the dishes."

Lauren's brows tug together. "Are you sure?"

"Don't ruin this for me, Mom. *Please.*"

"Ruin what?"

"This thing with Ava." He sighs happily. "She's . . . special, Mom."

"Tell me you brought condoms," I say, point blank. There's no point in dancing around the bush. I was seventeen once, and I know that look in his eye.

"Jack!"

I shrug. "He's seventeen, Lo."

"And she's *hot*," Michael says.

Lauren's head hits the couch cushion, and she covers her face with her hands.

"Mom, listen—she likes to bake. She rides horses. She knows what a double-leg takedown is." He beams. "And you'll love this—she's taking advanced chemistry next year. Like, there's nothing to not love about her."

"Just be smart," I say, trying to buy Lauren a minute to get her wits about her. "You're only going to be here for two weeks. Don't lead her on. Don't make promises you can't keep. Treat her with respect."

Michael flinches. "Of course, Dad."

"If you want to talk about this without your mother around—"

"Why can't I be around?" Lauren asks, sitting up.

Michael snickers. "Do you really want to hear . . . *things*, Mom?"

She gulps. "Maybe not."

"So can I have dinner with them? I'll eat with you guys tomorrow. I swear. Besides, Mads is staying at Pops's tonight."

"Why?" I ask.

"Well, for one, they're going blackberry picking tomorrow morning," Michael says. "And for two, Pops didn't act like he wanted to be alone tonight. It was kind of weird, but Mads was happy to stay with him."

I exchange a look with Lauren. "Should I go check on them?"

"I was just there," Michael says. "They're fine. But maybe check on them before you go to sleep. I'm sure if anything is wrong, Maddie will come screaming." He nibbles his bottom lip. "So, you aren't mad about the whole us-leaving-you-stranded thing?"

"Mad? No," I say. "You and your sister are going to go get the boat."

"Tomorrow?" Michael asks.

"Tonight."

"After dinner with Ava?" Michael counters. "I could totally take Ava with me and let Mads stay with Pops."

I know what you want to do, you little shit. I shake my head while my son fights a grin.

"Does Ava's varied repertoire involve boating?" Lauren asks.

"Probably. She's pretty skilled," Michael says, smirking.

Lauren points at him. "I'm going to ignore that."

"Go. Grab a gas can from the shed behind Pops's cabin. Make sure you tie it up in the right spot next to the boathouse—on the left of Pops's. Not the right."

"Got it," Michael says. "I'll see you guys later."

"Later," I say.

"Love you, little boy," Lauren calls after him.

"Love you, Mama," Michael shouts from somewhere in the darkness.

I open the seasonings and sprinkle them on the burgers. Lauren watches me carefully but stays silent. *Weird.* The fact that I've gotten this far without her interference is odd, but I'll go as long as she lets me. *I want to do this for her. I want to take this off her plate.*

I'm not sure whether to circle back to where we left off in our conversation before Michael showed up, or let it be.

"Can I ask you a question?" Lauren asks.

"Sure."

"What are you doing?"

She's grinning when I look up, an amused look on her face. *There it is.*

"I'm making you dinner," I say.

"You know how to do that?"

I narrow my eyes. "It's making hamburgers. I'm not getting fancy."

"What's gotten into you?" She laughs. "You're not poisoning me, are you?"

I chuckle.

"You've never made me dinner," she says. "Ever."

"Not true. I made you a roasted chicken once. Remember?"

She bursts out laughing. "That's a stretch. You tried to roast a chicken and burned that thing to a crisp. The fire department was almost called."

"Not my fault. Someone came in the kitchen looking gorgeous, and I forgot about the chicken."

"Blame it on me."

"I took the blame for our marriage dysfunction. The least you can do is take the blame for the burned chicken," I say.

She leans back against the pillows, feathering a finger against her bottom lip.

"Is that a sign?" I ask.

"What?"

"You're drawing attention to your mouth."

She drops her hand and laughs. "I was just thinking."

"What about?"

Her face sobers. "What happens when we go home?"

"What do you mean?"

"You say you want to change things . . ."

"I *will* change things."

"But the daily pressures aren't here. There aren't work schedules and kid schedules and life stress. We're going to be right back into our normal lives, and . . ."

"And you're afraid to take a step backward from the progress you think you've made toward leaving me?" I ask.

She nods again, more cautiously this time. *Yes, I've been listening.*

Billie's pep talk shouts through my head. I hear it in her voice, cheering me on. *You're a car guy, Jack, so I'll put it in your terms. Service that woman.*

"Well, I was thinking we need a maintenance plan," I say, hiding a grin.

"Like for a car?"

"Yeah, kind of."

She looks thoroughly confused. "Um . . ."

"We can create a checklist of things we need to check regularly. Like, cooking dinner together. And a date night every week."

Her eyes light up.

"Our life has been a lot about me," I say. "And you just said that your focus had become a lot about you. But this part of our life—the kids are going to be leaving for college. It's just going to be us at home. So, let's lean in to that. Let's make it unapologetically about *us.*"

"Do you mean that?"

I move toward her, my body humming with relief.

Her cheeks are flushed as I reach her. She stands, testing her weight on her ankle before committing to it.

"Are you okay?" I ask softly.

She grins. "Yes. I'm okay."

I touch the side of her face. The connection, the contact, melts whatever reservations remain between us.

"Does that maintenance plan require routine servicing?" she asks.

I smirk. "I'll give you the premium package."

A wash of hesitation clouds her eyes. I stroke her cheek with my thumb, afraid to press my luck. At the same time, all I want to do is take this woman in my arms and start making up for lost time.

"What do you need from me, Lo? Ask for it. Let me love you like you want to be loved."

She runs her palms around my waist, peering up at me with a love that makes it hard not to just kiss her.

"Don't make me regret this," she whispers.

"I promise."

My lips lower to hers, but she meets them in the middle. They press together simply, sweetly—for a moment. The kiss deepens immediately.

A warmth floods my veins, bringing me back to a place that feels a whole hell of a lot like home. *Like the way things should be.*

How did I go without this for so long?

I wrap her in my arms and pull her into my chest. She sinks against me as if she needs the contact as much as I do.

Her fingers go to my hair, urging me to kiss her harder. Deeper. Like she thinks I might pull away.

I straddle her feet with mine, tilting my hips into her so she can feel how hard she makes me. She breaks the kiss, moaning as I press kisses along her jaw and down her neck.

Blood pours through my veins. I can't think about anything except how badly I want her. My cock is so hard it hurts.

I need to fuck her. Reclaim her. Promise her.

Love her.

"What if the kids come back?" she asks, panting as I lift the hem of her shirt.

"They—"

"Mom! Whoa," Maddie says, giggling. The door snaps behind her. "Sorry to interrupt. Kind of."

I rest my forehead against my wife. Lauren laughs.

"What's up, Maddie?" she asks.

"Pops and Snaps are sharing a bag of beef jerky, and I wanted to see if we had any granola left because, well, I don't trust that Pops's fingers don't have Snaps's drool on them." She makes a face. "Cross contamination isn't my jam."

Lauren steps away from me and helps our daughter find a snack.

I watch them dig through the pantry and listen to their laughter fill the cabin.

This.

This is what I would've missed if I'd left.

Conversations with Lauren. Kissing her. Listening to my family's laughter while they make memories, just like the ones I made with my mom when I was growing up. *One of the things I can never replace.*

If I had gone when Tommy called, Lauren and I would be in the same place we were when we got here. Bitter. Angry. Complacent.

Is that the problem? That I've become so complacent? Proud of my work, but not invested in my family?

Maybe I have to *be* the change to facilitate the change.

A smile tickles my lips.

"I'm making burgers, Maddie. Do you and Pops want one?" I ask, coming into the kitchen.

Maddie balks. "Did you just say *you* are making burgers?"

"Yup."

She gives her mom a look. "Is he okay?"

Lauren leans against the wall and rests her gaze on me. She bites her bottom lip, a brightness on her face that makes her look ten years younger.

"I'm not sure," she says. "But I hope so."

I smile at her.

The sun has nothing on the smile she gives me in return.

CHAPTER SIXTEEN

Lauren

The sun sits on the horizon, putting on a spectacle. The most vibrant oranges, brightest reds, and richest streaks of purple light up the sky in what can be described only as nature's artwork.

Jack holds a beer bottle as he flips burgers on the grill just outside the kitchen window. The pepperiness floating through the air is concerning. I didn't have the heart to tell him that he was overseasoning the meat. Nor did I mention that salt, pepper, onion powder, garlic powder, *and* seasoning salt were overkill. He was so proud of himself while making our dinner. I didn't want to be a know-it-all . . . even if it means we'll probably not be able to eat it.

I give the pasta salad I whipped together a final toss. *At least we'll have something edible.*

We've worked in the kitchen shoulder to shoulder this evening, sometimes talking but working quietly too. It was nice having him next to me and wanting to help. But it was just as surprising how easily he managed to find his way around the kitchen.

A knot formed in my stomach when he fired up the grill.

Did it take me calling an attorney for him to want to do these things? Or would he have come around if I hadn't blocked him out of my life? Because I haven't exactly offered to be a part of his world, either, and I might have if he'd asked.

I've contributed to our toxic patterns more than I've realized.

Every Wednesday, I take the trash to the road to be picked up. Jack doesn't have a chance to do it. Instead of asking Jack, I ask Billie to pick up Maddie if I can't. I didn't ask him to help with the shelves, to mow the lot next door, or to help me with the laundry last week, when I was so overwhelmed with life that I wanted to cry.

I just did it. I did it all.

Sure, the reason I overfunctioned was because of his past behavior. But looking back on it now, I see that I made it too easy for him to drop the ball . . . and nearly impossible for him to pick it up again.

I glance at him through the window.

He says he wants to change, and I think he's really trying. But just like I had to make adjustments before based on the circumstances, maybe it's time to do that again.

As I'm pouring myself a second glass of wine, Jack carries in the burgers.

"I still got it," he says, setting the platter in the middle of the table next to the buns and vegetable toppings. "Check those babies out."

Ten burgers, a little singed on the edges but otherwise surprisingly okay, are heaped together in the center of a rose-printed plate.

Jack struts around the kitchen. "It appears I've missed my calling."

"Oh, really?"

"I mean, you can't deny that's impressive."

I giggle.

"What? Does it turn you on to watch a master chef at work?"

Laughing, I take two plates from the cabinet. "A master chef? You've cooked one meal. I hardly think you can claim master chef status."

"I understand how some people think food is an aphrodisiac." He smirks. "You're turned on just thinking about how talented I am on the grill, aren't you?"

"Well, if I was turned on thinking about you at the grill, it wouldn't be food that was the aphrodisiac, then, would it?"

He lifts a brow. "Are you saying *I'm* an aphrodisiac, Mrs. Reed?"

"I'm saying what you said doesn't make sense."

He rolls his eyes.

"Besides, I don't think hamburgers are on the list of things that up sexual arousal."

He takes another beer out of the fridge and meets me at the table. We sit across from each other.

"What foods *are* on that list?" he asks, taking a proffered plate.

"Oysters are the most popular, I think. Clichéd, yes, but I'm pretty sure they scientifically improve your sex life."

He screws up his face and places a huge stack of tomato slices on his burger. "How? They're slimy and gross."

"I think they have a lot of zinc, which amps up testosterone production."

"Huh. What else?"

I hold up my glass and swirl the liquid around, holding his gaze. "Red wine. It has something in it that increases blood flow."

Jack wiggles his brows, making me laugh.

"Watermelon is another one," I say.

"Does the water make you wetter?"

"No," I say, grinning. "It has something in it that increases the nitric oxide in the body. Somehow, that causes your blood vessels to relax, so your circulation speeds up. Hence, amped arousal."

"How do you know all of this?"

I layer lettuce and tomatoes on my sandwich. Then, thinking— hoping—that pickles will disguise some of the spices, I add a few of those too.

"You'd be surprised at some of the things I know," I say. "I listen to a lot of audiobooks."

"What are you listening to that is talking about aphrodisiacs?"

I laugh. "Romance novels aren't just smut, you know. You can learn things from time to time."

"And where do you listen to these?"

I put the top on my sandwich. "While scrapbooking. Doing laundry. Waiting in the carpool line. Lying in the bath. Mowing the lawn. Shoveling snow last winter."

Jack diverts his gaze to the table.

Crap. "I didn't mean it like that."

"No, it's okay. Even if you did."

I sit back in my chair and watch my husband rearrange his sandwich.

We can't keep doing this. If we want this to work out—and he says he does, and at the bottom of my heart, I do, too—this can't happen every time we have a conversation.

My breath stalls while my heart thumps, rattling my rib cage. I want to open my mouth and tell him I'll forget the past and we can go on from here and pretend like the last few years didn't happen.

But that wouldn't be fair—to me, to the kids, or to him. We *all* deserve better.

Fear streaks through me, warning me that I could end up right where I started when I got to Story Brook. But it's just as terrifying to think that I might have walked away from Jack when it didn't have to happen.

And maybe it doesn't.

"Jack?"

He looks up.

I swallow so roughly that my ears pop. "We have no hope if we're going to hold grudges."

He wrinkles his forehead. "What do you mean?"

"When I said that about mowing and snow shoveling, I honestly didn't mean it as a passive-aggressive slight toward you. It's just the truth."

He nods, evidently uncertain where I'm headed with this.

"If we're going to try to fix this—"

"*We are.*"

I smile as a bubble of hope rises inside me. "Then we can't be ready to find fault in each other. We can't expect the worst."

"Okay. That makes sense. So, you mean that when I come home, *because I'm going to come home*, I shouldn't expect you to be pissed automatically."

"Right. And when it's time for dinner, I shouldn't automatically assume you won't show up."

He grins. "Right."

He reaches across the table and takes my hand. His palm is warm and calloused. It's been a long time since I've felt it like this. His thumb strokes the top of my palm.

"I'll ask about the shop more," I say.

"And I'll ask all the questions about scrapbooking."

"I'll remember you're capable of taking the trash out, even if it piles up on the floor."

He grins. "And I'll make you go to lunch with me, even if you don't want to."

I'll want to.

I'm starting to speak when the door opens, and Snaps streaks through the cabin.

"Pops is asleep," Maddie says. "Snapsy kept licking his face and trying to bite the end of his nose, so I thought we should come back."

The puppy darts under the table and tugs on the edge of my sandal. *This fucking dog.* I kick gently into the air, hoping that'll dissuade him. It doesn't.

"Jack, get your dog, please," I say, moving my leg swiftly through the air.

"Snaps, come here, buddy," he says.

The dog drops my shoe and bolts to Jack.

"You want a hamburger, Mad?" I ask.

"No. It smells weird."

Jack's jaw drops. "Excuse me?"

"They smell weird. What's wrong with them?"

I cover my mouth to hide my laughter.

"Nothing is 'wrong with them,'" Jack says, holding Snaps back from lunging onto the table. "I made the burgers. They're great."

Maddie shakes her head. "Doubt it."

"Here." Jack thrusts Snaps toward his daughter. "Take him."

Snaps growls playfully as he lands in Maddie's arms.

Jack side-eyes Maddie as he gets his burger into a nice, neat stack. Then he brings it to his mouth and takes a large bite.

I grin smugly as I watch him start to chew.

"See? This is great," he says, his eyes beginning to water. His chewing slows. "Really great."

My chest bounces as I suppress a giggle.

"Really great," he says again, reaching for his beer.

"It looks like you're really enjoying that, Dad," Maddie says, laughing.

Jack tips back his drink.

"Give us a description of that bite," I say, smirking. "Was it decadent? Rich? Just plain ol' delicious?"

"To hell with both of you," he says, his face red.

Maddie and I laugh as Jack scoots his chair back. Then he unceremoniously dumps his food in the trash can.

"What's wrong, Daddy? Didn't you enjoy your *great* burger?"

My cheeks ache from smiling.

"That thing was . . ." He blows out a breath and reaches for his beer again. "Hot. And garlicky."

I snort. "You only put a half a pound of pepper on there."

"And chili flakes," he says.

"Chili flakes? I missed that."

He takes the burgers off the table and sets them beside the sink. "Be glad you missed all of it. I think my tongue is burned."

Maddie leans against my chair and pets the puppy.

My heart is full.

"Snaps and I are going to my room to text Daniel. I'm so happy we get some internet here this year. I mean, I have to stand at the window to get reception, but I'll take it."

"God forbid you go without internet," Jack says, fanning his tongue with his hand.

"Good night, Mom and Dad."

"It's still early," I call after her.

Her response is the padding of her feet against the staircase, followed by her bedroom door clicking shut.

"I don't know how we ever made it without cell phones growing up," Jack says.

"They'll never know the fun of having to drive around town to find your friends if they didn't answer the house phone."

"Or the sound of dial-up internet."

"Or Lisa Frank Trapper Keepers," I say.

"What about buying a pack of baseball cards for fifty cents? I loved walking down to Henry's on the corner and buying them with the little strips of bubble gum hidden inside."

"Well, I loved Hi-C Ecto Coolers myself."

Jack grins. "Walkmans were the pinnacle of tech."

"They had nothing on Lip Smackers. My Caboodle was full of them."

"Your what?"

"My Caboodle." I laugh. "I haven't thought about those for a long time."

Jack's chair creaks as he settles back again.

A warm breeze flows through the cabin, carrying with it the croaks of frogs outside. The curtains flutter as if they're dancing happily to the events of the evening. The wooden walls of the cabin itself seem to sigh with contentment.

The door opens again. Jack and I exchange a leisurely grin that fills in a small part of the hole in my heart.

"Hey," Michael says, walking into the kitchen. "Burgers? Cool."

"Don't eat that," Jack and I say in unison before bursting out laughing.

Michael looks at us like we've lost our minds.

"I made them," Jack says. "Have some pasta salad, or heat up some leftovers. Save yourself the pain."

Michael furrows his brows and sits next to us instead.

"Did you have fun with Ava?" I ask.

He sighs, his shoulders slumping. "You guys, I'm freaking out."

Jack lifts a brow. "Why?"

"We don't have much time left here," Michael says.

"And?" I prompt. "You have wrestling camp as soon as we get back."

Michael's face falls. "I know."

What? I look at Jack.

"What's going on, buddy?" Jack asks.

"When will I see Ava?"

I try to remain serious, considering my son's apparent midteenage crisis. But he's too adorable to keep from grinning.

"It's not funny, Mom."

"No, I know it's not. I'm not making light of the situation, Michael."

"I don't know what's going to happen," he says. "We go home, and she goes home, and—what? I never see her again?"

Jack leans forward. "She lives thirty minutes away from us. You can see her on the weekends."

"On the weekends?" Michael's jaw drops. "What if I have a tournament? Or if she has a recital or a . . . horse show or whatever horse people do. I don't know."

"Hey, it's going to be okay," Jack says. "You'll work it out."

Michael pushes away from the table. "This sucks, you know that?" He heads for the stairs. "I can't decide if it was better to meet her or if I would've been better off to not ever know her."

Jack chuckles. "Welcome to falling in love, Michael."

"Fuck love," he says.

"Hey, watch your mouth," I say.

He stops at the staircase. "Sorry. I'm just . . . frustrated. The older I get, the more frustrating things become. Putting together shelves. Getting a job. Not living close to Ava."

"You'll make it," Jack says.

Michael stomps up the stairs, punctuating his displeasure with life every step of the way.

"I don't think I can deal with Michael and Maddie in relationships at the same time," I say, reaching for my wineglass.

"Let's just focus on ours and let them fend for themselves."

"Jack," I say, laughing.

He shrugs, peering over my shoulder.

"What are you looking at?" I ask.

"Dad's light came on."

I follow his gaze. Sure enough, Harvey's bedroom light glows from behind his curtains.

"Should you go check on him?" I ask.

Jack hesitates but gives in. "Probably."

"Go. I'll clean this mess up and then reheat the leftovers."

He stands and kisses me on the head as he walks by. "Leave the mess. But please reheat the lasagna."

I laugh, my stomach fluttering.

The door shuts, and I heave a sigh of relief. Of contentment. *Of happiness.*

CHAPTER SEVENTEEN

JACK

"Do you remember that haunted house in Meigs County?" I ask. Dad chuckles. "Hell yes, I do."

"A haunted house?" Maddie asks. "What are you talking about?"

The three of us trudge through the forest with empty ice cream buckets in our hands. Dad has used these same buckets for blackberry picking for at least the last thirty years, but probably longer. One is splitting down the side. I tried to toss it in the garbage a few years ago, but like the bucket itself, Dad came apart at the seams. *Won't make that mistake again.*

"There was this old house in the middle of a cornfield by my home-place," he says. "My dad always said it was haunted, but I figured it was just to keep me and my brothers and sisters away from it. You know how kids do—they mess around and get hurt or in trouble. Probably just wanted us to stay away."

"Watch your feet, Mads," I say, moments before she steps in a mess of vines.

"But one day, I don't know—I must've been in my twenties, I had a dog. Named her Mop. She was a good dog, really. Followed me home one day from the stripper hills. I was out there mushroom hunting, and she stayed on my heels all day. I got in the car and she chased me about half a mile or so, so I loaded her up and took her home with me."

"What happened to her?" Maddie asks.

He shrugs. "She died."

"Pops!"

"What?" he says, scoffing. "Things don't live forever, Maddie Moo. Might as well get used to that now."

My daughter looks at me, horrified. I wink at her in an attempt at calming her down. It does little for her state of mind.

"Back to the haunted house, Dad."

"Oh, right," he says, pausing for a rest against a tall tulip poplar tree. "Well, me and Mop were out there, and she nosed around the house. She finally got her courage up and went in. Three, maybe four minutes went by, and that dog raced out of that house like she saw a ghost. Tail between her legs—the whole bit. She jumped in the bed of my truck and wouldn't get out."

Maddie's eyes widen. "What did you do?"

"I got my ass back in the truck and got the hell out of there."

I chuckle, watching my father tell my daughter the story.

It's been the same tale since I can remember, varying very little over the years. Dad is full of stories like this, and I grew up wondering if he was full of shit or if he'd had the most exciting life ever. Looking back, it's probably something in the middle.

Dad groans as he pushes off the tree, stutter-stepping a bit before he finds his balance. My heart leaps, and I reach for him. He swats my hand away.

"You okay?" I ask.

"I'm fine. You fucking okay?"

Maddie looks at me. I shake my head at her to leave it be.

"Come on," he says, plodding deeper into the woods with his walking stick. "The big patch is back here."

"Pops, Dad and I can go back and get them, if you want."

Dad stops and looks at me over his shoulder, warning me not to go along with my child. "Your dad will miss all the good ones. Trust me." He holds my gaze and then starts walking again.

I keep a few steps back from them to watch Dad's gait. There's something slightly off, but I can't make it out exactly. *I'm going to get to the bottom of this.*

"You got a knife on ya, Jack?" Dad asks.

"Yeah. Why?"

"Gimme it."

He holds his palm to the side. I take my pocketknife out of my jeans and lay it in his hand.

Dad ambles to a giant oak and taps it with the butt of the knife. "Here it is."

Maddie touches the scarred wood with a heart around it. "What is this? *H* and *R*. *M* and *R*?" Her fingers trail down the bark, reading the last name. "'Jack'?" She looks at me over her shoulder and smiles. "Is this you?"

"How many other Jacks do you know?" Dad asks. "Of course it's him."

I shake my head. "*H* and *R*—Harvey Reed. *M* and *R*—Myra Reed."

Dad offers her the knife. "Go on. Add your mark."

Maddie takes the handle and steps to the tree.

"Be careful," I say.

Dad sighs. "Will you let the girl live a little?"

Maddie giggles.

"What's gotten into you, Dad?" I ask, chuckling.

"I'm trying to make a memory here, but you're butting in."

I hold up my hands. "Sorry. Go on."

Maddie holds the knife up to the tree. "Just press the tip against it?"

"Just like this." Dad holds her hand and helps her create an *M.* "See?"

Maddie smiles. "I have to write Maddie, though. An *M* could be Michael, and he's not bringing Ava out here one day and acting like this was him."

"I'm sure that's what he would be wanting to do with Ava out here," Dad says.

Maddie's eyes go wide, and she looks at me, waiting for my response. "I got nothing," I say. "I give up."

Maddie giggles again and goes back to work on her name. Dad grabs a seat on a fallen tree.

My chest tightens as I watch him struggle for a breath. His cheeks are red, and a bead of sweat lines his forehead.

He's too old for this. *Will he be able to walk out? How would I get him help if he can't make it back to the truck?*

I take my phone out of my pocket. No service. *Great.*

Dad lifts a hand off a knee and points vaguely across the forest. "See those berries? Go pick 'em."

"Yes, sir," I say, heading off in the general direction of his gesture.

"How long ago did you and Grandma carve your names in this tree?" Maddie asks, still in earshot.

"Oh, hell. A long time ago."

"I wish I could've met her."

Dad exhales. "I wish you could've too. Your grandma wouldn't know what to do with you and Michael. You couldn't fit her head in the doorway she'd be so proud."

I pluck the ripened berries off the bush and drop them into my bucket.

"What was she like, Pops?" Maddie asks.

"Myra?" He gazes into the distance. "She was a good woman. Smart. A hard worker. As pretty as a picture."

Maddie grins, starting to work on the *R* in Reed.

"Your grandma was a catch," Dad says. "I had to work solid for a month to get her to go out with me. Then she turned me down twice when I asked her to marry me."

"She did?" I ask. *News to me.*

"Hell yes, she did." He chuckles. "I didn't have a damn thing to offer her, and she could've had anyone she wanted in a five-county radius. I didn't have a penny to my name. What would she want in a man like me?"

"Well, you're awfully handsome," Maddie says.

Dad smiles. "Yes, I am."

I snort. "And humble."

"But I finally got her to say yes," he says, stretching his legs out in front of him. "I promised her she'd never want for anything. I'd make sure she had everything she could ever need. *And I did.*"

His voice rises and then falls curiously. I glance over my shoulder. My eyes lock immediately with his.

A chill races down my spine.

His point is unstated, but it isn't necessary to be clear.

He knows about Lauren and me. *But how much does he know?*

Should I tell him we're okay?

We are okay, aren't we?

I replay everything from last night—our conversation and our kiss. Dinner. How we talked late into the night after we went to bed.

"He's absolutely guilty," she says, licking the spoon. Her eyes shine with talk of the latest celebrity trial. "There's a mountain of evidence against him."

"It's all circumstantial." I lean over her. "Give me another scoop of that."

She pretends to pull the ice cream away from me. I bury my face in the crook of her neck, making her squeal.

"Circumstantial or not," she says, giving me access to the pint, "the jury will never believe his story."

"They will if they're objective."

She rolls her eyes. "I objectively think you're wrong."

"Bet me."

"What do you want to bet?"

I think about it. "If he's guilty, I'll be at your beck and call for a week. If he's not, you're mine for seven full days."

Her eyes twinkle. "Deal."

Even though we didn't make love, there was definitely more comfort between us. I didn't feel as though a wall was barricading me from my wife—and the pillow wall was gone. I have to ask myself again, How long has it been since I felt *that*?

My stomach flip-flops as I pick apart our interaction for anything I missed. But the more I think about it, the more confident I am that there's nothing I'm forgetting to worry about.

"But what about Maine?" she asks.

"What in the hell is in Maine?"

She elbows me in the side. "It's beautiful there. And maybe the timing will be perfect, and we'll catch the leaves changing colors. I'm not sure when the kids are off on fall break, but maybe it'll work out."

I smile at her. "Or we could go alone, and we wouldn't have to coordinate any school schedules."

"You would do that for me, Jack Reed?"

I lean across my shoulder and kiss her nose. "I could be convinced."

"But what about the kids and fall break?"

"I don't know. How do you feel about South Carolina?"

I exhale a sigh of relief.

"I've seen pictures of Grandma," Maddie says, oblivious to the thoughts in my head. "She seems like she was really sweet."

"She was," Dad says. "I just wish I wouldn't have waited until she was gone to realize it."

Oof.

Maddie snaps the knife closed and turns to face us.

Dad takes it from my daughter.

"Good job, kiddo," he says. "Now you're immortalized in the tree with the rest of us."

"We just need Michael and Mom to come out."

Dad nods approvingly. "Yes. We do."

I clear my throat. The woods are suddenly suffocating.

"You ready to go back?" I ask. "It's getting awfully sticky out here."

"Pops says the best berries are always the farthest back," Maddie says.

"That's a lie," I say, winking at Dad.

He braces himself against the tree and slowly rises to his feet.

"It's still early enough that if we go back, I can probably swim with my friends at the lake," Maddie says, looking up at the sky.

"What are you looking at up there?"

"It's probably eleven thirty," she says, lowering her chin.

Dad balks. "Who taught you that?"

"Daniel. He sent me a link on how to tell time and direction when you're in the woods." She grins. "Isn't that sweet?"

Dad begins to walk back the way we came. "At least he's good for something."

"He's good for many things," she says.

"Name three," I say, unimpressed. *So, the boy knows how to tell time by the sun. I'm pretty sure wild animals can do that.*

"He knows how to tell time and direction in the woods," she says. "He's great at math. He can do sales tax in his head."

"Oh. He's basically a genius," I say.

She sighs dramatically. "And he knows just about every country in the world and where it's located."

Okay, that's slightly impressive.

"He's probably yanking your chain," Dad says.

"*He is not.* He plays this video game about conquering the world or something, and you must know geography to win." She shrugs haughtily. "I bet neither of you can do that."

I look at Dad and grin. "Think he can swap an engine in a car?"

"Think he can fillet a fish?"

"Bet he can't drive a stick."

"Wonder if he can piss standing up."

"Pops!" Maddie says. "I can never bring Daniel around the two of you. God knows what you'd say."

I chuckle, earning a grin from Dad.

"Maddie Moo, I can assure you that if you ever bring Daniel around me, I'll be the same man then that I am now."

She groans. "Oh, that's comforting."

"I hear that sarcasm," Dad says, shaking his walking stick at her. "But believe me, boys will just break your heart. You're better off without them."

"You didn't break Grandma's heart."

"Grandma's not here to defend herself. So, we're better off not making assumptions when it comes to her," Dad says.

I furrow my brow, but he ignores my unspoken question.

"So, you did break her heart?" Maddie asks the question I wanted to but didn't.

Dad sighs. "I didn't break her heart. But I could've done better by her. It's a bunch of shit that you don't learn some lessons until it's too damn late."

I keep my gaze focused ahead of us and not on my father.

"Well, I can't wait to prove you wrong about Daniel," Maddie says. "I'm gonna make you eat your shoe at our wedding."

"I won't be at your wedding. I'll be dead."

"Pops! Stop it." Maddie grabs his arm and rests her head on his shoulder. "Be nice."

"I am being nice, sweetheart. But there's no sense in lying to you."

Dad's face is blank, as if he's talking about the trees and not his ultimate death. He's a cranky old man most of the time. Lauren says it's part of his charm. But it's not just crankiness today; there's an element of acceptance. Like he's not only trying to get a rise out of his granddaughter but also trying to tell her something.

I shift my weight, giving my father a quick once-over. He has good color in his cheeks, and he's getting around about the same as always. But there's something off about him. I noticed it last night.

He scoffs. "I'm just tired, Jack. I'm an old man. Get out of here and let me sleep, and maybe I won't be so aggravating tomorrow."

"What are we doing with all of these blackberries?" I ask.

Dad hums. "Well, I guess we'll give them to Mrs. Shaw and see if she can make us a cobbler."

"Yum," Maddie says.

"Mrs. Shaw is a pretty damn good cook."

Maddie stands tall but keeps her arm locked with Dad's. "Is she a better cook than Grandma?"

"Oh, now you're playing with fire," he says. "I can't answer that."

The two of them banter back and forth about loyalty and the right answer to Maddie's question. I tune both out.

"It's a bunch of shit that you don't learn some lessons until it's too damn late."

I grin. *Thank God I learned mine while there was still time.*

CHAPTER EIGHTEEN
LAUREN

I hate hills," I mutter, groaning as I reach the top of the ascent into Story Brook.

The late morning is beautiful, the epitome of perfection. Birds chirp overhead, singing pretty songs and happily chatting among themselves. The breeze is a wonderful juxtaposition to the warming temps. The other residents of Story Brook mill in front of their cabins as I walk by, cleaning up from last night's campfire or throwing balls with their dogs.

"Hi, Gayle," I say. She married her husband the same year I married Jack. We were Story Brook rookies together. "How have you been?"

She steps off her porch and comes to the road. Her red hair shines in the sunlight. "I'm good, Lauren. How have you been?"

"Good. Thanks."

She grins. "You look wonderful. I've been wondering if you were up here this summer. I haven't seen you, but I thought I saw your kids run by the other day."

I laugh.

"They've gotten so big," she says, laughing too. "Do you get tired of everyone saying that? I don't have kids, as you know, but I would imagine comments like that would irritate you at some point. Like, 'Yes, I know my kids are growing up. Stop reminding me.'"

"I'm reminded every day. Maddie has her first boyfriend, and if that doesn't remind you that your kids are growing up, I don't know what will."

"Ooh," she says. "The first boyfriend, huh? How is Jack taking that?"

"About as well as you'd think."

She chuckles. "He's always been so much fun to watch with the kids."

I'm unsure what my face does, but her brows pull together in response.

"You know what I mean," she says. "You see so many fathers at the beach with their kids, or boating, or having a slice of pie outside of the Cupboard. But when you really look at them, they aren't paying a bit of attention. They're on their phones or striking up conversations with other people. So many of them don't even acknowledge their children, but that's never been Jack. If he's throwing a ball with Michael, he's throwing a ball with Michael. If he and Maddie ride bikes, they're side by side and chatting away. Quality over quantity. So important."

"Yeah. Absolutely."

I blink, wondering if things just seem to pertain to our situation because I'm thinking about it. Or if the universe will keep splashing things in my face until I finally notice.

No, I know Jack's an excellent father, and what Gayle has noticed when we're on vacation has been true.

But there have been unnoticed gaps in the other fifty weeks of the year.

I inhale a deep breath. *Don't hold grudges, Lauren. You promised you wouldn't.*

Gayle pats me on the arm and gasps. "I saw you on TV a while back. How exciting for you, Lauren! I bet you're over the moon."

"Yes, it's really exciting." I take a deep breath and refocus. "I never imagined that I would be scrapbooking as a career. But I wouldn't change it. I love it."

"You're very good at it. I looked you up online after the bit on the morning show, and your work is fascinating."

My heart warms. "Thanks, Gayle. That means a lot."

A clatter rings through the air, and a spattering of profanities comes from the shed beside their cabin. Gayle groans.

"I need to help Kevin," she says. "He was determined to clean out that mess of a building himself this morning, but obviously, that's not going well."

"Good luck," I say. "It was good to see you, Gayle."

"Good to see you too. And if you need a scrapbooking assistant—call me."

I laugh, giving her a final wave, and then start down the road again.

My shirt clings to my body as the breeze gives way to the humidity of the day. I mosey through the barely two-way streets winding through the cabin community and enjoy the peace in my mind.

Waking up and finding myself curled against Jack was not on my cabin bingo card. Having his arm scooping my head and holding me against his shoulder wasn't in the plans. I never imagined that he and I would see three in the morning together, sharing a pint of ice cream from the Cupboard while propped up in bed. I didn't dream that we would be laughing about our first road trip together, or our first night home alone with Michael—or the atrocious wallpaper I talked him into hanging in our first house.

"It had flowers and peaches, Lo. Flowers and peaches. It was horrible."

I laugh. "It was pretty . . . kind of."

"It was not pretty. Or easy to put up."

"Or easy to take down."

Jack looks at the ceiling, making me laugh harder.

I wipe my eyes. "Do you remember when we got to the wall by the table?"

"How could I forget? I had to put new drywall up on that whole fucking wall."

I grab his arm and rest my forehead against it, still laughing. "But you were so cute while you were doing it."

"You're lucky I love you, because that was a nightmare."

I grin as I wave to Charles, the retired mailman who lives on the corner.

Despite the last few years, Jack and I have had a lot of good times together. I haven't thought about so much of that lately. I've been hyper-focused on the present day—on how miserable I was. Did I forget what a good man he is at his core?

I've been so obsessed with Jack's perceived failures and all the things he does wrong. The things that annoy me. The things that hurt. When did I start assigning those things to Jack in lieu of the others?

"Maybe if you didn't act like you didn't want me around, I'd put more emphasis on coming around."

I kick a pebble and watch it sail across the street.

Our life used to be so simple. Our love was even simpler than that. Kids and jobs and bills . . . responsibilities, they all piled up.

We layered so much on top of what was important—us—that we couldn't see it anymore.

"Hi, Mrs. Reed," Ava says, breaking me from my thoughts. She's standing at the end of the steps leading to our cabin. "I just knocked and no one answered."

Her white-blonde hair is pulled back into a slick ponytail. It makes her blue eyes pop more than usual.

"I think Jack and Maddie are probably still with Pops. They probably stopped for a chili dog at Schmidt's," I say. "The last time I saw Michael, he was headed to find you."

Her cheeks flush. "We've been hanging out all morning, but he wanted to come home and put on his swim trunks."

"Well, I have no idea. Let's go inside and see."

We move up the steps and into the cabin. A note sits on the table.

"Looks like Michael headed to the Cupboard to pick up lunch," I say. "Did you look for him there?"

"No. I came here first."

"Do you want a glass of tea?" I ask, taking the jug out of the fridge.

"No, thank you, ma'am."

Such a sweet girl. "How are your parents? I need to go say hello to them, especially since my son is over there twenty-four hours a day."

Her smile could light up a room. "They just said the same thing about you. Well, not exactly. They just said last night that they needed to come by and see you and Mr. Reed."

"We will definitely have to meet up."

"Mike showed me your social accounts. You're really funny, Mrs. Reed."

"Ha." I pour myself a glass of tea. "That's all Maddie. She makes me look a lot more interesting than I really am."

"I'd love to see your craft room sometime."

"Aww." I smile at her. "We'd love to have you over for dinner once the summer ends and we all go home."

A flash of sadness streaks through her baby blues.

I take a seat at the table and invite her to sit with me. She goes to a chair across from a dirty plate that someone didn't put in the sink this morning.

"What do you have planned for the rest of the summer?" I ask.

"We'll be here until the end of July. Or, I will, anyway. I think my parents are heading back in the next couple of weeks, but I'm staying with Grandma. It's a lot for her to close up the cabins for the fall, since we won't be back up here until almost Christmastime. Besides, I like hanging out with her. She's fun."

I smile.

"But I'll miss Mike when you guys leave," she says.

I take in the vulnerability in her eyes, the genuine emotion in her voice. I remember that feeling.

"There's little doubt Michael will come to see you," I say. "He thinks you're pretty special."

"Really? I mean, I think he is too. He's really smart and funny. And, you know, cute."

I laugh. "He is pretty cute."

"I worry about what will happen when we leave," she says, tucking a strand of hair behind her ear. "I hope he doesn't forget me. I'm sure he has a lot of girls trying to get his attention."

It's hard to know what to say to that. After all, I don't want to get involved or speak for my son. But I do know one thing I can say that's safe.

"Michael is a lot like his father," I say. "You can't take him anywhere without him catching the eye of bystanders."

She smiles nervously.

"But, like his father, Michael is very loyal. I have no qualms with saying that, if he tells you not to worry about things, you shouldn't."

Ava sighs in relief. "Thank you for saying that."

We jump at the sound of the door opening and turn to see Michael walking in. He looks surprised to see us too.

"Hey," he says, his cheeks splitting into a grin. "What are you doing here?"

Ava's smile couldn't be bigger if she tried. "I was looking for you."

"I went and got us sandwiches." He holds his arms out, with bags dangling from them. "I thought we could take the boat out and have lunch."

"Where's Snaps?" I ask.

Michael grins. "You're starting to like him, aren't you?"

I give him a look, making him chuckle.

"I let him out to go to the bathroom and then took him to Pops," he says. "He likes to lie in the window and look at the birds that gather in the backyard."

Ava gets to her feet. "You are so sweet, Mike."

He blushes.

"You two be careful," I say.

"We will, Mama."

"Thanks for talking with me, Mrs. Reed," Ava says. "I'll tell my parents to come over and say hello."

"You do that."

Michael steps to the side so Ava can get to the door.

"Ava?" I say.

"Yes?"

"You are welcome here for dinner, too, you know," I say.

She grins. "Thank you."

Michael tosses me a quick wave before they disappear through the door.

The cabin is quiet once again, and I enjoy the silence while I finish my tea. I need a shower to rinse the sweat off me, but I'll just get gross again, so why bother?

I bet Ava would take a shower if Michael was coming by and she was sweaty.

My brain scoots through my relationship with Jack as I grab my computer from our bedroom. It's entertaining to think about our relationship mirroring Michael and Ava's. *Did it ever resemble Maddie and Daniel's?*

We've had the sexy honeymoon phase. *Romance.* The exhausted new-parent phase. *Adjustment.* The struggle of dealing with a thousand things. *Distress.*

What comes next?

I sit at the table and open my social media accounts. "Maybe it's reality," I say out loud. "Maybe the next stage of life is accepting reality and . . . commitment."

My brows pull together.

If we go forward together now, the commitment will be different. We won't be promising to take care of each other during new love and lust. It'll be us promising things, knowing every bump, bruise, and failure the other has to offer.

I smile softly.

My likes and follows have continued to increase despite my not being online for the last few days. As I sort through a few mentions, I stop in my tracks—and burst out laughing.

Almost every post, one after another, has some variation of the same comment.

From @jackreedauto: *I'm so proud of you. You made this? I love you. You're so beautiful.*

I blink back a wash of tears and keep scrolling.

"Things just might work out, after all."

CHAPTER NINETEEN

Jack

"Watch your fingers, Maddie," I say as she reaches a little too far across the fire.

Yellow-and-orange flames dance happily from the firepit. Nineties country music, Pops's favorite, plays from a speaker propped up in the kitchen window. Laughter and conversation surround us.

I sit back in my lawn chair, a beer in hand, and take in the scene unfolding in front of me.

Maddie works hard to either burn a marshmallow to a crisp or to get as close as she can to falling in the flames without actually getting hurt. I'm not certain what she's going for, really. Michael and Ava, with Snaps on her lap, sit beside her, lost in their own world. The topic of their conversation must be fascinating because they only remember the rest of us are here when we say their names.

Pops sits across from me and beside Lauren. He's been especially entertaining tonight. He had the kids rolling over hamburgers—that Lauren made—and he poked and prodded my wife until she broke down and baked a pan of brownies. He used the kids to lobby me to start a fire.

It didn't take much effort on his part. I was happy to do it.

Lauren's eyes meet mine over the flames, and a small smile graces her lips. I wink at her. Her cheeks turn a rosy shade of pink that reminds me of her when she was younger.

"Want a s'more?" Maddie asks, squishing the blackened sugar between two graham crackers. A drip of chocolate falls off the side. "It's delicious."

"It looks like it's going to taste like the hamburgers I made."

She laughs. "Wrong. You have to burn the marshmallow a little to get it toasty and caramelized. Otherwise, it's a warm blob of goo."

"I'm good. Thanks, though."

She shrugs. "Suit yourself." She takes a bite of her concoction. The marshmallow forms a thin strand from the graham crackers to her mouth.

"How does it taste?" I ask.

"Delicious."

I shake my head and chuckle.

"What did you do with all of our blackberries, Pops?" Maddie asks, wiping her mouth with the back of her hand. Chocolate streaks across her cheek.

"I gave 'em to Mrs. Shaw."

"When did you see her?" Maddie asks.

"What? Do I have to give you a copy of my schedule for the day?"

Maddie giggles. "No. I was just wondering."

"I think my grandma is making Harvey a blackberry cobbler," Ava says. "Isn't that what you asked her for?"

"I didn't *ask her* for anything. I merely suggested that a homemade blackberry cobbler sounded mighty fine, and I conveniently had a few pails of them sitting on the porch when she drove by in her little buggy."

Ava grins.

"You and Mrs. Shaw aren't fooling around, are you?" Michael asks, teasing Dad.

Dad smirks. "What's it to you?"

Michael holds out his hands as if he doesn't have an answer.

"She's a looker, you know," Dad says before switching his attention to Ava. "I shouldn't probably be talking about your grandmother that way. I apologize."

Ava strokes Snaps's head. "Oh, don't worry about me. I kinda think my grandma is sweet on you, Harvey."

Lauren and I exchange a smile.

"What in the world would she want with him?" I joke.

"Excuse me," Dad says, sitting up in his chair. "I'm damn good looking for an old fart. Charming too. And I might have a little money in the bank. What do you know?"

I take a drink and shake my head. *The man is a hoot.*

"Would you even want a girlfriend?" Maddie asks, licking her fingers. "Is that what you would even call it at your age? Or would it be a 'lady friend' or something?"

"I ain't dead yet, Maddie Moo."

She drops her hand. "Will you stop talking about dying, please?"

"I think it was less about him being dead and more about him still being alive," Michael says. "Right, Pops?"

He points at my son. "Right, Michael."

Maddie takes another marshmallow out of the bag and shoves it on her stick. "Would you get married again, Pops?"

I lean forward, resting my elbows on my knees. My drink dangles between my legs.

I've never considered Dad getting remarried—and I'm not sure why. He's been alone for a long time. Maybe it's because he's never brought it up or made it an issue. Still, it seems odd that he hasn't, now that I think about it.

"Yeah, Dad," I say. "Would you get remarried again?"

He runs a hand through the air. "Nah, I'm not interested in all that jazz. I was married once. Glad I did it too. But it's different when you're my age."

"Why?" Maddie asks.

"Well, when you're young and you want to get married, it's because you have your whole life ahead of ya. You're gonna set out to build your life together. For a lot of people, for your grandma and me, it made us feel like a team to have the same last name. And back then, times were different. It gave your grandma security that she would be taken care of, if that makes sense."

Maddie shrugs, turning her stick over to burn the other side of her sugar.

Lauren clears her throat. "Did it give you security too?"

"Sure. And it gave Jack that also. It was the three of us—*the Reeds*," he says, dragging out our last name. "But I'm not having more kids at this point. Not saying my guys wouldn't swim."

I smirk as I watch Maddie look bewildered.

"But relationships at this age aren't about physical attraction and desperation to find a mate," he says. "It's companionship. Someone to relate to. Someone to sit around with in the morning and have a glass of coffee because we don't have to go to work."

"Good," Ava says. "Because I don't want to hear about my grandma getting freaky in the sheets."

Lauren chokes on her wine, making the rest of us laugh.

"Speaking of . . ." I nod toward the road as a purple golf cart comes chugging toward us. "Isn't that Mrs. Shaw there?"

"Well, I'll be," Dad says, twisting in his chair. "She must've heard us talking about her."

Ava waves. "Hey, Gran!"

Mrs. Shaw drives her cart through our yard. It comes to a stop just behind Dad and Lauren.

"Well, isn't this a group," she says.

"Want to join us?" I ask.

"Thanks, Jack. That's sweet of ya, honey. But I was coming by to tell Harvey that his cobbler is finished."

Dad looks impressed. "Is that so?"

"That's so," she says smugly. "Thought maybe you'd want to catch a ride over to my cabin and give it a taste?"

Lauren's gaze connects with mine. I cover my mouth with my hand and try not to laugh.

Dad jumps to his feet with more nimbleness than I've seen in years. "I'd be delighted to."

"What about you kids?" she asks. "Do you want to go get some cobbler? We can bring your parents back some, if you want."

Maddie props her stick against Michael's chair. Michael takes Snaps from Ava and brings him to me.

"Are you all going?" Lauren asks.

"We'll be back, Mama," Michael says as they climb on Mrs. Shaw's cart.

"I didn't mean to ruin your evening, Lauren," Mrs. Shaw says. She winks at me. "I'll bring them back later."

I nod, holding Snaps tight so he doesn't dart off after them.

With a little tooting of her horn, Mrs. Shaw zips off toward her cabin with our kids and my dad in tow.

The fire crackles as I stare at my wife through the flames.

A heat begins in my core and stretches through my body, making me feel like I've had more than one beer tonight. Lauren bites her lip, as if she's hesitant to break the silence.

It's like we're dating again. It's been this way for the last few days. I'm not walking on eggshells around her, but I am always trying to put my best foot forward.

I've let her lead. She's in charge of showing me what all she feels comfortable with. Last night, it seemed to be talking and almost getting to know one another. And as badly as I wanted to touch her, kiss her, have sex with her—I didn't. Not only do I not want to push her, but I don't want to miss any of the pieces we need to put back together. Because when we get home and things aren't this easy, I want us to be as strong as we can be.

My stomach ripples with anxiety from the thought of going home. In some sense, I'm excited at the prospect of having a life with my wife again. But on the other hand, it's going to be hard to balance my work life and my home life. A lot of things are going to need to be rearranged and redistributed—new habits made.

"I hope I'm as nimble as she is when I'm her age," Lauren says, getting to her feet. "She just bebops around here like she's in her thirties."

"You're only as young as you feel."

"Not sure if that's good or bad."

I put Snaps on the ground. Then I stand and help Lauren collect the paper plates, cups, and wrappers from Maddie's s'mores. Snaps chases after me, nipping at everything I pick up.

"Well, I can't vouch for how you feel," I say, following her into the cabin, "but I can tell you that if I saw you somewhere, I'd get your number."

She laughs. "You would, huh?"

"Yup. Hell, I might even order a scrapbook, just to get you to talk to me."

She deposits her collection in the sink while I throw away the garbage. Snaps bolts into the living room, leaps onto the couch, and snuggles up in a nest of blankets Maddie arranged for him this morning.

"I doubt you'd have to go that far to get me to talk to you," she says, prepping the leftovers to go in the fridge.

My heart races as I look around the kitchen. I need to help, but I'm not sure what I'm supposed to do.

I scan the room until my gaze settles on the dishes.

"A man standing at the sink, shirtless, doing dishes. That image stirs something inside me that I thought was dead."

Bingo.

I strip my shirt off and toss it onto the counter. "The burgers were great tonight. Thank you for making them."

"You're welcome."

I grin as I turn on the tap. She wasn't expecting that thank-you.

"You did a great job of grilling them," she says.

"Thanks. Glad I can do something helpful in the kitchen."

We chuckle at the memory of my disastrous attempt at dinner.

I plug the sink and add some dish soap. The hot water creates bubbles immediately. I begin to place the dishes from dinner in the basin.

"I was on your social media stuff last night," I say.

She laughs. "I saw."

"There were so many comments on there about people wanting to hire you," I say. "How many of them contact you?"

"*A lot.* Like, a *lot*, a lot."

"Do you make good money from it?"

"Way more than you would expect." Her voice is filled with confidence and joy. "I can't believe it sometimes. Well, I can, actually. Preserving memories is important, and I think after the last decade or so, when everything's gone digital, people are wanting tangible things again."

Makes sense. "Is that something you want to do full-time? Or do you just want to pick projects up as you can fit them in?"

"Right now, I'm booked solidly through the end of the year. I've been careful to pace myself, though. I'll have a lot of time at the gym with wrestling season coming up this fall, his senior year, and Maddie's cheer practices and fundraisers—yada yada yada. But I keep telling myself that it's just two more years, and then I can have a bit more freedom."

I force a swallow. "If you didn't have all of that, what would you do?"

"Cry, because that means the kids are gone." She laughs. "No, I'd probably really lean in to the whole thing and see what I can do with it. It's exciting to be . . . what did they call me on the morning show? A 'scrapbooking trailblazer'?"

"I think they said you were 'blazing the way for future hobbyists.'"

She stills behind me.

Guilt swallows me, reminding me of everything she's had to give up for our family.

"I'm happy that I've been able to stay at home with the kids, Jack. It's a privilege."

I glance at her over my shoulder. She's standing at the table with a softness in her eyes that melts my insides.

"Thank you for giving me that opportunity," she says.

My hands drip water onto the floor as I turn to face her. "Thank you for giving us the best of you."

She leans against the table, her lips twitching. "I know what you're doing."

I furrow my brow, playing clueless. "Whatever do you mean?"

"You're doing dishes shirtless."

"Ah, that I am." I look down at my abs. "Does it stir something inside of you?"

She laughs, making her way across the kitchen. "Maybe."

I hum.

She stands in front of me, peering up into my eyes. I hold my hands up, bent at the elbows, while sudsy water trickles down my forearms.

"How badly do you want to do those dishes?" she asks.

"I don't know. What are my other options?"

She slides her fingertip around the waistband of my shorts. I suck in a quick breath.

"I'll tell you what," I say, licking my bottom lip. "I'm going to wash these dishes the fastest that anyone's ever washed dishes before."

She giggles.

"And while I'm doing that, you're going to go lock every door and window in this cabin," I say. "The kids can go to Dad's tonight."

Her eyes widen. "How fast can you do dishes?"

"We're about to find out."

She turns toward the door, and I spring into action at the sink.

Who even am I?

I snort.

A man who's about to reclaim his wife. That's who.

CHAPTER TWENTY

LAUREN

"Did you lock the doors?" Jack asks, his voice leading him down the hall.

My stomach clenches as I run a toothbrush around my mouth. "Yeah."

"All of them?" The door closes with a snap. "And the windows?"

"Yeah." I spit in the sink. "Think we should stick a note on the door to please leave us alone?"

He stands in the doorway, one hand gripping the top of the frame. A smirk that's as decadent as it is sexy is planted on his lips. *My God, this man is something else.*

His body is strong—fit. Muscled from days working in the shop. There are scars and marks on his tanned skin from various sports injuries or accidents at work that add an air of strength to his appearance.

A full-body shiver rips down my spine.

It feels like I'm twenty-one again, accompanying Jack to his apartment after our date at the Italian restaurant that was one step more upscale than fast food. It was all our college budgets would allow—Jack's, mostly, because he wouldn't let me pay for anything.

After dinner, he asked me back to his place with a twinkle in his eye. I accepted, with three condoms and an emergency toothbrush kit tucked away in my purse.

I rinse my mouth, my hand trembling, then pat my face dry with a towel.

"What's the matter with you?" he asks cheekily.

I set the towel on the sink. "Nothing."

"Are you nervous, Mrs. Reed?" he teases.

He saunters across the room with a confidence I only wish I could attain.

"Why would I be nervous?" I ask.

He wraps one arm around my waist and pulls me into his chest. The motion is quick yet smooth, and my heart flutters at the contact with his body.

His eyes hood. Darken. His lips are full, as if they've already been kissed. I wrap my arms around his neck, feeling the heat of his skin against mine, and let the scent of my husband comfort me. Relax me. *Excite me.*

"I need you to do something for me," he says, his palm splayed against the small of my back.

"What's that?"

"I want you to tell me exactly what you want—what you like."

My face flushes. "Jack . . ."

"Lauren . . ." He grins, brushing a strand of hair out of my face. "I'm on a quest to deliver the best experience I can offer. But to do that, I need to know what that means to you."

I giggle. "You sound like an infomercial. Are you trying to sell yourself to me?"

"Pretty sure that's illegal."

I feather the hair at the nape of his neck, grinning. "Is this a limited-time offer?"

"I'd say the warranty expires in forty, maybe fifty years. It depends on how long Maddie stays with Daniel."

My laughter fills the small bathroom.

Jack sways us back and forth. "I mean it, Lo. I've operated too long, assuming I knew what you were thinking and what you wanted. You're going to have to tell me now."

I start to pop off a joke, sure he's kidding. But as I begin to speak, something in his tone stops me.

He's not kidding.

"What does the best experience mean to me?" I ask. "It's pretty easy."

"And . . ."

I grin. "It's *this*."

He places a kiss on my forehead, and I melt in his arms.

"I just want this," I whisper. "I want you." Pulling away, I look up and into his beautiful eyes. "Last night was one of the best nights I can remember. And it's so . . . goofy, almost. Sitting in bed, eating ice cream, laughing about things that probably aren't even really that funny."

He smiles.

"You weren't just my husband last night," I say softly. "You weren't my adversary. You weren't the father of my children or the guy that's on the bank account. *You were my friend, Jack.* That's what I want more than anything."

"I have some bad news, then."

My brows tug together. "What?"

"Billie is about to lose her best friend's job, because I'm taking over."

I laugh, running a finger down his jaw. "She'll probably fight you, you know."

"I can take her."

"You do have an advantage."

He opens his mouth as I drag my fingertip across his bottom lip. "That's good to hear. But may I ask what that is specifically?"

I grin. "I don't want to have sex with Billie."

Jack's eyes darken even more.

"You see," I say coyly, "I'm in a dry spell, and I really, *really* hope you'll help me find my way out of it."

"I thought you'd never ask."

He wets his lips and then kisses me. It's with a gentle, sweet reverence. He combs a hand through my hair, pushing my locks away from my face as if he needs to have complete access to me. Then, as his fingers reach the back of my head, he tilts my mouth upward.

The kiss deepens, his tongue parting my lips and exploring my mouth.

I moan against him. Gripping his shoulders, I pull him toward me—needing all the contact I can acquire to combat the growing ache between my legs.

He cups my cheeks, walking me backward until my back hits the sink. The glass containers holding cotton swabs and dental flossers rattle against the counter.

Our kisses grow more frenzied, Jack's body heating against my hands as I roam my palms over his shoulders, down his arms, and onto his chest. The lines of his body, the cuts of his muscles, ripple in my hands. It is a form of foreplay all its own.

He skims his touch down my neck, then my shoulders, before sliding his fingers down my sides in a slow, intentional movement. He grips the top of my shorts and draws them down over my hips.

They unceremoniously hit the floor.

Jack grips the curve of my ass cheeks before pulling away. He drags in a lungful of air, his eyes wild. "Damn, Lo."

I can barely fit my hands between us to undo the button on his shorts. He steps away long enough for me to force them to the floor.

His cock is hard against my stomach as he grinds his hips into me. The pressure in my groin is nearly unbearable.

"You still want me to tell you what I need?" I ask, panting as Jack presses kisses down my neck.

"Yeah."

"I want you to fuck me."

He stills for a long moment before chuckling against the bend of my shoulder. "Hearing you say that almost makes me come."

I laugh, the sound turning into a shriek as he lifts me up. My legs wrap around his waist just before he turns us toward the bedroom.

"When did you start dirty talking?" he asks between kisses.

"Today."

"It turns me on."

I laugh as he nibbles my bottom lip. "I'll note that for later."

He tosses me on the bed. The mattress dips with my weight, and some of the pillows topple to the floor. Before I can get my bearings, Jack is crawling across the bed to me.

I part my legs, letting my knees fall to the side. He wastes no time settling between them.

My breath goes in and out at an obnoxious pace, keeping up with the erratic beat of my heart. I can feel my pulse throbbing in my wetness. It takes everything I have in me not to touch myself to relieve the pressure.

Jack strips me of my shirt, discarding it off the side of the bed. His lips find mine immediately, desperately—his hands roaming my body as if he's never touched it before.

"I dream about you almost every night," he says, planting kisses across my jaw. "Sometimes I lie awake and look at our old pictures together. Or I'll come home and peek into your room and watch you sleep."

"That's creepy," I say, gasping as his kisses trail across my collarbone.

He chuckles against me. "I want to climb in bed with you, but you look too peaceful to disturb."

I moan as he grips my shoulders, then digs his fingers into my hips. My back arches as he caresses my breasts and rolls my nipples between his fingers.

Every touch is a reminder of how long it's been since I've been in this position. *It's long overdue.* Every gasp is a reminder of how good we are *at this.*

Our lips reconnect as he reaches between my legs. He drags a finger through my wetness, grinning against my mouth.

"I need you, Jack," I say, groaning as he rubs my swollen clit.

"Not as much as I need you."

A ripple of heat washes through me, spreading across every inch of my skin.

He spreads my legs apart with his. Air blasts against my flesh, making me shiver. He grabs his cock and inserts the tip into my opening.

Teasing me. Taunting me. *Promising me.*

"Ah!" I suck in a hasty breath. *"Please."*

I roll my hips, dying for contact. When he doesn't move, I open my eyes to find his trained on me.

I stop moving. "Why are you looking at me like that?"

His smile is soft and slow to grow.

"This is not the time for jokes, Jack."

He chuckles. "There's nothing to joke about here."

"Then what?" I circle my hips again in a futile attempt at making him slide into me. "What's the holdup?"

"I was just taking a second to absorb this."

I blink. "I want to absorb you too. *Now.*"

He grins. "You're funny."

"No, I'm wet, and there's an ache throbbing between my legs that only you can fix."

He exhales a leisurely breath. "If you could see yourself right now, you'd understand."

I flush.

The way he's looking at me is heady. Intense, yet tender. Intoxicating, yet sober. Hungry, yet satisfied.

I still as a warmth stemming from love instead of simply lust flows through my veins.

"You're so pretty, Lo. *Beautiful.* Sexy. I wish you could see you the way I see you right now."

"I'm kind of glad I can't."

He laughs. "You'd be very impressed."

"I'd be very impressed if you'd—*yes*," I groan as he slides all the way inside me. "*Just like that.* Damn it, Jack."

I hiss, the sensation of being completely and utterly filled.

"I like you demanding things from me," he says, his voice rough.

"Well, I quite like you giving in to the things I demand."

"Can you demand sex more often?"

I grin, bracing myself against the headboard. "Daily too often?"

He chuckles, and the sound echoes through me.

My muscles clench, my body molding around him with ease. I lift my knees and tilt my pelvis to give him even more access.

He grits his teeth and shoves inside me again. One long, smooth motion ends with the head of his shaft hitting the spot inside me that drives me wild.

I reach for his face as he picks up the pace, finding a rhythm that is nothing but bliss.

He lowers his mouth to mine, kissing me greedily this time, as if he can't get enough.

I've worried so many times that Jack and I would never find this again. That this connection, this form of communication, was a thing of the past.

"You feel *so good*," he says through clenched teeth.

"Keep going. Don't stop."

I hook my ankles at the small of his back and lift my hips off the mattress. He grips my hips with both hands. The pressure against my skin burns.

"Don't stop, Jack," I beg, tears from the intense pleasure wetting the corners of my eyes. "*Please.* Don't stop."

My senses are overrun. The sound of our bodies slipping against one another. The taste of Jack's mouth. The smell of his sweat mixed with his cologne blends with the sting of his hands.

And the absolute vision of the gorgeous man watching me like I'm some kind of prize.

This. I've missed this.

Being his. Being craved and adored. Being loved.

Then he hits *that* spot.

My eyes fall closed as I begin to topple over the edge.

"There you go," he says, guiding me down his length. "Give it to me, Lauren. Give yourself up for me."

"Oh, my . . . *ah*!"

I grip the blankets in my hands and jerk. My body shakes furiously around Jack, trembling in an explosive bout of ecstasy.

My body goes limp as I feel Jack begin to swell inside me.

A guttural groan rips through the air. He pounds into me harder and harder.

The sound prompts me to open my eyes and watch him fall apart.

And fall apart he does.

His Adam's apple bobs in his throat as his head falls back. The corners of his eyes wrinkle as his body shakes.

"Fuck," he says, hissing between his teeth.

Watching him release is almost as satisfying as getting off myself. Almost.

Slowly, he comes back to earth and lowers me gently to the mattress. He slides out of me and then collapses on the bed at my side.

My heart swells as I take in the look on his face.

"How was that?" he asks, resting his head on his arm.

"I give it five stars."

He grins. "I'm glad."

"How was it for you?"

"Ten stars."

I laugh. "I'm glad."

He reaches for me, pulling me so that we're lying side by side. He feathers a finger up and down my arm.

"Our maintenance plan needs to include that at least five times a week," he says, peering down at me with amusement written all over his face.

"I don't know."

His brows shoot to the ceiling. *You don't know?*

"No. I don't know. I happen to remember a few other things you used to do that I really, *really* liked. I might want to swap some of that out."

He smirks. "I think we have a problem."

"Oh, really?"

"I don't know what you're talking about." He presses a loud, wet kiss to my lips. "Looks like we're going to have to take a bath—then I'll probably need a snack and maybe a nap. But then you're going to have to go to all the trouble of explaining *exactly* what it is you want me to add to the plan."

I smirk back. "I'm not sure I can describe it. We might need a run-through to make sure we're on the same page."

He rises and hops off the bed. "Then I'm going to get the bath started so we can get back to show-and-tell."

I laugh as he disappears into the bathroom.

There he is. There's the man I married. The selfless, fun, loving, absolutely beautiful man I fell hopelessly in love with.

I've missed that man so much.

CHAPTER TWENTY-ONE

LAUREN

I stretch, feeling the pull in my muscles all the way through my toes. Jack sits beside me, propped up against his pillows, holding a book. His hair is a mussy, wild mess and still damp from our bath. A contented smile stretches across his lips.

I've dozed off and on since our second round between the sheets. The follow-up wasn't as frenzied as the first. There was more kissing, exploring, and talking. Playing. *Teasing*. It was carefree and fun in a way I'd forgotten sex could be.

"What are you reading?" I ask, yawning.

"*The Great Gatsby*. I found it in my middle console. Forgot I slipped it in there before I came."

"Interesting choice."

He closes the book and sets it on his lap.

I move onto my side, laying an arm across his stomach.

"Maddie asked me a question a couple of weeks ago about it," he says. "They were reading it in school, I think."

I nod. "Yeah. She had to do a paper on it."

"Right. Well, she asked me something about one of the characters' motivations, and I had no clue what she was talking about. She started breaking it down for me, and it sounded interesting. So I bought myself a copy."

I grin, narrowing my eyes. "So you're a bookworm now?"

He laughs. "I wouldn't start labeling me anything yet. I'm on chapter six."

"There's something super sexy about a man with a book."

"Is there?"

My fingers stroke his skin. "Yeah. It doesn't matter what kind. Classics or historical dramas or books about car parts." I laugh. "It shows that you have interests outside of yourself. That bodes well for the future."

"I haven't read a book in a long time. I think the last one was that yellow parenting book we read together when you were pregnant with Michael." He chuckles. "We spent so much time memorizing all of that shit and didn't use any of it."

"No, but it made us feel more prepared."

He slides his arm under my head and pulls me into the crook of his arm. I nestle against him, lacing one foot over his.

"You got a new freckle," he says.

"What?"

"You have a new freckle." He touches the side of my nose. "Right there."

I laugh. "How would you ever know that?"

"I know every freckle, mole, and scar on your body, Lo. I've committed every inch of you to memory."

I grin against him.

"That's the shitty part of this whole thing," he says. "You think I don't find you attractive—that I don't want to be with you. That I don't appreciate you. But you couldn't be more wrong." He strokes my side. "Assumption is the mother of all fuckups. Maybe I assumed you knew, or maybe I just got lazy with telling you. But I'm going to tell you all the things, all the time now. You'll get sick of hearing it."

My heart swells so big I think it might burst.

"That runs both ways, Jack."

"How do you mean?"

My stomach twists so hard that I squirm. "I feel like a jerk."

"Why?"

"I've made it clear that you didn't tell me things or make me feel certain ways. But I probably didn't tell you things or make you feel certain ways either. And I never considered that."

He strokes my arm. "It's okay."

"It's not okay. I need you to be honest with me. Did that ever hurt your feelings?"

"Maybe not in those words."

"Then how?"

He flexes his feet, causing his legs to tense. It's clear he's as uncomfortable with this as I am. The easy solution would be to change topics and not address this one at all. Besides, we're already on the same page.

But if we want to leave Story Brook with clear air and a fresh start, we need to leave all this here.

"I haven't exactly been the supportive wife lately," I say. "I can't think of the last time I told *you* that I appreciate you. Because I see all you do—I know the hours you put in and the time it takes you away from us. Would I rather you see us some too? Yes. Sure. Do I think you need to be gone so much? No. But you've never mishandled our finances. I've never wondered if you were having an affair." I blink back a surge of feelings. "I might've given this family the best of me, but so did you. Just in another way."

He pulls me close and kisses the top of my head. "I'd do anything for you. You are my life, and I'll listen and change and work on whatever I need in order to keep us together and happy."

I love you so much, Jack Reed. "I will too. It'll be a team effort."

He chuckles.

A scratching sound rattles the door.

"Sounds like your friend needs to potty," I say.

Jack kisses me again and then climbs out of bed. He throws on a pair of boxer briefs. "I'll let him out. Need anything from the kitchen?"

"I'm good."

He starts toward the door and looks at me over his shoulder. "That you are."

I straighten the blankets and pull my hair out of my face, securing it with an elastic despite its wetness. *I'll deal with it in the morning.*

Jack's voice drifts through the cabin as he encourages Snaps to venture into the dark yard to do his business. Soon the door clicks shut, and Jack's footsteps grow closer as he comes down the hallway.

Snaps leaps from Jack's arms onto the bed. He races in a full circle once, twice, three times before sitting on my leg and barking.

"I think he wants me to move," I say.

Jack slips in the bed beside me and, despite a protest from the puppy, pulls me into his side once again.

"Take that," I say to the dog.

His head cocks to the side.

"What are you going to do with that thing when you come home?" I ask.

"Well, Snaps is a part of the family now. We're a two-for-one deal."

I laugh. "You're telling me that if I don't let the dog live with us, you won't either?"

"I'm saying that if you don't want the dog to live with us, I'll offer you *lots* of incentives to change your mind."

"Well, I do love a good incentive."

He chuckles. "Come here, Snapsy."

The puppy jumps from his sitting position on top of my leg all the way across the bed and into Jack's arms. He nuzzles against him.

"Let's figure this out with the two of you," Jack says. "Snaps—what are your grievances with my wife?" He looks at the puppy and nods. "Okay, that's fair."

I giggle. "What did he say?"

"He said that he thinks you associate him with a bad time in your life, so you're really not giving him a fair chance."

"Smart dog."

Jack winks. "Now, Lauren, what are your problems with our dog?"

"Our dog?"

"Our dog."

I roll my eyes. "He judges me."

"How?"

"He looks at me like I'm in his way."

"Okay. What else?"

I laugh, not sure what's happening but finding it entertaining nonetheless. "He tries to intimidate me. He sits on me. Barks at me when I look at him. Chews on my shoes—*while I'm wearing them.* It's rude, to be honest."

Jack sighs. "Snaps, Lauren isn't like the guys at the shop. She doesn't find your alpha-dog routine amusing."

Snaps stares at my husband like he's unimpressed with his reaction. He's also obviously smitten with Jack.

The little thing is adorable. Even I can't deny that. When his little nub of a tail wags back and forth, I can't help but smile.

"Look, *I'll try*," I say. "I'll give the little shit a shot. But he's going to put in some effort too."

Snaps looks at me and barks.

"You're not helping things with that," Jack says, tapping him on the head.

I hold out a hand. Snaps is suspicious but leans toward it anyway. After giving me a thorough sniff, he licks the tips of my fingers.

Jack sets the dog between us. I'm wholly unsurprised when the dog presses his back paws against me and lays his head on my husband. *Now that I won't tolerate.*

"He's not sleeping between us," I say. "Hard limit. I only just got you back . . ."

The last sentence comes out as a whisper. My heart is still tender, fragile, from everything that's happened between us.

The look he gives me fills me with a warmth, a love, that soothes me.

"Well, we can't have that," he says, placing Snaps at the end of the bed. Then he draws me closer and snuggles me into his side. "I left the front door unlocked in case the kids come home in the morning."

Snaps barks, pawing at my feet before plopping down next to Jack with a huff.

"Can you imagine leaving our doors unlocked at home? Even in Maple, where nothing bad ever happens, I would still be scared to go to bed without locking the place down."

Jack gets situated. "We didn't lock our doors when I was little. I mean, I do remember Mom doing a final sweep of the house some nights. She'd check the doors and windows, and then the pilot light on the stove, because it was gas and she had a fear of a gas leak while we slept."

"Well, between her fear of a nighttime gas leak and mine of a night-time fire, we would be besties."

He laughs. "She would've liked you. I imagine she would've thumped me in the head for behaving the way I have." The levity falls from his face. "I continued the same cycle with you that my father did with her. And the thing is, I knew better. I watched my mom grow lonely and saw the hit it took on her confidence. And then I did that to you."

I take his hand in mine. He laces our fingers together.

"I probably disappointed her, wherever she is in the universe," Jack says. "She's probably thinking that she didn't raise me this way."

"Actually, I think your mom is watching you and is proud of the man you've become."

"You think?"

"Yeah. Imagine if Michael was you," I say. "Would you be proud of him?"

Jack nods slowly. "Yeah. I'd be disappointed in myself because he would've learned all of that from me."

"And *I'd* be disappointed in *myself* because my behavior told him it was okay. But then, once he has it pointed out to him, it's on him."

Jack brings our hands to his lips and presses a kiss on the top of mine.

"How was your dad today?" I ask, slipping my hand from his. "Did he seem okay?"

Jack groans as he lifts Snaps and puts him on the other side of him. I scooch closer until I'm against his hard, warm body.

My husband blows out a hasty breath that's filled with concern.

"I don't mean to worry you," I say. "But he was a little off tonight."

"I know. I'm trying to figure out how to bring it up to him, because you know my dad. He'll posture up and fight against me."

"Has his blood sugar been stable?"

Jack nods but also shrugs. "I think so. He's been eating better than he usually does, and he's not really giving off bad blood sugar vibes. He usually gets dizzy and wants to drink all the time. But that's not really been the case."

I kiss Jack's rib.

"He's just . . . what is it?" Jack asks, thinking it through. "More abrasive, maybe? Talkative? More open?" He looks down at me. "That all sounds normal when you say it out loud."

It does sound fine when it's spoken aloud. Honestly, if that's what Pops thinks he's being with his sharp responses and willingness to talk about a lot of things he usually avoids, it doesn't sound like he has an issue. It sounds normal.

But it's not. It's not Harvey Reed. And like Jack, I don't know what to make of it.

"He had a hard time in the woods today," Jack says. "And a couple of times, he started going the wrong way. My dad doesn't go the wrong way. He knows those woods like the back of his hand."

"I noticed when he was talking to me around the fire that he kept going off on tangents. Or, maybe it was that he kept losing his place in the story he was telling me. But it was very odd, and I wanted to mention it to you."

Jack nods. "I'll talk to him about it tomorrow. Prepare for fireworks, I'm sure."

I laugh. "Oh, that's a guarantee."

He rolls over in one fluid movement and pins me to the bed. I yelp, my heart pounding in anticipation.

"In the meantime," he says, eyes blazing, "let's make some fireworks ourselves."

I lift my legs and wrap them around him. "What are you waiting for?"

He captures the rest of my words with his mouth, making it clear he's not waiting for anything.

Which is good. Because I'm tired of waiting too.

CHAPTER TWENTY-TWO

LAUREN

"Mom!" Maddie's cry pierces the air. *"Mom!"*

I sit straight up in bed, struggling to get my senses together. I have no idea what time it is, nor what day. All I know is that my baby girl is screaming my name.

"Madeline!" I shout, yanking the blankets off me.

Her steps smack against the floor in a rush. Sobs tear through the air, sending a cold chill down my spine.

Jack's out of bed before me and across the room before my feet hit the hardwood.

My heart thunders, adrenaline spiking at the sound of my child in panic. *What's wrong? Where has she been? Is she hurt?*

A million thoughts cross my mind in the ten seconds it takes Jack to open the door.

Jack left the door unlocked last night. Maddie and Michael went to Pops's. Michael texted us that while we were in the bath.

Did they go out on the boat after that? Is she hurt?

"Mom," Maddie sobs, the syllable extended to three.

She rounds the corner, passes Jack, and launches herself on the bed. Snaps yelps from under the blankets and scurries out from beneath her.

"Maddie, what's wrong?" I ask, taking her in my arms. She curls onto my lap with such force that it knocks me back into the headboard. "Honey. Talk to me. What's going on?"

Her body is racked with sobs. Her long, sun-streaked hair is matted against her face. She heaves air into her lungs in between long stretches of crying, and I have no idea what to do.

"Maddie, talk to me," I say, detaching her from my chest.

A steady stream of tears falls down her rosy cheeks. Her pupils are wide, and her bottom lip quivers.

"Mads, answer your mother," Jack says, still standing in the doorway.

I search her face for injuries. Her pajamas are fine, her arms and bare feet clean and seemingly perfect.

"Where is Michael?" I ask.

She sniffles, her chest shaking. "Daniel broke up with me."

The words open yet another dam of tears, and she howls into my chest. I wrap my arms around her and hold her tight.

Then, with a ton of reservation, I look up at Jack.

Arms crossed over his chest. Jaw clenched into a tight line. Eyes narrowed. *Protective Daddy Mode engaged.*

"It's going to be okay, Mads," I say, rocking her back and forth. "It's going to be okay."

Jack lifts a brow. I fire him a warning look.

"He . . ." She hiccups. "I got a text when I woke up this morning."

"He broke up with you in a text?" Jack asks, his voice much calmer than his demeanor.

"Shh," I say, rubbing Maddie's back.

"No man breaks up with a woman by text," Jack says. "That's not okay."

Maddie sits up, her tearstained face glistening in the morning light. "Well, he's fourteen, so there's that."

Snaps jumps up, resting his paws on Maddie's arms, and tries to lick her face. She swats him away.

"I don't care if he's fourteen or forty," Jack says. "If he doesn't respect you enough to have a conversation with you, then he doesn't deserve your time."

Her bottom lip trembles again. "But I don't want to let him go, Daddy."

The stoic *Fuck that kid* on Jack's face melts away as his baby pulls at his heartstrings. The love that he has for her pulls at mine.

"Mads . . ." Jack comes back to bed, picking up Snaps and then sitting next to me. "You're gonna be all right. You know that, right?"

She shakes her head.

"You will," I say, tucking her hair behind her ears. "I know it hurts right now."

"I feel like my heart is in a bunch of pieces," she says. "It's the most painful thing I've ever felt."

Jack catches my eye. I'm not sure if he's ready to load up the troops to go find Daniel or celebrate that Daniel has extracted himself from Maddie's life. Either way, it's hard not to laugh.

"He's your first love, sweetheart," I say. "First-love breakups are always painful. You never forget your first heartbreak."

She looks at me with watery eyes. "Who was your first heartbreak?"

"Yeah. Who was your first heartbreak?" Jack asks with a cocky brow.

"His name was Shane," I say, running my fingers through Maddie's hair. "We were in eighth grade. He had this great blond, surfer-style hair and bright-blue eyes."

"Makes sense for Ohio," Jack says.

I grin at him. "Stop it."

"Did you feel like you were punched in the chest?" Maddie asks.

"Yeah. I think I locked myself in my room and cried for a whole weekend."

"I don't think I'll ever stop crying. It burns right here." She places a hand between her breasts. "It's even hard to breathe."

"It'll get better. I promise," I say.

She picks up the edge of our sheet and wipes her face.

I take a long, deep breath and try to regulate myself. The adrenaline that shot through me earlier has begun to wane now that I know no one is dead. *It's only heartbreak.*

I glance at Jack and catch him watching me. He reaches for my hand and gives it a gentle squeeze. I'd give anything to know what he's thinking, to understand what's prompted the pensiveness on his face. Something tells me it's not Maddie's situation alone.

"The weird thing is that I don't even know what I did," she says during a moment of calm. "Everything was fine yesterday. What could I have done to make him mad while I was asleep?"

"You didn't do anything," I say.

"Then why would he do this to me?" Her voice breaks. "How fair is this?"

"Here's the thing, Mads," I say. "You can't assume that you have anything to do with the way someone else behaves."

She furrows her brow. "But if I didn't do anything, then why would he break up with me?"

"What your mom is trying to say, but I'll put it more bluntly, is that sometimes people are just assholes. That's it. There's no other reason," Jack says.

"He's not an asshole, Dad. Don't say that."

"He's certainly behaving like one. If your brother pulled this on a girl, we'd be having a talk. So, if you think I can just swallow that Daniel acted this way to you . . . I'm sorry, Mads. I expect a boy to treat you better than that." He leans closer. "And I want *you* to expect them to. Sometimes your mother even has to demand better of me. That's what strong, smart women do."

I reach out and take his fingers in mine.

Snaps walks across the bed and makes himself at home on Maddie's lap. He nestles against her stomach and sighs. *Don't use my daughter to win my favor, Snapsy.* Maddie almost smiles. *Then again, go ahead.*

"You're at an age where kids have a lot of emotions and hormones," I tell my daughter. "It's a lot to control. And, sometimes, people act on a flood of one or the other, when they shouldn't."

Her ears perk up. "So, what you're saying is he might realize he made a mistake?"

"What I was hoping you'd take from that is that it's not your fault," I say.

"Why would you want to be with someone that makes you feel this way?" Jack says. "I'm not just saying that because I'm your dad and know you're the second-smartest, prettiest, most amazing woman in the world."

Maddie looks at me and smiles softly through her anguish. "At least you two are back together, right?"

I turn my attention to my husband. It's my first time really looking at him since last night.

There's something different in the way he's looking at me this morning. I'm not sure what it is, but I feel it inside me. It's as if the wall we've built—intentionally or by accident—between us has been torn away. The vulnerability that either Jack has hidden from me or I've refused to see is there again. I wonder if he can sense mine too.

I no longer feel like my life is a thousand-piece puzzle that's strung out and missing the corners. It's all snapped together, right where it should be. It's complete.

We're complete.

I hope.

Maddie lies across the bed with her head on Jack's legs and her body across mine. Snaps tries to sit on her head but is quickly dissuaded. Instead, he climbs onto Jack's lap and goes back to sleep.

"I don't know how you guys were thinking of divorce if you love each other even a little bit as much as I love Daniel," she says, tears falling down her cheeks again. "This is unbearable."

"You're telling me," Jack mumbles.

I smack him on the arm.

The front door opens and closes in the distance. The footsteps fall hard and quick—*definitely Michael's.*

"Hey, what are you . . . *o-kay.* What's going on here?" he asks, taking in the scene before him.

"Daniel dumped me."

Michael's gaze snaps to mine.

"She's going to be okay," I say gently. "Your sister just isn't over the shock yet."

"What did he say to you?" Michael asks, looking every bit as angry as Jack did at first.

"Nothing." She turns her face toward him. "He broke up with me by text."

Michael's brows shoot to the ceiling. "He broke up with you *by text*? Who does that?"

"That's what I said," Jack says.

"You better not ever bring that little creep around again," Michael says.

"Well, we're broken up, so that's apparently not a concern."

Michael laughs angrily. "Oh, he'll come back. He'll go out and see if he likes anyone else any better, and when he realizes that you're the best, he'll mope around and try to get you to take him back."

"Don't say that." She sits up. "He's not trying to find a new girlfriend already." She turns to me, panicked. "Is he?"

"Michael, let's leave it alone for a while," Jack says.

"What? Someone has to tell her the truth."

I touch Maddie's cheek. "Michael is just being protective."

"No, Michael is being honest," he says of himself. "I'm a guy. Granted, I attempt to be a little more upstanding than that little screwball."

"Michael," I say at the same time as Maddie objects.

"But I know how these things work," he says. "You do, too, Dad."

Jack sighs. "Easing your way into this would probably have been a better tactic. Maybe note that going forward."

Michael shakes his head, clearly disgusted by the entire situation. "Well, you guys keep telling her what she wants to hear, and I'll be at the lake with Ava." He starts to leave but stops and looks at his sister. "Daniel better watch himself."

"You're going to be eighteen soon," Jack says. "*You* better watch *yourself.*"

"Yeah, because I totally don't know people that will be underage after my birthday."

"Can we not do this?" I ask, blowing out a breath. "It's . . ." I glance at the clock. "Eight in the morning. I haven't had coffee. Can we not start a war until I've at least peed?"

Jack gets to his feet. "Speaking of peeing, I probably need to let Snaps out before he pees on the floor."

Michael comes back into the room. "Give him to me, and I'll put him out before I go."

Maddie hands her brother the dog. Michael takes the puppy but doesn't move.

"I'm not trying to be a dick or make this harder for you," he tells his sister. "But it pisses me off to think that that kid thinks he can just be mean to you for no reason. You're nothing but a sweetheart to him."

Maddie grins softly. "Thank you."

He backs away. "But I do know people."

"Get out of here," Jack says, laughing.

Michael disappears down the hallway.

Maddie scoots up beside me and buries herself under the blankets. "Can I lie in here with you for a while, Mom?"

I look at Jack.

"I'll start a pot of coffee and then go check on Dad," he says, slipping on a pair of shorts and a shirt. "Does that work?"

"Make it strong."

He darts into the bathroom and brushes his teeth before heading out. Once he's gone, I lie next to Maddie.

The pillow is wet with her tears, but the hysteria of the breakup seems to have eased. Little does she know it, but the crack in my heart from seeing her hurt will remain much longer than hers.

What a way to start the day.

CHAPTER TWENTY-THREE

Jack

"Why are you here so damn early?" Dad rocks back and forth in his recliner, a cup of coffee in his hand. "Did you roll out of bed and come straight here?"

I scrub a hand down my face. "Do you have any more coffee?"

"You know where the pot is."

I make my way into his small kitchen. I find a white mug with orange-and-brown mushrooms on it and fill it with liquid energy.

"You didn't answer my question," he says.

"I was woken up this morning by my daughter screaming bloody murder."

Dad stops rocking. "Maddie? Why?"

"Daniel broke up with her." I sit on the sofa next to him. "By text."

"That little prick."

I grin and take a sip of coffee.

"She okay?" Dad asks.

"She'll be fine. Eventually. There could be a few more days of dramatics before that happens, though."

He chuckles as if he expected as much.

We sit together in silence. The only sound is the occasional squeak from the chair. Dad rocks steadily, watching the birds out the window.

I fall back against the cushions, the same ones that have occupied this cabin since I was a boy. Mom used to prop colorful decorative pillows and brightly colored blankets on the sofa. I never understood why, but I didn't argue either—they were great for making forts.

"You know what?" Dad says. "Good."

"Good?"

"Yeah." He takes a drink. "It's good that boy broke up with her."

I sip my coffee. "I can't say I'm torn up about it. But she's over there crying her eyeballs out. That's what gets me."

"To hell with that kid."

I place my mug on the table in front of me. "What's gotten into you, Pops?"

"Nothing has gotten into me, Jack. She just doesn't need no damn boyfriend."

"Well, I happen to agree with you. But she had one, and now she's upset. There's nothing *good* about that."

He chuckles.

His nonchalant attitude about this situation surprises me. *And it makes me mad.* Maybe it's because I'm tired—after a fantastic night with Lauren—or that I haven't processed seeing my daughter truly cry for the first time, but his indifference to this topic gets under my skin.

My baby girl is hurting. *Am I similarly glad she's no longer dating Daniel?* Yes, especially after he had the audacity to break up with her by text. But I think I'm more surprised by the two unexpected reactions—Michael jumping to Maddie's defense and my father's apathy.

Today is making no sense at all.

"You know what's wrong with people these days?" he asks.

"I'd love for you to tell me."

"They get too focused on shit that doesn't matter in the end."

What? My brows pull together as I try to make sense of the old man.

"Oh, come on, Jack. It's not that hard to understand." He takes another drink. "How many times a day do you get so absorbed in something that you won't even remember the next day?"

"What does this have to do with anything?"

He stops rocking. "It has something to do with *everything*."

I lift my coffee and then stand, needing to move before I crawl out of my skin.

"Maddie's sad," Dad says. "I'm sorry to hear that. But she'll be all right, and she'll probably be better later because she's gotten this out of the way. It's a stepping stone of life, to lose your first love. It'll happen at some point. Might as well get it over with."

"When did you become so coldhearted?"

"It comes with age. You stop giving a shit about things that don't matter. I don't have enough energy to use worrying about everything anymore."

I stop next to my mom's bookcase and observe my father from across the room. His hair is lighter than I've seen it. I'm not sure if it's the time of day or the shadows in the room, but his skin looks pale. Lines gather along his forehead and around his mouth, and I can't help but wonder, *When did he get so old?*

"I sit here, or at home, and watch people scurry around like little ants," he says. "They hurry over here to do something. Then they run over there and do something else. They're always moving, always in a rush to go on to the next thing. Why be in such a frenzy to do more when you're so damn busy that you don't get to really do any of it?"

"What are you getting at?"

He sighs and shakes his head. "When I was growing up, we didn't have all the opportunities you kids do now. There wasn't that much to do. Our lives were simpler back then, and I suppose they were less fancy and all that. But you know what? We may have been playing dominoes and not computers, but we *played dominoes*. The neighbor kids would all come together on the sidewalk or someone's porch, and we'd play all afternoon. *Together*."

The sun moves in the sky, coming through the window at a different angle. Dad squints against the sudden brightness.

"Now you all have so many things you can do that you think you have to try them all. But you never get to really experience any of them," he says. "And you're so inundated with information and possibilities and connections that you lose sight as to what life really is."

I take my seat on the couch and look at my father. I'm beginning to worry about him. What Lauren said is resonating with me and—

"I worry about you, Jack."

He what? "You worry about me? Why?"

He pulls the handle on the side of his chair and lowers his legs. Then he gets to his feet. "You're a better man than I ever was. Smarter. More intuitive. More like your mother, thank God."

What?

"Don't do what I did," he says, walking gingerly across the room. "Don't tie up who you are with what you can accomplish. I did that. I killed myself for a company that didn't give a shit about me. Missed out on so much—practically my whole life—because I thought that the paychecks, the promotions, the accolades were somehow worth it."

I can barely breathe. "You're a good man, Dad."

He scoffs. "I have a lot of regrets. A lot of them." He stops at a rollback desk in the corner. "My biggest one, though, is that your mother missed out on living her life because of my choices. I kept thinking we'd travel when I retired. We'd come up here and stay all summer together. We'd make up for lost time. But then she died . . . and the time was already gone."

I've never heard my father talk like this before. *Where is it coming from?*

Harvey Reed has always been a juggernaut of a man, loud and gruff. Not one to be messed with or mislabeled as weak. So to hear his voice on the cusp of breaking almost breaks me.

He rummages around the desk with his back to me. "Don't you tell your kids that I told you this, but I know Lauren was going to file for divorce."

My heart drops.

"Maddie called me one night crying because Michael found a card on Lauren's desk," he says matter-of-factly. "I wasn't surprised. I figured as much was coming."

"You did?"

"Well, sure I did. I was paying attention." He glances over his shoulder to drive home his point. That *I* wasn't.

I want to yell at my father; I'm so angry. *Why did everyone simply figure it was coming and not bother to say anything to me?* I glance back at Dad, knowing he's not finished.

"So, when you called off this trip," he says, "the kids and I figured out how to get you both up here."

Okay, well, at least he's taking some of the blame for that.

"I want to be pissed that you would work in tandem with my errant children. But, in light of the way things have worked out, I can't be mad."

"No, you can't." He flips his attention back to the desk. "You really owe me a favor, if we're being honest."

I roll my eyes but can't help but grin.

"I want you to try to slow down a little, Jack. Don't get caught up in this performance-based lifestyle the world demands nowadays. The only performance that matters is the one you do with your family."

"When did you become a philosopher?"

"There it is," he mumbles, closing the desk. He turns to me once again. "I watch a lot of television. There's some good advice on there from time to time."

I nod toward his hand. "What do you have in there?"

He thrusts an envelope in my hands before going back to his recliner. "I had that drawn up a while back. Thought this was the time to go ahead and give it to you. I finalized it before I came up here."

I pull open the tab. "What is it?"

Dad sits silently while I pull a stack of white papers from the envelope. I take one look at the top sheet and gasp.

"What the hell, Dad?"

"It's gonna be yours anyway."

I skim the wording on page after page of documents that put everything my father owns into Lauren's and my names. My hands shake.

"Now, I just added you to my checking account," he says. "So that's still mine. I'll keep paying the property taxes and utilities and stuff, of course. And I trust that you won't kick me out of my house."

I drop the papers on the table. They hit with a thud.

My heart pounds as I try to make sense of all this. "Why did you do this?"

"My attorney said it was best if I put it all in your name. Easier transfer when I die."

I force a swallow. "Is there something you're not telling me?"

"I had some tests done last week. Got a knot on my liver. Doctor didn't like the look of it, so he did a little biopsy."

"What?" My jaw drops. "*Dad.* Why didn't you tell me?"

He groans. "Because I didn't want this to happen."

"What? You didn't want me worrying about you?"

"Exactly." He narrows his eyes. "I don't want you coddling me or babying me about it. I'm probably fine anyway."

"When will you know?"

He shrugs. "The test results are probably in."

"So, call and get them."

"I told them I'll come in when we go home."

I spring to my feet in disbelief. "You could be sitting here with cancer or something else, and you're all nonchalant about it? What's wrong with you?"

"What's wrong with me? Probably cancer. You're right."

I glare at him. "This isn't funny, Dad."

"No, it's not. But I'm gonna have to die sooner or later. And we don't really get to plan our exit strategy, do we?"

My head is ready to explode.

"How can you just not know?" I ask.

"Because I want one more summer with you and the kids and Lauren without knowing, Jack. I want one more stretch of beautiful weather and berry picking with the kids and Lauren's cooking—I want one last summer to live and make memories without being an old dying fart."

Slowly, I sit back down. I can feel the color draining from my face as his words sink in.

My father is dying? He might be dying?

That's not true and I know it. I've known Dad was frail for a while now. But the fact that he's been this sick—having a fucking test—is a blade right to my heart.

My head spins as I try to wrap my mind around what's happening. Too much has been thrown at me too quickly today to process it all. I do know that something has to change between me and my father . . . whether he likes it or not. I'm going to be there for him. I'm going to take care of him.

I just have to figure out how to make that happen without ruining everything else I'm trying to do. I certainly can't just spring another responsibility on Lauren. *Fuck.*

"Look," he says, taking pity on me. "I've been doing a lot of thinking. Apparently, when you get news that you might be dying, it makes you start reevaluating a lot of shit."

I hold my head in my hands.

"Promise me that you won't make the same mistakes that I did. Tell me that you'll remember to live your life while you're living it," he says, his tone rough and raw.

"Yeah," I say, dropping my hands. "I will."

"I mean it, Jack. I fucked my life up and your mom's. Don't let me screw up yours and the kids' too."

The man sitting in front of me isn't the same man I grew up with. He's wise, in a strange way, and considerate. I knew my father loved my children, but I didn't know he had that much true affection for anyone else.

Maybe we're all changing.

"Got any questions?" he asks, teasing me. "Need me to give you a hug?"

"Don't be a dick."

He chuckles. "Now, let's keep this between me and you. All right? Lauren has enough on her plate, and those kids of yours will drive me straight to my coffin if they hear a word about this."

"Too soon for coffin jokes," I say, shaking my head.

"Promise me you won't tell them, then."

My brain is a mess of inputs, overwhelmed by the data it's had to process already this morning.

Promise I won't tell my family that my father might have cancer?

How did this happen? What happened last night to make everything screwed up this morning?

"Yeah," I say, the word hollow. "I won't say anything."

"Good. Now, back to Maddie. Are we going to egg this kid's house or what?"

A smile slowly trickles across my face. It pulls the corners of his lips up too.

What a day.

What a fucking day.

CHAPTER TWENTY-FOUR

LAUREN

*E*motional exhaustion is entirely worse than physical exhaustion. Wishing for a pain reliever to ease the ache in my head, but too tired to get up and get one, I stretch out on the sofa with a sigh.

Where did the day go? Didn't I just wake up? Wasn't I in Jack's arms, basking in the afterglow of a night of perfection ten minutes ago?

Nope. Somehow, we went from coffee with the morning dew to dinner after a storm—both theoretically and literally.

Maddie's devastation has swallowed my whole day. There was no way I could leave her to her own devices when she was listening to music one minute and sobbing the next.

Trust me, kid. I understand heartbreak.

I lay a hand on my chest and focus on the steady beating of my heart.

Jack has been gone most of the day. He popped in for a quick shower after visiting his dad. Seeing that Maddie and I were settled, he took off shortly after. *Where did he go?* I either didn't hear him tell me or I forgot in the chaos of the day.

Being face-to-face with the aftermath of Maddie's breakup, coupled with Jack's absence, has left me vulnerable. My brain keeps throwing up flags. *Am I being smart, sliding right back all in with Jack?* I had managed to get on the other side of this in my own life. I made it out of the heart-break and became someone I really liked. *Should I really reverse that?*

Is that a good decision for me?

Yes. Yes, it is, and I'm certain this is the way forward. For me. For us. For our family. But I can't shake the memories of feeling similar at home. Alone and sitting in the middle of a pit of sadness.

The door opens and I turn my head, cringing at the stab in my temple. Jack comes in with a distant look in his eyes.

"Hey," I say.

"Hey." His voice is hollow. "How is everything here?"

I sit up.

"Is Maddie doing okay?" he asks.

"She just went up to get a shower. I think she cried herself out."

He nods.

"I kept her from texting Daniel a hundred times," I say. "She just wanted to ask him why he did this. Just to say hello. To tell him she'll wait on him."

Jack lifts a brow.

"I know," I say, sighing. "I did my best to convince her that was not the way to go."

He sits on the edge of the chair next to the fireplace and blows out a breath. The soles of his shoes are muddy, and there's a stick stuck to the side of his shorts. Although curious, I don't ask him about it.

"Are you okay?" I ask instead.

"Yeah. Why?"

I shrug. "I don't know. You seem a little preoccupied."

He scrubs a hand down his face. But before he can answer me, Maddie joins us in the room.

"I feel a little better now," she says, curling up beside me.

With a side-eye pegged on Jack, I smile at her. "I'm glad. Are you hungry?"

She shakes her head. "My belly feels rotten."

"You have to eat, Maddie."

"I will. Just not now."

She leans her head on my shoulder and curls her legs up beneath her. I blow out a breath and watch my husband over the top of her head.

My stomach ripples at the sight of him, elbows rested on his knees and a frown on his handsome face. Something happened today. *But what?*

The scene triggers a million thoughts in my head. In turn, those set off a billion internal reactions that have me shifting from nausea to panic to anger to desolation.

I wish my marriage were solid enough that one wonky afternoon wouldn't be enough to make me second-guess everything, but it's not. Suddenly, I'm afraid I bought into the second-honeymoon phase a little too soon.

Of course our problems are still present. It's ludicrous to think they could disappear because we want them to.

But what is the problem now?

"I'm surprised my heart is still beating," Maddie says.

I fight a grin at her melodrama. "Well, it is, and you're still here."

"He's just another boy. There will be more of them," Jack says.

"I'm only interested in him."

"Expand your interests, then." He reconsiders. "Or don't. Actually, don't. Just be your mom's best friend and forget all about boys."

Maddie makes a face and scoops up Snaps from the floor. She curls up with the puppy on the other end of the couch.

"I can't be Mom's best friend," she says. "Mom has Billie, and Billie gets territorial."

I laugh.

"One time, I walked in the kitchen to ask Mom to take me to the mall," Maddie says, a sparkle returning to her eye. *Thank God.* "And Billie was there, and she tried to fight me because she said I had taken up enough of Mom's time that week."

"She was kidding," I say.

Jack lifts a brow. "She probably wasn't."

"I don't think she was," Maddie says, making a silly face.

I tap her on the leg. Snaps growls at me.

"Every girl needs that one friend that she can relate to, someone whose core values are the same. Someone she can vent to without causing familial damage." I wrinkle my nose at her. "That you can call and bitch about your mother and know she'll always take your side and never say a word to anyone."

"Billie always takes your side. Even when you *forgot to pick me up from cheer practice.*"

I drop my jaw. "I did not forget. I got stuck in a parents' meeting for Michael's senior class and somehow got elected secretary for the group. If I forgot you, I wouldn't have called Billie to get you, now would I?"

She rolls her eyes playfully.

Jack's phone rings. The sound surprises all of us because, much to the children's dismay, our devices haven't worked great in the living room. He furrows his brow and pulls it from his pocket.

"Yeah?" he says without looking at us. But he also doesn't get up from his chair. *Probably afraid he'll lose connection.* "Seriously? They fined us?"

Maddie looks at me and grimaces.

Jack's face pales. "What? Tell me you're kidding."

I sit up taller.

"Is the door still there? Does it close?" He listens intently. "So can you secure it for the night, or is it too banged up?"

Jack holds his forehead, his eyes closed.

Maddie nudges me with her toes. I look at her and wince.

"I don't know. You're a mechanic. There are three other mechanics there—or there's supposed to be," he says, frustration dripping from his voice. "Can't you figure it out?"

Jack stands but then sits immediately.

"Yeah. Good." He nods slowly. "No, don't do that. Those are for Vegas. I had them made to pass out." He nods again. "Thanks. Bye."

Vegas?

My stomach swirls at the hint of a trip I know nothing about—and the reminder of real life awaiting us on the other side of this village.

Snaps nips at my fingertips. *I'll be left with this little responsibility to care for while he's away.*

"Mom?" Maddie asks, breaking me out of my thoughts.

Ignoring Jack's gaze on the side of my face, I turn to our child. "Yeah?"

"Do you think we can come back here for Labor Day like we did last year? Ava said they're coming and the Schottenheimers too. We're on a different schedule from them this summer, and I'd really like to see Christina."

"Sure," I say, blowing out a shaky breath. *Vegas?* "I don't see why we can't."

"Great."

Snaps jumps to the floor and whines at Maddie.

"I'll take Snapsy out, and then I'll go check on Pops," she says.

"Okay," I say, my blood pressure rising.

She walks out with the puppy on her heels. The door slams behind them.

The cabin grows eerily quiet. Jack hangs his head, elbows back on his knees. I sit awkwardly, stuck in the middle of knowing a little but not enough.

"What's going on, Jack?" I ask.

"Nothing."

He's lying. Between his behavior and Vegas, something is obviously going on. *Why won't he tell me?*

"What's wrong with you?" he asks, lifting his head. "Are you okay?"

"Just emotionally drained from drying Maddie's tears all day. Where did you go this morning?"

His shoulders slump as he sits back in the chair. "I'm sorry. I did a little hiking down by the lake. Sat with Dad for a while. I've just had a lot on my mind. You know how it is."

Do I?

"Is everything okay at the shop?" I ask, poking around for the crux of the problem.

"It'll be fine."

The dismissal hits a nerve. *It'll be fine.*

Am I too unimportant to know what's going on?

"Didn't we have a discussion about being involved in each other's lives?" I ask, trying to hide my annoyance. "Because I feel like there's a lot happening in your world, and that world is most definitely not interfacing with mine."

He groans. "We got fined. I'll deal with that when I get home. Someone—I don't know who, because Tommy was being elusive about the name, so it's probably him—drove a car into the roll-up garage door."

My eyes go wide.

"They're going to get it secured for the night and then call a guy in tomorrow to take a look at it," he says. "No idea what that's gonna look like or cost."

"I'm sorry, Jack."

He chuckles in frustration—in defeat.

I pause, uncertain whether I should ask about his trip. He's upset. Maybe I should let it go. But if I do, it'll eat at me, which wouldn't do either of us any good in the long run.

"You're going to Vegas?" I ask.

He wipes his palms down his shorts. "Yeah. We talked about it a few months ago."

"I don't recall having a conversation with you about Las Vegas."

"Well, we did. You were standing at the refrigerator holding an empty milk jug, to be exact. And I told you we got an invite to the CBA show in Vegas this summer. One of our suppliers got the shop two tickets. It's a big deal—the biggest car show in the country."

This is all news to me. Maybe he did mention it, but if he did, I didn't hear him.

A lump settles in my throat as I struggle to internalize this trip. I'm sure it'll be great for his business; that's a good thing. But the more his business booms, the more our family time dwindles—and I'm left holding everything in our lives together.

Just like always.

My stomach churns, exhaustion from the impending situation already sinking deep in my bones. "When is it?"

"The week after we get home from here."

My eyes widen. "So . . . we go home and then you leave? For how long?"

"Four days."

I force a swallow. "Okay."

What else is going to confront us as soon as we're home?

I'm panicking. I'm falling into old habits, and the resentment I carried for so long is creeping back up. It's happening all too easily. *But how do I fight it when it's so fresh in my mind?*

"Will you go with me?" he asks.

I stare at him blankly. "Jack, no. I can't go with you—especially not on a moment's notice."

"Why?"

I blink. "*Why?* Is that a serious question?"

"Yeah."

The room buzzes with energy. It's a dry forest waiting on the match to strike. I'm dumbfounded by his question. *Has he not listened to anything I've said?*

It's a nice sentiment—that's not lost on me. He's never asked me to go with him to work events. That's a step in the right direction. But I've spent the past few days explaining that his time away from the family puts a heavier load on my shoulders.

Doesn't he get it? Is he really that out of touch?

I stare at him, confused. *I'll break it down for you.* "If it's the week after we get home, I'll have to unpack all this stuff. Do laundry. Go to the grocery store. Go through the mail. Figure out what we're going to do with your dog."

He swallows hard.

"Michael has wrestling camp," I say, mentally sorting my day planner. "We still need to prep for that. Someone is coming to look at the sprinkler system because it hasn't worked all summer, and our grass in the front yard is getting crunchy. The HOA has already sent us a notice about that. Maddie is not only going through her first breakup, but she's supposed to fundraise two days a week, starting when we get home, to raise money for their cheer trip to Florida."

"Oh."

Does he think I'm done? "I have a doctor's appointment on the twenty-second. Maddie sees the dermatologist on the twenty-fifth."

"What for?" he asks, brows pulled together.

"She has a weird mole on her back that I want looked at. I'm sure it's fine, but I'll feel better if someone with a medical certification tells me that."

A pregnant pause fills the space between us. We look at one another as if we're both afraid to proceed.

He did ask me to go. But I assumed the worst.

Is this progress or a slippery slope back to the way it was before?

He's trying, and that makes my heart swell. But this conversation proves we are far from fixing our problems. And the solution feels so out of reach.

The past few days with Jack and the kids, and Harvey, have reminded me of just how wonderful things can be when we're together. But the problem is, and has always been, that we aren't together—that I'm alone. And as I look at my husband and the wariness in his eyes, the real question is sitting right in front of me: *Is being alone better than being with him?*

Jack rolls his head around his neck and blows out a breath. The sound breaks the silence. "I won't go."

"Why?"

214

He sighs. "Because you're obviously slammed, and I want to stay and help you."

If I thought he meant it, I'd be touched. But the way his eyes narrow and the edge to his tone make me think otherwise. *He's saying what he thinks I want to hear.*

That isn't at all what I want. I don't want to be made to think that this is all my fault, that these issues are mine alone. That my needs in this relationship take a back seat to practically everything and everyone else.

I steel myself to him. "Don't make me feel guilty."

"I'm not. But I don't know what you want me to do, Lo. I'm in between a rock and a hard place here."

We both are.

I study him—the lines on his face and the trepidation in his eyes. As much as I want to get up and walk out of the room, which is what I would've done before this trip, I don't. He's willing to talk this through. I will too.

"I want you to talk to me about things, Jack. About whatever's going on with you today that you won't share with me." I hold his gaze. "Tell me about trips to the other side of the country. About . . . getting dogs."

He shakes his head. "I'm telling you—I told you about the trip."

"Fine. But what about the rest of it?" *What's wrong with you right now?*

He watches me for a long moment before he gets to his feet. His jaw pulses as frustration rises from his chest and colors his face a fiery shade of red.

"You can't just blame this on me," he says, ignoring my question. "You're out here making plans without talking to me too."

I jump to my feet. "What are you talking about?"

"You didn't ask me if I wanted to come here for Labor Day. Hell, I didn't even know you came here last year for Labor Day."

"I wonder why," I say, standing my ground. "Or maybe I mentioned it at a wholly inopportune time, and you didn't hear me."

Air moves around us in a hasty swirl. My body is tense, prepping for a battle with my husband.

"But I think going to our cabin is a little different than going across the country," I say. "You could easily come up here with us *on a holiday*."

"If you don't bring your *best friend, Billie*."

I throw up my hands, the swell of emotions from the day finally starting to tip over the edge. "*My best friend, Billie*. Right. You want to be pissed about that? Am I not allowed to have friends now? I'm not allowed to bring a friend to shoulder some of the single parenting that, although I've become quite adept at, I didn't want for yet another fucking weekend? Is that it?"

"That's not what I said."

"Then what did you say, Jack?"

He takes a step toward me. "I'm just saying that you're accusing me of living my life without you when you have clearly been living one without me—"

The door slams shut.

"Because I've had to, Jack."

"Dad?" We whirl on our heels to see Maddie holding Snaps. She looks at me and then her father. "Where's Pops?"

Jack's face turns white. "What did you say?"

"Where's Pops? He's not home."

He starts toward the door. "I'll be back, Lo."

Okay . . .

CHAPTER TWENTY-FIVE
JACK

"This fucking day can just be over," I mutter, marching to my dad's cabin.

His truck is gone, but that's not wholly unusual. He's been known to loan it out in exchange for firewood and baked goods. He likes to portray this as him getting one over on everyone else. In reality, he likes being nice. He just doesn't want that label.

I take the steps two at a time and rap my knuckle against the door. As expected, no one answers. So I walk on in and call for him.

"Dad?" I yell, wandering through the rooms. "Are you here?"

My voice echoes through the hallway, but there's no response.

A pit of bile sloshes in my gut as I clear each room like I'm some kind of private investigator.

Living room.

Kitchen.

Hallway.

Guest bedroom.

Bathroom.

Laundry cove.

Main bedroom.

Main bathroom.

A chill spirals down my spine as I make my way back up the hall.

There are any number of reasons why my dad isn't answering, and he sure as hell isn't required to tell me where he's going. He's a hard-headed old fucker with a teenage rebellious streak. If I told him to tell me if he was leaving, he'd leave and explicitly not tell me because I'd asked him to.

I sort through the table by his recliner for any indication of his whereabouts. There's a half-smoked cigar in an ashtray. A crossword puzzle. The remote to the TV sits next to a box of tissues with a melted butterscotch candy on top.

"Where are you, Pops?" I ask, gazing across the room for a clue.

I suppress a wave of nausea and fight against a streak of panic.

There's nothing to panic about. This is my dad. He's probably at the Cupboard with Mrs. Shaw.

But even as I think it, I don't quite believe it.

"I had some tests done last week. Got a knot on my liver. Doctor didn't like the look of it, so he did a little biopsy."

I take a deep breath, calming myself. He's fine. He's . . .

"But I'm gonna have to die sooner or later. And we don't really get to plan our exit strategy, do we?"

No. Don't think about that now.

I turn to go back home. My gaze slides over the hooks by the door, and my blood runs cold.

Where are the blackberry buckets?

The clear ice cream buckets from decades ago hang by the door unless they're being used. It's one of the few rules around here. Those containers were saved by my mother, and Dad thinks they're plated in gold—he acts like it, anyway.

Did he take Michael with him?

The thought eases my concern enough to make it easier to breathe. Still, I make it back to my cabin quick.

Lauren is standing at the sink when I walk in. Maddie is sitting at the table with a glass of juice.

"Hey, Mads," I say before the door closes behind me. "Did Pops ask you to go berry picking with him today?"

"Yes. Well, I was supposed to. I told him last night that I would. But then . . . *Daniel . . .*" She frowns. "I went over there to get my phone charger this morning and told him I couldn't go. Why?"

Fuck.

"Jack," Lauren says, her voice rising. "What's going on, damn it?"

"Probably nothing. But Dad is gone and . . ." I turn to the door. "Something tells me . . . I just need to find him. I'll be back."

"Jack . . ."

I hate leaving like this. I really want to turn back and fix things with her. Explain it all. Tell her that my dad might be dying, but he's sworn me to secrecy, and the burden of it is swallowing me already, and I've known for only a handful of hours.

My truck sits a few feet from the cabin. I hop inside, turn it on, and jet onto the street.

I'm not the reason my dad might have cancer, but I'm culpable all the same. I've not spent nearly enough time with him. I've been detached from him just like I have been Lauren, burying my head at work and pretending everything else was fine. Because it was fine. *For me.*

What else have I missed? What else have I been blissfully ignorant about? Who else have I let down because of my misplaced priorities? How many times has Lo brought the kids here, and I haven't even known?

Fuck.

"I'm not allowed to bring a friend to shoulder some of the single parenting that, although I've become quite adept at, I didn't want for yet another fucking weekend?"

Shit. And now Dad could die.

I slap my hand against the steering wheel as the engine roars down the lane.

It's a complete mindfuck that I could be doing what felt right, what was so easily justifiable, and have it be all wrong. Or partly wrong. Wrong enough to have let the seams in the fabric of my life fall apart.

Nodding to Gayle as I drive by, I set my sights on the top of the Cupboard. Mrs. Shaw's purple golf cart sits by the back door, and I pull in beside it, a puff of dust filling the air around my truck.

The store is empty, aside from the lady of the hour behind the bar.

"Well, hello, Jack," she says sweetly. The smile on her face slips as she takes me in. "What's the matter?"

"Um, nothing. Just wondering if you've seen my father."

"No. Not since this morning. He came in for a piece of rhubarb pie. Why? What's wrong?"

I don't want to worry Mrs. Shaw—especially because I'm not certain there's anything to be worried about. *Especially because I hope there's nothing to be worried about.*

"Everything is fine," I say. "I just haven't seen him this afternoon, and he's not home. It's just odd. That's all."

She takes off her glasses. "That *is* odd for Harvey. The children haven't seen him?"

"No."

"Huh." She sets the glasses on the counter. "Well, he was in here just before lunchtime. I'd say around ten thirty or so. He seemed fine—just ornery like usual."

I smile. *That's Dad.*

"You know what?" she asks. "He did mention going berry picking today."

My stomach sours.

"I only remember because he asked me if I'd be up for making him another cobbler this evening," she says. "He promised to help me fry fish tomorrow night if I'd make him another dessert."

I tap the counter. "That's really helpful, Mrs. Shaw. Thank you."

"Can I do anything to help find him?"

"No," I say, walking backward toward the door. "Just have him check in with me or Lauren if he happens to come in, okay? I don't care if he gets pissy. *I'm pissy.*"

She grins. "The apple doth not fall far from the tree."

I stop at the doorway and look at her. Her smile grows as if she's just bestowed the greatest compliment on me.

"The apple doth not fall far from the tree."

I don't know how I feel about that, but I'll have to sort it out later. Right after I give him a piece of my mind.

CHAPTER TWENTY-SIX

LAUREN

Jack bursts through the door. "Hey."

I whirl around, my heart in my throat.

I've paced the length of the kitchen since he tore out of here twenty minutes ago. Maddie's been sitting quietly at the table, the puppy at her feet, watching me like I'm two steps away from snapping.

The kitchen is full of shadows from the early-evening sun. The majority of the rays are blocked by the lingering storm clouds from this afternoon. A chill ripples through the room from the breeze coming through the open front door.

"Jack . . ."

He sighs. "Dad's not home, and no one has seen him. His truck's gone too."

"Where do you think he went?" I ask.

"Maybe he's with Mrs. Shaw," Maddie says.

He shakes his head. "I just talked to her. She hasn't seen him since this morning."

My heart drops to the floor.

Harvey doesn't go missing. He doesn't leave without one of us, usually, but definitely not without telling someone.

But our day has been chaos. Maybe he decided to stay out of it and go on with his day.

"Oh," Maddie says, frowning.

Jack walks to the tiny closet by the door and takes out his boots. "Where would he have gone? Did he say anything to you, Mads?"

"No. Not specifically."

"Maybe he drove to town," I offer. "He might've been out of the cigars he doesn't smoke."

Jack slips on one boot and then the other. "I hope, Lo, but I don't think so. His berry buckets are gone."

My husband stands, facing me. The severity on his face—the somber lines etched across his forehead and around his mouth—kills me.

I forget my irritation with him. *Would Harvey go into the forest on his own?*

"What can we do?" I ask. "What are *you* going to do?"

"Maddie, can you go get Michael? Tell him I need him to come home now."

She stands. "Do you know where he is?"

"I'm guessing with Ava."

She nods. "I'll go there first. If not, they're probably at the lake."

"Thanks, sweetheart," Jack says as she scoots out the door.

Snaps raises his head and looks at us. Finding us uninteresting, he lays his head back between his front legs and closes his eyes. *Lucky.*

"What do you know that you're not telling me?" I ask. "I feel like you're keeping something from me."

His chest rises, filling with oxygen, before he blows it out slowly.

I have no idea where this is going. And with the plethora of events that have happened today, it could very well be anything. That might be the worst part of it all—not knowing.

"Lo," Jack says, sucking in a breath again. "Dad is sick."

We knew Harvey was sick, but the way Jack says it puts it on another level. That makes it hard to breathe.

"I don't know anything for sure," he says carefully. "But we had a conversation this morning that leads me to believe that he might be worse off than I thought. So, the fact that he's not here . . ."

My husband holds my gaze, his beautiful brown eyes cloudy.

I'm uncertain where Jack is going with this line of thought. Harvey is sick, so he's not here because . . . *why?*

Does he think he went to the doctor? Did he go home? Did they get into an argument today, and Harvey said "Screw it" and took off under duress?

I cover my mouth with my hand and fight back a wash of tears.

Jack heads to the bedroom. He returns with a thick envelope that he drops unceremoniously on the kitchen table.

"What's that?" I ask as a chill slips down my spine.

His jaw sets. "Everything my father owns is now in our name."

"What?"

He just looks at me.

"Jack. *What the hell?"*

"Said it would be ours anyway. It'll make it easier when he dies."

My mouth hangs open as tears lick the corners of my eyes. *Oh, Harvey.*

"His headspace is fucked up, Lo. He took a turn somewhere, and I didn't notice. I'm kicking myself in the ass for not picking up on it sooner."

"No, Jack. Don't do this to yourself."

I push the envelope away and wrap my husband in my arms. He pulls me into his chest and presses a kiss to the top of my head.

My heart breaks for Jack—and for Harvey. It's one of the things I'm eternally grateful for. I never had to see my parents suffer. But it also isn't going to be easy to watch the old man who took me in as his own suffer—not to mention his son, the man I love with my whole entire heart.

It might break me too.

"He probably just needed some space," I say, pulling away and wiping my eyes. "You needed a bit of time today, right?"

Jack nods.

"Your dad probably did too. I can only imagine how painful it was for him to admit he's a mere mortal like the rest of us."

A smile flirts against Jack's lips.

"We'll find him," I say. "He's probably sitting somewhere with a bucket of berries and a bacon sandwich."

Michael, Maddie, and Ava come inside.

"That didn't take long," I say.

"My grandmother called and talked to Mike," Ava says, holding on to my son's arm. "We hurried over on the golf cart. We met Maddie halfway."

"Dad—where's Pops?" Michael asks, his eyes wide.

"Not sure."

"It's gonna storm. The dark clouds are rolling in again."

Jack peeks out the window. "Shit."

"If he was going to find blackberries, he's probably either gone out by Asher Cave or Old Bear Cave," Maddie says. "He mentioned those yesterday."

"We should check the boathouse," Ava offers. "Even if he's not there, they may have seen or heard something."

I smile at her. "That's a good idea."

Michael places a hand on Jack's back. "What do you need, Dad? I got you."

Jack forces a swallow as he looks at our son. He pulls him into a hug that takes Michael by surprise. The whole scene does nothing for my emotional stability.

My heart.

I grab a tissue box from the top of the refrigerator and pull a few tissues out to dry my eyes.

Jack pulls back. "Okay, here's what we need to do. Michael, can you take Maddie and Ava with you? Make sure the boat is still at the boathouse. Ava—good call."

She grins.

"If the boat is gone, take ours and look for him. Tell the boathouse to call me if he turns up. Check all the peninsulas and inlets where he likes to fish. Okay?"

Michael nods. "Got it."

"If he's not there," Jack says, his voice more confident, "head to Asher Cave. If not there, try Old Bear Cave. Maddie is right—those are two of his favorite haunts. But remember—check all the service roads and parking lots for his truck. Hopefully, he's in it and didn't let anyone borrow it today."

"Got it, Daddy," Maddie says.

"Stay together," Jack says. "If you don't have any luck in an hour, come back here, and we'll regroup, okay?"

They nod.

Jack looks at me. "Your mom and I are going to head out by the iron furnaces, and we'll check the fields out that way. Again, we're looking for the truck. If there's a reason for you to go exploring on foot, stay together. And if you find the truck, Maddie and Michael, you go look for him. You know where he'll be. Ava, can you drive my truck back here and let us know? The phones probably won't work that far out."

"Yes, Mr. Reed."

"We'll see you in an hour," I say. "If we're not here, we've found him. Sit tight until we get back."

"Keys are in my truck, Michael. We'll take your mom's car."

Michael and Ava head for the door. Maddie turns but pauses. "Daddy?"

"Yeah?"

She smiles. "We're gonna find him, and he's gonna be fine. Trust me."

"I love you, Mads."

"I love you, too, Daddy." She grins at me. "You too, Mom."

"Love you, baby girl."

She tosses open the door. Snaps bolts down the stairs and stops at the screen. He barks for Maddie to come back, but she doesn't hear him. Jack's truck is already headed down the road.

I jog into the bathroom and return with an emergency kit. Jack eyes it nervously.

"It's just in case," I say.

He tears his eyes from the white plastic box and brings them to mine. The fear, the anger—the determination in them strengthens me.

"Let's go find your dad," I say.

Jack holds the door open for me, and we head for the car.

CHAPTER TWENTY-SEVEN

JACK

"I keep thinking his truck is just going to be parked around one of these corners," I say, slowing Lauren's car as we round a gravel curve. "He has to be somewhere."

"We'll find him." She touches my forearm gently, causing Snaps to bark from the back seat. "Heck, he might not even be lost. There's still an off chance that he went to town to get ice cream or something."

I smile for her benefit. Theoretically, there's a chance. Realistically, there's not.

"He's going to be the death of me," I say, gripping the steering wheel as a blast of rain pelts the glass.

"At least it's not me for a change."

I glance at her over my shoulder.

"He's going to be fine, Jack. He's tough. Even if he is out there by himself, he's walked every bit of this forest a hundred times. He knows it better than anyone. He probably stumbled upon a patch of berries and couldn't help himself. He'll be riding your ass about getting everyone riled up as soon as he gets home."

I sigh. *I hope.*

"Oh, you know where we should look," Lauren says, taking her hand away from me. "There's that waterfall on the side of the hill where everyone fills up their jugs. Do you remember what I'm talking about? I don't know how to get there or where it is for sure, but he swears that water grows the best blackberries around."

That's right. "Yeah, I know what you're talking about. Let's head out there." I pull the car onto the shoulder of the road and then do a quick three-point turnaround. "How much time do we have?"

"About twenty minutes. We'll need to head back to the cabin in about fifteen."

"We could drive right by the truck now and not even see it. This fucking rain."

I'm not sure if I'll be less mad if he's stranded out here or if he went to town and didn't tell anyone. It's a toss-up.

"I had some tests done last week. Got a knot on my liver. Doctor didn't like the look of it, so he did a little biopsy."

My heart sinks in my chest.

"I don't want you coddling me or babying me about it. I'm probably fine anyway."

Too bad.

"Promise me that you won't make the same mistakes that I did. Tell me that you'll remember to live your life while you're living it."

An invisible band stretches so tightly around my chest that it's hard to breathe.

"Need me to give you a hug?"

I laugh. *Yeah, I do. I really fucking do, you son of a bitch.*

"What are you laughing about?" Lauren asks just loud enough for me to hear her over the sound of the rain.

I look at her over my shoulder. "Dad doesn't want you to know he's sick."

She balks. "Why?"

"He said you have enough on your plate. He doesn't want you or the kids to know."

"So he's keeping that from us, like we tried to keep our problems from him."

I grin. "Guess so. It's ironic, isn't it? We're all trying to protect each other while we fall apart. When, in reality, if we would've just opened up about it all, we could've helped each other."

"This family has major communication issues."

Together, we chuckle. Snaps steps onto the middle console and paws at me.

"Not now, buddy. I'm driving," I say.

He turns to Lauren and cocks his little head to the side. She mimics his reaction. That must be enough of a welcome banner for Snaps because he climbs onto her lap and sits.

"Don't pee on me or anything," she says to the dog. "I mean it."

"He's not going to pee on you."

"How do you know? He doesn't exactly have the best manners, and he can be quite rude."

I shake my head. "I think he's starting to accept you as higher in the pack than him. The whole 'putting him at the end of the bed at night' thing broke a part of his spirit."

Out of the corner of my eye, I notice Lauren scratching under Snaps's chin. *Progress.*

"Damn it, Dad. Where are you?" I ask, slowing the windshield wipers now that the rain has eased.

"Maybe he's back at the cabin by now."

I glance at the clock. "We're going to have to head back there soon. We'll do one quick pass by the waterfall, and then we'll go home."

"What's the next step if we don't locate him? Do we call the police? What do we do?"

"I think we have to. I don't know where else to look, and it's going to be getting dark really soon." My stomach sours. "But I don't know if they'll even look for him in the dark. And if the temperature keeps dropping and he *is* out there somewhere—all wet from the rain . . ."

"He'll probably finagle a campfire and be fine."

I hope you're right.

"That's what you would do," she says, peering out the window and down a side road. "You'd figure it out. Michael would too. You both get that from Harvey."

I regrip the steering wheel. I'm not sure if I need to get a grasp on the car or on my thoughts.

Both, probably.

"Do you think I'm a lot like Dad?"

Lauren moves Snaps to her other leg. "Is that a serious question?"

"Yeah. It is."

"Then, yes, I think you're a lot like your dad."

I bite my bottom lip and mull that over.

Gravel crunches under our tires, mud puddles sloshing as we drive over them. Trees dripping with rain hang heavily over the road. But there's no sign of him.

I imagine him lying on the ground, having slipped in the mud, with no way to get up. He could be in pain. Scared. Injured.

My blood pressure goes up again. It's so high I can feel it in my neck.

Keep your mind busy. Don't panic. That's not going to help anything.

Instead of using my brain space to think of all the ways this could go wrong, I think of all the characteristics of my father.

He's abrasive. Ornery. A giant pain in the ass. *He might be dying of cancer and doesn't bother to tell anyone.*

He's loyal. Capable of anything. Would jump the moon for his family. *And is out trudging around the forest because we were all too busy with our bullshit to take care of him.*

"Your dad is one of the best men I've ever known," Lauren says softly, staring out the window. "He's unapologetically him. What you see with Harvey is what you get, and there's something really precious about that."

"'Precious,' huh?"

"Yeah. Precious." She wipes the fog off the window with the sleeve of her shirt. "I didn't know him when you were growing up or when your mother was alive, so I can't vouch for anything then. But I know that when he looks at you, and the kids, and even me, I never doubt— not for a second—that he loves us all."

Does she think that about me too? Am I like him in that way?

I sink against my seat.

"I've been thinking about him being sick and that he didn't tell us," she says, her voice thick with emotion. "It kills me that he was going through that alone."

Her voice breaks, and that breaks something deep inside me. I reach for her hand. She grabs mine, holding it for dear life.

"I kept thinking we'd travel when I retired. We'd come up here and stay all summer together. We'd make up for lost time. But then she died . . . and the time was already gone."

A rock settles in my chest, making its presence known.

And I keep losing more time.

"Jack! Look!"

I follow Lauren's gesture to a parking area on the side of the road. Next to a picnic table and a tall oak tree is Dad's truck.

My spirits fly so high that I hit the brakes a little too hard. Snaps growls at the intrusion from his nap.

I pull in front of the truck so it can't move without plowing through our car and then cut the engine. Lauren meets me with Snaps in her arms at the truck.

"He's not in here, and the doors are locked," she says, trying the passenger-side handle.

I look around the area. It's one I'm not familiar with—I haven't been here for years—and I have no idea where to begin looking.

Lauren turns a circle and takes it all in. "Do we just start shouting his name?"

"Maybe." I shrug. "Maybe one of us should go back to the cabin and get the kids? We could cover more area that way."

"Yeah. I'll take—*Snaps!*"

Lauren's voice borders on shrill as the dog leaps from her arms. He lands in the center of a mud hole but bounds out of it immediately and makes a circle around the truck.

"Come here," I say, frustrated. *"Snaps."*

Lauren starts to grab him, but he backs away with his little tail wagging like it's a game.

"This is not funny," she says, reaching for the dog.

He scoots back and barks at her.

"He just jumped out of my arms like a freaking rabbit," she says, lunging for him.

Snaps is too quick. He's on top of the picnic table before Lauren knows what's happening.

"Fuck it," I say, scanning the wood line. "There's a path over there. See it?"

Lauren abandons her futile attempts at reining in the dog and follows my gaze. "Yes."

"I'm going to—*that fucking dog!*"

Snaps bolts toward the path as if he comprehends English. His leaps and bounds would be impressive if I weren't so frustrated.

"Snaps!" I shout, chasing after him.

Lauren struggles to keep up at my side. "This is why you ask your wife before you buy a dog."

"I didn't buy him. I told you—I rescued him. Snaps!"

"Whatever. Semantics," she says, gasping for air as we enter the woods. "Would you say the same thing if I 'rescued' a cat?"

Fuck no. Cats are evil. "If I wasn't staying at the shop, I wouldn't have considered a pet."

"Oh, so we're back to this?"

Her cheeks are flushed, and her hair is matted to her head from the humidity. I'd stop and kiss the hell out of her if my life weren't spiraling out of control in every other way at this exact moment in time.

The path is uneven, with roots popping out of the ground every few feet. Trees have fallen across the dirt, making it difficult to get through.

Unless you're a small terrier.

"Snaps!" I shout, my voice echoing through the forest.

His bark is far in the distance.

"Do we yell for the dog or your dad?" Lauren asks, hustling next to me. "This would be really funny if it wasn't happening to us."

I hold a tree branch back so it doesn't smash her in the face.

"Such a gentleman," she says, sliding by.

"Dad!" I shout. "Harvey!"

"Snaps!" Lauren adds, the word barely audible over a crack of thunder.

We slow our pace and listen. There's no response.

Damn it.

"Should I go back and get the kids?" Lauren asks. "I feel like we got away from our game plan."

"I'm not letting you out of my sight now. We're already this far in. *Dad!* Can you hear me?"

Lauren gasps for air. "Jack, I'm worried. Wouldn't he be answering us?"

Snaps's bark sounds in the distance.

"I would think so," I say, moving forward. "I don't know whether to follow the dog or to start looking around the pathway."

"Well, let's be honest here—Snaps is no Lassie."

I look at her. "If we're really being honest—the dog is the only thing helping us right now."

"Not sure I'd call it help. Harvey!"

"Dad!" I shout, slowing to listen.

"If he's out here picking berries and he doesn't need your help, he's going to be pissed," Lauren says. "And I'll never be happier to see a pissed-off Harvey."

"Me too. Dad!"

We go around a bend and hop over another fallen tree. The sky has just enough light to see, but it won't be light for long.

We're without a flashlight. Our phones. The emergency kit.

We have nothing.

"Lo, I think one of us is gonna have to—"

"Look!"

I pull my attention from her and to the path. Snaps is running toward us with something in his mouth.

"Come here," I say, crouching down.

He runs full blast until he's a few feet from me. Then he stops on a dime and sits.

Gently, Lauren reaches down and plucks the item from Snaps's mouth. She turns to me, her eyes twinkling.

"Jack." She holds out Dad's red handkerchief he keeps in his pocket. *"It's your dad's."*

I stand, my heart racing. "Hell, maybe I should've named him Lassie."

Lauren looks at me, her chest rising and falling in big movements.

"Snaps. Take us to him, buddy," she says.

He yelps and races back down the path.

Lauren and I follow, our hearts in our throats.

CHAPTER TWENTY-EIGHT

LAUREN

I can barely breathe as we race down the path. Jack pulls ahead of me, trying and failing to keep up with Snaps.

Harvey's bandanna—what does that mean? Is he lying somewhere hurt? Did he drop it and Snaps just happened to find it? Is he . . .

No. Don't go there.

My heart pounds, sending tremors through my body with its force. A bead of sweat dots my forehead in response to the humidity and the adrenaline coursing through me.

Jack hops a fallen tree ahead of me and then disappears to the left into the trees.

"Please, God. Please let him be all right," I whisper through the clog of emotions in my throat.

I make it to the spot on the path that shows Jack's shoe prints detouring off to the side. I step into the grass and over a small stream of running water. Then I step under the canopy of trees.

My eyes adjust to the much dimmer light. I can't see anyone, but I hear Snaps's bark.

"Snaps," I call out.

"Over here, Lo."

I spot the top of Jack's head next to a tree and sprint through the vegetation—getting whacked by sticker bushes in the process. As soon as they come into view, my feet fail to move.

My hand covers my mouth as I take him in.

Harvey is sitting with his back against a tree. His clothes are soaked, his hair drenched. One of his shoes is missing, and his blackberry buckets are strewn on the ground around him.

There's a slice above his right eye that seems to have stopped bleeding. Dried blood crusts against his hairline next to his ear. A purple welt rises from the top of his right hand, and a matching one grows on his cheek.

"Harvey," I say, dropping to my knees beside Jack. "Are you okay? What happened? Are you hurt?"

"One question at a time. What is this—a speed round?"

I giggle, leaning my head on Jack in relief. He wraps a hand around my waist and squeezes.

"First question—are you okay?" I ask.

"Yes, I'm okay. Don't I look all right to you?"

"Well . . ."

"No, Dad. You look like shit, to be honest."

"Well, nobody asked you." Harvey's tired smirk grows into a smile. "It took you long enough to find me. I've been sitting out here forever."

Jack tries to touch Harvey's forehead but gets his hand swatted away.

"If you'd told me where you were going, we would've come sooner," I say.

"That would've been a good plan, wouldn't it?" He shakes an unsteady finger at me. "But if I'd told you I was coming, one of you would've come with me. And everyone had something to do today instead of farting around with an old man."

"Looks like we're farting around with you anyway, doesn't it?" I ask.

Snaps paws at Harvey's arm. "You. You're the hero of this story, young man."

"Don't build his ego. I can barely live with him the way it is," I say.

Harvey chuckles, but the movement makes him wince.

"All joking aside, are you all right or not?" Jack asks. "What in the hell happened?"

He slumps against the tree. "I don't really know. I came out here, and it was just fine. I've been out here a million times. But a storm rolled in, and I got turned around and . . ." He looks up at me with watery eyes. "And I couldn't find my way out."

Tears fall down his wrinkled cheeks.

"Oh, Harvey," I say, pulling him into a hug. "We're here now."

He lays his forehead on my shoulder and cries.

Jack's hand touches the middle of my back as tears fall down my face too. I can't risk looking at him. If he's crying, I'll lose all my sensibilities and fall completely apart.

Harvey lifts a shaky hand and taps around until he finds mine. He pats the top of my hand until I turn my palm over and let him hold it.

The emotions of the day—from Maddie's breakup, Jack's distance, my second-guessing my choices, and Harvey's stunt—pile too high.

I crumble.

Jack's arms cover me from behind, enclosing his father in his hug.

If something had happened to Harvey, nothing would be the same. *Nothing would ever be the same.*

Suddenly, everything comes into perspective.

My life may not be perfect. My marriage certainly isn't. But my life with these people, with Jack and Harvey, is infinitely better than my life would be without them. I don't need them—I've proven that.

But I want them.

Over the last twenty years, we've built a foundation of trust and loyalty. The blocks are mortared together with laughter and tears. Our bond tells a story of a family going to wild lengths to ensure it stays together—because *together* is the only way.

I can feel Jack's love for me and his father as he holds us, and Harvey's love for us is evident in the way he leans on me and his son. We've all been through shit, both separately and together. And through it all, we've built something special.

We love each other.

And this kind of love—this deep, layered, genuine love—isn't something to be taken for granted. Almost losing Harvey has made me realize just how lucky I am to have found it once, and how much I'm willing to fight to keep it.

It makes me think back to what Mrs. Shaw said about the watershed moments of her marriage. We all have them.

"The thing that got us through them was simple—we wanted *to get through them. It's amazing how far that one little thing goes."*

It's time to stop fighting that and embrace it, because I *know* with absolute certainty that Jack *wants* to get through this. He wants us.

There is no out to this. Only an in.

Harvey pulls back and wipes his eyes with the backs of his hands. "If you ever tell anyone I cried, I'll call you a liar."

I chuckle, pulling the top of my shirt up and wiping my nose.

"I don't know why I got so confused," he says, looking bewildered. "I couldn't find north. Nothing looked the same to me anymore. And I got . . . scared." He gulps. "Then my feet got all tangled up in some vines, and I fell."

Snaps whines, digging at Harvey until he lets him on his lap.

"Well, no more berry picking unassisted," I say. "I mean it."

"You don't tell me what I can do."

I snort and get to my feet. I start collecting his buckets. "That's what you think. No more berry picking alone. No more keeping secrets from us."

"Jack, you snitch."

I look at my husband and grin. "Don't be mad at Jack. He did the right thing."

Harvey scoffs. "You two were hiding stuff from me too. How's that any different?"

Good point. "I guess it's not."

"Damn right, it's not. What's good for the goose is good for the gander," Harvey says.

Jack sighs. "Where's your shoe?"

"The hell if I know."

"Do you think you can stand?" Jack asks.

"I got two legs, don't I?"

An idea comes to my mind. It's pretty wild and big—big enough that I should probably talk to my husband about it before I offer it up to the world. But when I look at Jack, I already see the answer. It's in his soft smile. It's in the shine in his eyes. It's in the tenderness of his touch against the small of my back.

There's no reason for any of us to do this alone. Harvey battling his health issues by himself is asinine. Jack sorting through his emotions alone breaks my heart. And although I can do life by myself—I've proven that—I don't want to.

Our life might be imperfect, complicated, and frustrating, but it's better together. There's no other choice for me. Maybe there never was.

"Harvey, no more doctor's appointments alone," I say.

He groans.

"I mean it." I stack the buckets on the ground and brush the mud off my hands. "Also, you're going to move in with us."

I hold my breath as I absorb their reactions. I'm not sure whose jaw drops more—Harvey's or Jack's.

"You two can get over it," I say, putting a hand on my hip. "I'm tired of this. We're falling apart, boys."

Surprisingly, neither of them speaks. They don't argue—but they certainly don't agree with me either.

"I can't be going back and forth from your house to the doctor and back to your house before coming home for every appointment," I say. "And I'll be damned if you'll go alone, Harvey."

A ghost of a smile tickles his lips.

"And who's supposed to help me around the house if you're just going to take off to Vegas on a whim?" I ask, winking at Jack. "And, hey—I won't have to bring Billie along for Labor Day. I can bring Harvey."

"I'll be coming on Labor Day, thank you very fucking much," Jack says, grinning.

My heart warms, flooding my veins with . . . happiness.

"I know this sounds out of left field and maybe like I've lost my mind," I say, "but this is the way it needs to be."

Jack doesn't say anything, but he doesn't have to. The look of relief on his face says it all.

"We all need to work together," I say. "So, Harvey—you can take the bedroom downstairs by the garage. You can have your own little space out there by the sunroom. No one uses it anyway. Besides, Snaps likes you. It'll keep me from having to mess with him."

Snaps barks.

"Does the dog understand English?" I ask, making everyone laugh.

Jack tucks me against his side and lowers his mouth to my ear. "You are unbelievable. Do you know that? I love you so fucking much, Lauren."

He rests his head against mine. I love this man. *So fucking much.*

"Are you going to fight me on this?" I ask Harvey.

He sags against the tree. "I wanted one last summer. One last chance to make memories with you kids and the grandkids. I just wanted to give everyone a last bunch of memories to remember me by in case there's not another summer for me."

Harvey runs his hand over Snaps's head and looks at Jack. My bottom lip quivers, and the tears begin to fall again.

"I've sat around for a few weeks now, maybe months, and wondered what I could do to make up for some of my misgivings," Harvey says. "Then the kids called and told me about the two of you, so I thought that was it." He nods. "I could help the two of you come back together."

"So, was this little missing-in-action thing a part of your stunt?" Jack asks, teasing.

"Why do you care? It worked, didn't it?"

I watch two of the three men I adore more than any others in the world exchange something between them that words could never say. It's an emotion, a respect. An agreement. An understanding.

And I think they've both needed this moment equally.

Maybe I've needed it too.

"I have one caveat," Harvey says, turning his attention to me.

"What's that?"

"Make it two."

I roll my eyes. "Go for it."

"First, you can't coddle me," he says. "I'm only moving in to help you out. To make it easier on you. There won't be any babying me or that kind of bullshit. Got it?"

I nod. "Mostly."

"Second, if I bring chicks home, you have to pretend not to hear a thing. If the door is rocking, don't come knocking."

I burst out laughing, much to Harvey's amusement.

Jack chuckles beside me. "Dad, you're a fucking fool."

Harvey's chest bounces with laughter. "Now help me get off this ground. It's cold, and my ass is soaked."

Jack takes one of Harvey's arms, and I take the other. Snaps bounces around like a rabbit as we help Harvey to his feet.

"Oof," Harvey says, taking a second to straighten himself out. "I'm not as young as I used to be."

"Let's try to remember that when you're wanting to play Lewis and Clark," Jack says, picking up Snaps. "And you, little guy, are the real winner today. Good job, Snapsy. Good boy."

"Hand me that bandanna," Harvey says, holding his hand out.

I fork it over.

He ties it around Snaps's neck. "There you go. You can show off now. You saved Grandpa."

Snaps barks, wagging his tail. I swear the dog smiles.

But that's fitting. Because we're all smiling too.

"All right," Harvey says. "How in the hell do we get out of here?"

I pick up his blackberry buckets and lead the way.

CHAPTER TWENTY-NINE

LAUREN

P ops!"
   The kids file out of the house before racing toward Harvey's truck. Jack insisted that he drive his father home. Harvey put up a resistance, I think mostly because he thought it was expected, but gave in quickly.

Michael pulls open Harvey's door. He gets shoved to the side by Maddie.

"What happened to you?" she says. "Oh, Pops. Are you hurt?"

"Are you okay?" Michael asks, taking Snaps from his grandfather.

"I would be if I could get out of this truck," Harvey says.

I climb out of my car and grin, making sure I grab the first aid kit. Harvey's wounds, while ugly, are only superficial. Still, they need to be cleaned up and bandaged once we get inside the cabin.

Jack moves the kids out of the way and helps Harvey to the ground. He complains the entire time.

"Hey, Michael," Jack says. "Will you run over to Pops's and get him some clean clothes and a pair of slippers?"

"Sure thing." Michael sets off across the lawn toward the other cabin.

"Is he okay, Mrs. Reed?" Ava asks.

"He's going to be fine, sweetheart. Thank you for your help tonight."

"Oh, of course. Um . . ." She glances over her shoulder. "I hope this is okay, but there's really nothing I could do to stop her."

"What?"

"My grandmother came and brought dinner. It's warming in your oven."

I wrap an arm around her shoulder. "Ava, that's the best—second-best—news I've heard all day."

She beams up at me. "I made the cornbread. It's from a box and nothing fancy, but I think it turned out pretty good."

"I can't wait to try it."

She smiles and rejoins Maddie in their joint effort to get Harvey to the porch despite his protests. The only one who seems to be having a good time is Snaps, in his new red bandanna.

Jack reaches behind me and shuts my door. Then he leans against the side of the car. A look of relief is etched on his handsome face.

"How are you doing?" I ask.

"Fine."

"That had to be scary for you."

He takes a deep breath. "I've had a lot of shit scare me lately. It's just another thing, you know?"

I hum.

"I want to talk to you about some things later, once this whole thing dies down," he says.

My brows pull together. "About what?"

"Stuff."

"Stuff?"

He grins and stands tall. *"Stuff."* He walks around me and toward the cabin.

"Jack, that's not fair."

"Stuff," he says again without breaking stride.

If I didn't love him so much, I'd hate him.

I walk to the cabin, which is all lit up from the inside. Laughter and voices drift through the screen door and the open windows. Scents of cake and spices float along the breeze, and suddenly, I feel like I might cry. But instead of crying for someone else, or crying out of relief or heartbreak, this time, it's for me. For my happiness.

Things between Jack and me aren't perfect. Hell, we argued today. But the truth is that they may never be. They probably won't be. But I'd much rather have imperfection with him than perfection with someone else.

He's always there when it truly counts. He's willing to do whatever it takes, even if that means carrying me on his back for a mile through the forest or following his gut when he suspected something was wrong with Harvey. He never stops loving us, even if he gets sidetracked sometimes. *But I do too.*

I can't shake the look on Jack's face when I suggested Harvey move in with us. How happy he was—how much he trusts my judgment. He's never tried to control me or tell me what to do. And he's always believed in me as a wife and mother, supporting me in my decisions . . . even if he didn't bother to weigh in on them. He hasn't second-guessed me. Ever.

I'm staying in this marriage not because he's the perfect partner or because I'm trapped in a life with him. Neither is true. I'm staying because what he brings to my life, and what I hope that I bring to his, is better than anything else out there. And when we work together, it's pretty close to bliss.

Maddie sits at the table in front of the window. Her smile isn't quite as bright as it was yesterday, but it'll return. And Michael and Ava will certainly have moments when they aren't as sweet as they are tonight. They might not even be together tomorrow. Then there's Harvey and Mrs. Shaw and whatever they are. They're fun and flirty and make each other laugh.

We're four different stages of love—all beautiful, all difficult, all *real.*

"You coming or what?" Jack asks from the porch.

I wipe my eyes and join him by the front door.

"Thank you," he says, rubbing his thumb along my jawline.

"For what?"

He shrugs. "For any number of things. Patience. Forgiveness. Patience. Resiliency. Patience."

I chuckle. "I'm noticing a theme here."

He chuckles too. "You amaze me, do you know that?"

"Well, yeah. I am pretty amazing."

He grins. "I can't believe you asked my dad to move in with us. Have you thought about that? Did you mean it because . . ." He whistles between his teeth. "That might be a lot."

"Is that okay? I know that's probably one of those things I've been telling you that you need to ask your spouse about before you do it. But I did it."

He laughs.

"But you got a dog!" I laugh. "So there's that. Now we're even."

"So you're equating my father to a puppy?"

I lean forward. "They're eerily similar. I'll have to clean up after them both. They both growl at me, need to be fed, and can be really damn loud."

Jack's forehead wrinkles as he laughs. His eyes are filled with light. "I just never want to hear you say a word about me rescuing a puppy again. You just rescued a senile old man."

Laughter bursts from my lips.

"Excuse me," Michael says with a stack of clothes in his hands. "Just need to sneak by here to give these to Pops. Don't need to hear or see anything else."

Jack pulls me close to him and looks down at me with his clear brown eyes.

"Want to tell me what 'stuff' is all about?" I ask. "Because it's been a damn day, and I don't think I can worry about anything else."

"It's nothing to worry about."

"Easy for you to say," I say as he sways us back and forth. "Also, as soon as these people leave, I'm probably going to pass out. I've cried a lot, and crying makes my eyes sleepy."

"I don't think your eyes can be sleepy."

"Then you've never experienced sleepy eyes. I assure you, it's a thing."

He hums, grinning.

I wait for him to break down the meaning of "stuff." When it's clear he's not going to, I fist his shirt in my hands and shake them. "Tell me."

"Fine." He widens his stance and takes a deep breath. "Dad and Snaps aside, we're going to have to make a lot of changes to our lives going forward, Lo."

I still. "How?"

He looks around the porch and sighs. "When you look back on our marriage, we've always lived for something besides the two of us." His attention returns to me. "We were planning a wedding, buying a house, trying to have a baby. Having a baby. Then another one. And I was trying to find a way to feed us and pay the mortgage, and you were keeping everyone alive."

"Yeah."

"But it's time to live for *us*, Lauren. Me and you. More than just dates and sex and dinners. A whole upheaval of our marriage."

I stop moving. "I'm not sure I follow you, nor am I sure I want to."

He grins. "I want to spend time with you. Taking trips to Maine to see the leaves. Coming up here to Story Brook for weekends so we don't have distractions. Starting every morning and ending every night with a kiss—at least."

"Okay . . ."

He shifts his weight. "I don't want to put any pressure on you. I had an idea and was going to just start making things happen, but I realized that wasn't fair to you. So, I want to run something by you."

"English, please."

He dips his chin. "You have supported me and my business for the last fifteen years. I want to support you now."

I can't believe I'm hearing what I think I'm hearing. I'm also afraid to hope I know what he means.

"I don't want to put any burden on your shoulders that you don't want," he says. "I can keep working as much as you want me to, as much as I need to. But I'm ready to step back. I've already talked to Tommy and the guys, and they know we might be changing the structure around at the shop." He leans forward. "Because I'm going to be helping my wife. It's your turn to shine, Lo. It's your turn to live *your* dreams."

My lips part. I try to speak, but I don't know what to say. I'm also afraid to talk because then I might cry—again—and I'm tired of crying today.

"We can work it out later," he says. "We have the rest of our lives. But whatever you need me to do to support you and Story Books—I'm in."

I collapse into his arms and hold him as tight as I can. He presses kisses to the top of my head and whispers things I can't hear.

But that's okay. I understand what they mean.

"I love you, Jack."

He kisses my head again. "I love you more, Lo."

The door creaks open behind us.

"Mom? Dad? Do you want to come in and eat?" Maddie asks.

I pull away from my husband and smile. "Yeah. We're coming."

Jack takes my hand and leads me into the cabin.

Harvey sits in the recliner with a giant bag sitting on the couch beside him. Snaps is perched on his lap, watching every move Mrs. Shaw makes. Mrs. Shaw, for her part, fusses over Harvey, a cotton ball and a tube of some kind of ointment in her hands.

"Harvey, sit still," she says.

"Or what?"

She smacks him on the shoulder.

Michael, Maddie, and Ava are gathered around the table with plates full of food. They're engrossed in their own stories. What are they talking about? I don't know. But Maddie seems to have forgotten, at least temporarily, that her life was in shambles this morning.

"Think we could just sneak back off into the bedroom?" Jack whispers in my ear.

"I wish."

"We do need to get cleaned up." He steps away and holds his arms out. "I think we smell like the woods."

"Jack, Lauren—there's a pot of beef stew on the stove and a pan of cornbread. Lauren, I had to use your oven to bake my cake. I hope that's all right, sweetheart."

I laugh. "Yes, Mrs. Shaw. That's fine. You didn't have to go to all this trouble."

"Oh yes, I did. I knew you would be back wet and tired. It's the least I could do."

"Well, thank you. It's very appreciated."

Jack walks across the room to his father. "I see what you're doing now."

"What are you talking about?" Harvey asks.

"You probably pulled this whole stunt on purpose just to get Mrs. Shaw over here, fawning all over you."

Harvey snorts. "I don't have to pull a stunt to get her to fawn all over me."

"Harvey Reed, you better stop telling fibs."

"What's that mean, Mrs. Shaw?" I ask, winking at Jack.

She sighs. "He acts like it's just me fawning over him. This father-in-law of yours goes out of his way to fawn all over *me*. He's the biggest flirt I've ever seen."

Harvey's chest puffs out. "Yeah. That's me."

Everyone in the cabin laughs. Harvey quickly quiets and holds his ribs.

"You need to see a doctor, Dad?" Jack asks.

"No, I don't need to see a doctor."

"You're holding your rib cage."

"Yes, I know where my rib cage is, Jack. Thanks for checking to see if I knew."

Jack shakes his head. "Why do you have to be such an ass?"

"Must not be too big of one." Harvey grins. "Your wife asked me to move in with you."

"You're moving in with us?" Maddie asks.

I turn around. "How did you hear that when you're in the middle of your own conversation over there?"

"Talent. So, is Pops moving in with us?" *And yet, she can't hear when I ask her to take out the trash. Ironic.*

"I am. Your mom said I can have the room by the garage."

Maddie beams. "This is great news. I love it."

"Finally," Michael says. "I'll have someone around to watch football with."

"Hell yeah," Harvey says. "Wings and football every Sunday. It's on."

My heart explodes with warmth. *I'm so glad we're here.*

"Dad and I need to wash up," I say. "We smell like moss and dirt."

Jack's eyes shimmer, and I feel it in my core.

"Good," Harvey says. "Get out of here, and let Mrs. Shaw fix me up. I'm starting to get some other pains that I'd like her to tend to in private."

"That's my grandmother," Ava calls from the table.

"Ava, your grandmother is a fox," Harvey says.

Mrs. Shaw swipes at him again, but he easily ducks it.

Jack starts down the hallway, and I begin to follow. But Harvey motions for me.

"Yeah?" I say, standing next to him.

He takes my hands in his and pats them. Snaps tries to bite them, but Harvey keeps them far enough away. "I love you, Lauren."

"I love you, Pops."

He winks, giving my hands another squeeze before letting them go. "Now, go wash up or whatever you're calling it. Then come back, and we'll play some euchre."

"You're going down," Michael shouts from across the room.

"You wish," Harvey shouts back.

I shake my head and slip down the hall and into my bedroom. I shut and lock the door behind me.

Jack's things are scattered around the room. Shoes are on the floor. Clothes are lying everywhere. His bottle of water from last night is on top of the dresser. But instead of being irritated by it, I'm somehow comforted.

"There you are," he says, coming out of the bathroom. "I started the shower for you."

"Are you getting in with me?"

He grins. "I was hoping you'd ask."

We face one another, neither of us saying a word. It's a relief to be able to breathe while in each other's space without feeling strangled or pressured or prodded.

It's a relief to have my friend back—*my best friend.* I just won't tell Billie.

Jack is happy when I allow him in my life—from burgers to baths to decisions. I'm happy, and excited, at the opportunity to get more involved in his world too.

I fight a grin. "Hey, when do you go to Vegas?"

"Next week." He looks at me warily. "Why? Do you want me to stay home? Because I can."

"No. I was thinking that maybe I could fly out for a couple of days, and we could hang out."

Jack's grin turns into a wide smile. "Really? Are you serious?"

"I have a lot of stuff to move around, but I can swing it for a couple of days." I swoon as he takes me into his arms. "You only live once, right?"

He presses a sweet kiss to my lips. "If you live more than once, I hope I get to live them all with you."

Me too, Jack.

Me too.

EPILOGUE

LAUREN

Eleven months later . . .

"You promised me you wouldn't be late, Jack."
Sun streams through the kitchen windows. The glitter covering the banner tacked above the archway into the living room sparkles in the light. Balloons in green and gold cover the ceiling in Maple High's school colors.

Friends and family will be arriving at any moment, ready to celebrate Michael's high school graduation. A cake sits proudly on the console table in the eat-in kitchen, and the main table is prepped for gifts and cards. The island is packed with finger foods and hors d'oeuvres.

The only thing missing is my husband.

"Jack?" I ask, sighing into the phone.

"Lo, *I'm sorry.*"

"I know, but—"

"But this isn't my fault." He chuckles. "You kept me up all night with your sexy little ass. Then you had me take your car this morning. I went by the shipping depot and sent your boxes to California. Then I picked up ice for the party, and I'm now leaving the shop because I

haven't been there in a week, and I still have their payroll checks. Oh, and your car is empty. I have to make a quick stop to fill up the tank."

God, I love this man.

"Being your personal assistant is tough. I want a raise," he says.

Could be fun. "Can I pay you in sexual favors?"

"Mom. Really?" Maddie comes into the kitchen, rolling her eyes. "I almost liked it better when the two of you didn't like each other."

I laugh. "I'll see you when you get here, Jack."

"Love you, Lo."

"Love you, Jack." I end the call. "Where's your grandpa?"

Maddie picks up a baby carrot and slides it through the veggie dip. "He and his bestie Snaps are out for a walk. Did you know Pops bought the dog a green bandanna to match the party today?"

I grin.

"Also, please remind Daddy not to embarrass me when Theo gets here. He doesn't need to mean-mug him or anything. Theo is a nice guy."

"I'll see what I can do."

"Thanks." She bebops out of the room, evidently satisfied with my answer.

I pour a glass of tea and wander around the house. It's quiet, which is unusual. Between me, Jack, Harvey, the kids, and their friends, there's never a dull moment. And now that my business has picked up even more and Jack is spending two days a week at home helping out, it's even more chaotic.

But so amazingly perfect.

I worried that Jack's stepping back from the shop would make him resent me later. I tried to talk him into staying there, riding it out until the kids were out of school. We'd make it, I promised. We'd figure it out.

But he was having none of it. His mind was made up, and I eventually caved. To my surprise, he seems to revel in his new role in the family. He calls himself my "trophy husband," which I find hilarious.

Yet it's also kind of true.

"What are you doing?" I ask, laughing at Billie as she comes through the back door. "My lord, woman. What did you bring?"

She sets four bags on the table and sighs. "I didn't know what kind of a gift to get Michael, so I got four."

"Um, that's overkill."

"He's my godson—unofficially. Sort of." She waves a hand in the air. "I'm the one he'll call if he gets arrested while in college. Or if he's drunk. I have to keep those lines of communication open, even if I have to buy his love."

"He'll be fine. Ava will keep him in line."

Michael and Ava were thrilled to get accepted into the same college. They'll both be living on campus in the fall and have lots of plans for their first year living away from their parents. I'm relieved that they'll have each other there to lean on. What the two of them have is really special. I love it for them.

I grin. But I love *that* for me.

"Hey, gorgeous," Jack says, making a beeline for me. He plants a loud, wet kiss to my lips. "My God, you're stunning."

"Get a room," Billie says, pretending to gag. "How are you, Jack? Miss me?"

"Like I miss having kidney stones."

She glares at him, making him laugh. "Okay, all joking aside, what do you guys need me to help with? I know you've been busting your ass on the scrapbooks for your new hotshot actress friend."

I blush. "She's not my friend. She's a client."

"Whatever. The star of *Melomie* knows your home address and sent you flowers last week. You're friends."

"But not best friends," Jack says, inserting himself into the conversation. "That's me. Then you. You're second place, Bills."

"I accept begrudgingly," Billie says. "Shit. I left my makeup bag in the car. My lipstick will melt. I'll be right back." She jogs to the door. "Shit, shit, shit."

Jack shakes his head. "She's a mess."

"But she's consistent."

He grins. "So are you, my boss wife. Do you need anything else from your executive assistant?"

"I do. But nothing you can deliver right now."

"*Oh, Lo.* I can deliver *anywhere.*"

The glimmer in his eye sends a bolt of energy to the apex of my thighs.

Jack can deliver *anywhere.* He's proven that over and over again the last few months.

That's not the only thing that he's proven, though. He's proven that he's an even better version of the man I married twenty years ago. He listens and pauses when I speak—and rather than turning away or lashing out when we disagree, he absorbs my words.

Jack is present. He's not only home for dinner, but he's a part of the process. *Except for hamburgers. Never again.* He's generous with everything and free with his time, acknowledgments, and love. He's been delivering on all those things.

I've been trying my best to deliver too.

That's the thing, really. I was so focused for so long on all the things that were wrong with Jack and our marriage that I forgot to see the good. The reasons why I fell in love with him in the first place. The ways I might have been failing him too.

I'm more patient than before, and more kind when frustrated. I stop by the shop a few times a week to say hello, and I bring dinner there on the rare occasion that Jack can't make it home.

Most importantly, I make a concerted effort to always see the silver lining—even when things aren't great. *Especially when things aren't great.*

Our marriage isn't perfect, but it's better than ever.

There's an adage that says not to sweat the small stuff. In some ways, that's true. To stay happily married, I must accept that the bathroom toilet seat will never be down, and there will never be a day I can walk in my house and not trip over Jack's shoes.

But, in other ways, that advice is wrong.

It's the small stuff that makes or breaks our marriage. It's the coffee in bed, the getting gas for the other person because they hate doing it. It's making sure to buy her favorite brand of cotton swabs, and we always have his favorite brand of barbecue sauce in the pantry.

The small stuff—keeping your socks together in the laundry basket and shutting cabinet doors when you're finished—is important. The magic is taking the time to have a conversation about something that seems insignificant and sending texts throughout the day, just to connect.

It's about ensuring that you give nothing but it all to your marriage, that you say "I do" every single day.

ACKNOWLEDGMENTS

It is still unbelievable that I get to tell stories for a living. It's an awesome part of my life, and I would be remiss if I didn't begin my acknowledgments by thanking my Creator. I'm so grateful for this wild journey.

At Montlake, I'm blessed to work with such an amazing, patient, and thoughtful team.

Many thanks to Alison Dasho for believing in me, and to Lindsey Faber for the joy she brings to her edits. Thank you to Bill S. for the tremendous help in cleaning up this manuscript. And to the countless others who have used their skills on this project—your efforts are truly appreciated.

I would like to thank my family for their love and support. My wonderful husband, four brilliant sons, and bonus parents are the best cheerleaders ever. I love you all endlessly.

Thanks to my friends who lend an ear, or an eye, every time I need it. Mandi Beck, S. L. Scott, Michele Ficht, Anjelica Grace, Kaitie Reister, Brittni Van, Jessica Prince, Kenna Rey, and Kari March teach me every day what friendship is all about. And a huge thank-you to my assistant, Tiffany, for keeping the ball rolling.

My deepest gratitude to Marion Archer for her encouragement and keen eye.

I also have to acknowledge Chupie, our Jack Russell terrier, who provided the inspiration for Snaps. He's part snuggle bug and part menace—and we wouldn't have him any other way.

Last but certainly not least, thank you for picking up this book. I know you have a million choices, and I'm honored that you chose to spend a part of your day with mine.

If you liked this book, try *Written in the Scars*, which features a blue-collar marriage in trouble similar to this book.

ABOUT THE AUTHOR

USA Today bestselling author Adriana Locke writes contemporary romances about the two things she knows best—big families and small towns. Her stories are about ordinary people finding extraordinary love with the perfect combination of heart, heat, and humor.

She loves connecting with readers, fall weather, football, reading about alpha heroes, everything pumpkin, and pretending to garden.

Hailing from a tiny town in the Midwest, Adriana spends her free time with her high school sweetheart (who she married more than twenty years ago) and their four sons (who truly are her best work). Her kitchen may be a perpetual disaster, but if all else fails, there's always pizza.

Learn more at www.adrianalocke.com.